"Sophie Renwick cooks up a s_____ any appetite. Fans of friends-to-lovers stories will especially enjoy this tasty treat." —Megan Hart, author of *Tempted*

"Sophie Renwick has created a most delectable recipe with her debut novel: Take one scrumptious, sexy chef, add a smart, sensual heroine, blend with scorching love scenes, whip in an exotic setting, then top with decadent desserts, and you have one orgasmic read! No matter how spicy you like your dish, *Hot in Here* serves up the heat on a decadent platter. I ate it up! Bon appétit!"

—Karin Tabke, author of *Master of Craving*

HOT IN HERE

Sophie Renwick

HEAT

NAL Accent
Published by New American Library, a division of
Penguin Group (USA) Inc., 375 Hudson Street,
New York, New York 10014, USA
Penguin Group (Canada), 90 Eglinton Avenue East, Suite 700, Toronto,
Ontario M4P 2Y3, Canada (a division of Pearson Penguin Canada Inc.)
Penguin Books Ltd., 80 Strand, London WC2R 0RL, England
Penguin Ireland, 25 St. Stephen's Green, Dublin 2,
Ireland (a division of Penguin Books Ltd.)
Penguin Group (Australia), 250 Camberwell Road, Camberwell, Victoria 3124,
Australia (a division of Pearson Australia Group Pty. Ltd.)
Penguin Books India Pvt. Ltd., 11 Community Centre, Panchsheel Park,
New Delhi - 110 017, India
Penguin Group (NZ), 67 Apollo Drive, Rosedale, North Shore 0632,
New Zealand (a division of Pearson New Zealand Ltd.)
Penguin Books (South Africa) (Pty.) Ltd., 24 Sturdee Avenue,
Rosebank, Johannesburg 2196, South Africa

Penguin Books Ltd., Registered Offices:
80 Strand, London WC2R 0RL, England

First published by Heat, an imprint of New American Library,
a division of Penguin Group (USA) Inc.

First Printing, June 2009
10 9 8 7 6 5 4 3 2 1

HEAT and logo are trademarks of Penguin Group (USA) Inc.

LIBRARY OF CONGRESS CATALOGING-IN-PUBLICATION DATA:

Renwick, Sophie.
Hot in here/Sophie Renwick.
p. cm.
ISBN 978-0-451-22691-4
1. Cookery—Fiction. I. Title.
PS3618.E64H58 2009
813'.6—dc22   2009000727

Set in Centaur MT
Designed by Alissa Amell

Printed in the United States of America

For all the women out there who love good food, hot men and sexy romance books, this one is for you!

Acknowledgments

Special thanks goes to my awesome editor, Tracy Bernstein. I learned a lot from you, and thank you for your time and excellent edits. What a pleasure it was to work with you, and what a joy it is knowing we will be working together again. You really helped make this book live up to its title!

HOT
IN HERE

One

"*I like my women the way I like my recipes: fast, easy and full of variety.*"

There was a pregnant pause, followed by a raised brow and a flash of blue-green eyes above the spine of the glossy magazine. "Did you really say that?"

The look that greeted him from across the table momentarily gave him pause. Then he smiled, turning on the renowned charm that now came automatically to him. "Of course not."

The brow went up again—*a challenge*—before her gaze lowered once more to the magazine. "The sexy chef was then overheard saying, 'Marriage? God, no. The only housewives I'm into are the ones who tune into my cooking show hoping to add some spice to their dreary lives. I *have* to like *them*. After all, they're the ones who've made me rich."

Again with the questioning brow. This time, though, there was an unavoidable air of disapproval as she stared him down. "I did not say *any* of that," he exploded.

"But you did say the first bit, about how you like your women?"

Bryce felt his face heat up. "OK, I said that. But not the other part. I would *never* say something so demeaning."

"Because it would cost you your career, or because you don't really feel that way toward the poor, overworked housewives the world over?"

Tossing his napkin onto the table, Bryce slid deeper into the plush velvet seat of the booth. He surveyed his dinner companion, not entirely certain he knew her.

Jenna McCabe.

Bryce scrutinized the familiar long strawberry blond hair and the smattering of freckles over the bridge of her nose. He saw her blue-green eyes flash beneath copper-colored lashes, and watched the way she toyed with the plastic sword that held the slice of banana and the cherry in her drink.

She looked like Jenna McCabe, pretty in a girl-next-door sort of way. She was dressed as she usually was, tailored, simple. Nothing risky. Nothing sexy. The black wide-legged pants and red blouse she wore spoke of professionalism and intelligence.

She was dressed like Jenna. She looked like Jenna. But this air of confidence, this undercurrent of distaste and, dare he say, disapproval was most un-Jenna like.

"Bryce, did you really say you liked your women fast and easy?"

Damn him, he blushed. He never blushed. But the way Jenna was staring him down, like he was a Neanderthal dragging his knuckles on the ground, made him feel ashamed.

And why should he? He was a rich bachelor. He played the field. Big deal. He had nothing to be ashamed of. He had no ties, and no desire to make them, either. Playing the field was what he wanted out of life, and he was not going to be embarrassed about it, nor was he going to be cornered into anything permanent. No way.

Shit. How many guys his age were doing the very same thing, scoring a different chick every night? Hell, it was a rite of passage for his generation. And he wasn't fucking apologizing for it, either. Not even to sweet, little country-faced-girl-next-door Jenna McCabe.

Bucking up, he sat straight up in his seat and pressed forward, catching and holding her gaze above the dinner candle that flickered gently. The sooner she realized that the guy she'd known in high school was long gone, the better it'd be for her, and him. Because, truth be told, he was damn tired of seeing that sad, disappointed look in her eye whenever she saw him. More than that, though, he hated the feel of the gut rot that gnawed his insides whenever he thought of being a failure in Jenna's eyes. Not that her opinion meant shit, of course.

Keep telling yourself that, and one day you might actually believe it.

"You know I'm easily bored. It takes a lot to capture my notice, and even more to hold it."

Something flickered in her eyes, but she didn't back off. "And the other?" she asked, her voice dropping, giving it a husky tone he'd never, ever imagined she possessed. "Did you flaunt the fact that you've made millions on your cookbooks and your cable TV show, and all from the hard-earned cash of those housewives you secretly mock?"

A muscle worked in his jaw. How could she even ask him such a thing? Yeah, he was a horn dog, but he wasn't a complete asshole. Had he really sunk that far in her eyes?

"I can't believe you're buying into everything that rag mag is saying, Jenna. You of all people should know me better than that. We've been friends for a decade."

"Have we?" Her expression appeared startled and the look in her eyes made his gut churn even more. "I wouldn't exactly say we were friends for all those years. More like acquaintances."

Well, wasn't that a kick to the middle?

Startled by his sudden, violent reaction, Bryce reached for his beer and chugged it back, using the seconds to try to find his footing, while attempting not to examine his feelings. But it was no use. One look into those soft eyes and he was thinking—remembering. Yes. He'd thought of her as a friend—hell, his best friend. And she . . . she had thought of him as what? An associate? A social contact?

What the fuck?

"Look, just answer the question, Bryce. I'm not here to judge you. I'm on your side, remember?"

"Yeah, you are on my side. And you're on it because I'm spending an outrageous amount of money to cover your fee. So you're damn straight you're on my side."

The old Jenna would have shrugged and dropped the topic like hot coals. She might have even gotten a little teary-eyed—she had always been such a sensitive thing. But the new, confident Jenna didn't so much as blink at the arrogance he heard in his own voice. This new Jenna wasn't going to be cowed by his asinine show of male dominance.

Every woman he had dated in the past five years had been the polar opposite of Jenna. All of them had been self-absorbed, stunningly beautiful and sexually experienced. And all of them couldn't have cared less about him. They wanted to see and be seen. Those women didn't talk to him—not really. Not about anything more meaningful than "What are we doing tonight and what should I wear?"

And none of those women had been more heartless than Chrissy Smithson. Chrissy and her conniving ways had pretty much ruined him for any other woman—most especially the nice, settling-down types.

But Jenna was different. A different kind of woman from Chrissy and all the nameless others. Jenna was comfortable. Someone you could just hang around with while tossing back a few beers. She wasn't one of these high-drama diva types. She was as low maintenance as a woman could be. But what he liked the most was that Jenna was nonthreatening. She wasn't out for a slice of his financial portfolio, and she didn't use her body to get him into bed. Jenna was just Jenna. With Jenna he didn't have to be on guard, always wondering what her underlying motives were. With Jenna he was just Bryce, and for once he could be himself.

"Okay," she muttered, licking her lips before taking a sip of her chocolate martini. "I know that *Celebrity Gossip* is infamous for taking stories and exaggerating them. And truthfully, 'he said, she said' no longer matters. What matters is your business empire. It's pretty much going to hell in a handbasket."

She didn't even blink as she trashed his ego with her analysis. This definitely was not the Jenna he had known since junior year of high school. This was the powerhouse marketing genius, confident in her abilities, glowing with the ideas of some brilliant plan she was secretly masterminding.

And, God, what a turn-on to watch her like this.

The mad thought broadsided him and he stole a look at her over the rim of his beer glass. His cock suddenly stirred behind his fly, testament to the fact that watching Jenna like this, all confidence and brains, was having an unsettling effect on his dick.

If he hadn't poured the beer himself, he would have sworn someone had slipped some libido-enhancing drug into his glass, because now he was as hard as he'd ever been in his life, and he couldn't keep his gaze from slipping down to her lips and imagining what that plump red mouth would feel like wrapped around his cock.

"What?" she asked, her brow creasing. "You're frowning. I'm sorry if I ticked you off with that last comment about your empire going down the toilet, but let's be truthful here."

Yeah. Truthful. That was what he needed to be. And the truth was, Jenna wasn't his type of woman. She was sexually inexperienced (as far as he knew) and a little too heavy for his tastes. Not that she was big, but compared to the size zeros and ones he was used to getting naked with—well, Jenna wasn't exactly small. She had much more tits and ass than what he normally went for.

"Wholesome" was how he would describe her. And he definitely wasn't into wholesome. He wanted the sex bomb, not the milkmaid.

No, the truth was, he admired her brain and her success. She'd made herself a name in the world of marketing and PR, despite the cutthroat industry and her lack of finances when she had started up. She was a force to be reckoned with in business. But the business of being a woman had never come easily to Jenna. And as a consequence, Bryce had never had a *serious* sexual thought about her.

Until tonight.

Until she sat up straight and made him take notice. Until she picked up that damn plastic sword and pulled the glistening red cherry, dripping with its juice, into her mouth with the tips of her perfect white teeth.

Oh, hell, yeah, he was taking notice.

Bryce almost choked, watching her tongue flicking along the tip of the red plastic, lapping at a rose-colored drop of maraschino cherry syrup.

His raging hard-on burst to life in his pants, rearing up as if trying to connect with her mouth so it, too, could feel what it was like to be cleaned up by Jenna's flicking tongue. Suddenly the thought of his dick drenched in syrup had merits, but only if he could watch Jenna lap it clean like she was doing with that innocent bit of plastic. Bryce swallowed hard, trying to get a hold on his rampant, surprising lust, not to mention the naughty visual of Jenna on her knees sucking him off.

He tried to remind himself that this was Jenna McCabe, high school friend. Jenna was not a sex kitten hidden behind a red wrap blouse. Jenna was safe, and he liked temptation. Jenna was . . . *Shit*, he thought, watching her run her tongue along the sword in slow, erotic flicks. Jenna was hot as hell and he was getting singed.

"What?" she asked, her voice husky.

He reached for his napkin and fought the urge to wipe his brow with it. Jesus Christ, what was happening here? Jenna showed him a bit of a spine and a dose of feminine self-confidence and he was ready to throw her down on the table and get sweaty with her? What the hell was the matter with him?

"Bryce?"

A hallucination came out of nowhere, of Jenna sliding onto his lap, straddling his legs, her voice a husky purr. Hell, he could almost feel the weight of her body on his lap, of her heart-shaped ass filling his hands. And suddenly he knew that fleshy ass would feel so fucking good in his palms as he kneaded her while she rode him.

"Bryce? Are you okay?"

Blinking, he looked around. The vision of Jenna naked, riding his cock, slowly dissipated until all he saw was the familiar sights of his restaurant. Turning his head, Bryce expected to see the woman he'd invited to supper. Instead, he saw someone else. Someone totally new. Someone totally hot and completely wrong for him.

"Is it getting hot in here?" he croaked.

Caving, he snatched the white linen square from the table and mopped his sweating brow. She shifted and leaned across the table, her breasts pressed provocatively together, giving him a tease as they inched up over the neckline of her blouse. She was well endowed—he'd always known that—but damn, he didn't know how much he liked it or the silky cleavage he couldn't stop staring at.

He found himself imagining what her bra was like beneath the soft fabric. Imagined getting his hand up it, feeling her up as he whispered something naughty in her ear.

"If this is too much for you," she said, "we can talk about it in the morning."

Too much? Little Jenna McCabe too much for *him*—for Bryce Ryder, the man who had any woman he wanted? The man who never wanted for sex?

His mouth tried to work, tried to make a sound. But he couldn't. He just sat there like a mute idiot, still wondering if the bra beneath the blouse was soft and silky, or sexy and lacy. And that was when he realized that maybe she really was too much for him. Because for the first time since he'd been a virgin, he felt awkward and unsure around a woman.

"I'm hot as hell," he finally managed to choke out, his gaze drifting along her body. He shook his head. Blinked. And still saw Jenna sitting across from him, looking totally sex kittenish, totally kissable. Totally doable.

"I'd better get to the kitchen," he muttered, trying to shimmy out of the booth and still hide his massive hard-on from her.

"Yeah," she drawled. "You better. It *is* getting kind of hot in here."

Kinda? Ten more seconds, and he would have lost all sanity and tossed her on top of the table, tasting her mouth and pussy like they were the finest chocolate in the world.

And he fricking loved chocolate.

"Tyson," he barked, as he plowed through the swinging kitchen door. "Where's the appetizer?"

"I'm just coming out with it."

"Good. And, Mark, get a move on with the main course."

"What?" his sous chef said with a teasing smile. "The wining and dining not going so well?"

No, it was going too well. Hell, on his present course, he'd be eating dessert off of Jenna's tits. An image came to him, of chocolate and warm caramel trickling between her cleavage, and him licking it off, offering it to her on his tongue for a taste.

That was the way dessert was meant to be eaten—off a body and shared with tongues.

The fly of his trousers grew tighter. *Friends,* he reminded himself. *Just friends.*

Steeling himself, he went back to the table, where Jenna was just reaching for a bread stick. This dinner was a business meeting. Pure and simple. He needed Jenna and her remarkable PR skills.

He did *not* need her in any other capacity.

As he slid into the booth, his cock twitched in his pants, once again growing hard and stiff—damn achy, and just a tad spiteful. While his brain told him he didn't need Jenna, his hard-on was telling him the complete opposite.

"Everything okay now?" she asked.

"Everything's fine."

"You cooled off yet?"

Hell no! He gazed at her, still confused and aroused by what he was seeing. "So, let's talk business. Because that's what I invited you here for."

His tone was too brusque, leaving no room for her to misinterpret what this dinner was all about. He saw something flicker in her eyes—hurt, embarrassment? He didn't know, but he wanted to kick himself after those words flew out of his mouth. "Jen, look, I'm sorry—"

"Nothing to be sorry for," she said, as she reached into the brown leather bag beside her. "It's business. And that's what I've come prepared for. Damage control. So, let's get to it before dinner arrives."

He nodded, relieved that he hadn't hurt her with his words and that they were at last on the right footing. Talking business.

"Jenna, you do understand that I'm not going to stand by and allow myself to lose everything I've worked so hard for, right? I can't go through that again. I'm not going to let some incompetent asshole reporter ruin my reputation and my livelihood just so he can sell a few copies of a second-rate magazine."

"I understand. I know what this restaurant means to you. I know what you've had to do, and what you've had to sacrifice to keep it."

Yeah, Jenna knew. He felt a bit embarrassed that she did know all the sordid little details. Man, he'd give anything right now to take back that afternoon he'd paid Jenna a visit at her apartment. It was hard to believe that four years had passed since he'd spilled his guts out about how Chrissy had only dated him because he had money, and how much of a fool he'd been to invite her to live with him, and how, three months after their common-law status had been sealed by law, Chrissy was taking him for half of everything he owned—including the only thing he had truly loved: his restaurant.

It had taken some finagling and fine work on Jenna's part to get Chrissy to leave things out of court. Nearly two hundred grand later, the bitch had departed, leaving Bryce in debt up to his eyeballs, not to mention a sour taste in his mouth about women.

Never again, he'd thought as he signed the papers for the bank loan to pay off Chrissy, would he ever get himself seriously involved with a woman. Not at the risk of his career and his restaurant. One-night stands and one-week flings were all he wanted. No strings, no payoffs and, most important, no more losses of any of his assets.

Four years later, he had come out smarter, and richer, and damn him, he was *not* going to lose everything now because of some so-called remark in a gossip rag.

The restaurant and his TV show were his life. Nothing in the world could make him give up the two things he loved most.

"You might want to have a look at this," Jenna said, drawing him out of the bad memories of Chrissy. She handed him the legal pad. "This is my plan. I'm going to refresh my lip gloss. Have that read when I get back."

Bryce didn't read a word. Instead, he watched Jenna walking toward the restroom, her hips swaying. Man, she had a fabulous ass. Why hadn't he noticed it before? And why the hell was he thinking it now?

"Hey, Ty," she said, waving at his waiter. Tyson nodded and smiled. When Jenna had passed him, he turned his head, stealing a peek. Whistling, he shook his head.

"She's fine," Tyson said. "Man, that ass."

"If you want this job, you'll keep your eyes to yourself and away from her ass or any other body part you might find *fine* on her."

Tyson laughed. "Yeah, like you're gonna fire family."

"Don't tempt me."

"C'mon, big brother, what's your problem? You don't like chicks like Jenna. Besides, you wouldn't know what to do with a woman like her."

"And you would? You're all of what, twenty-five?"

"So, I'm the baby. Doesn't make me stupid, just younger. And yeah, I'd know how to treat a woman like Jenna."

"All right," Bryce said, slapping the legal pad down on the table. "I'll bite. What would you do with a woman like Jenna?"

"Inside that kitten is a tigress. She just needs someone special to bring it out. With a woman like that, a man can be anything he wants—complete, fulfilled."

Bryce didn't need a woman to make him fulfilled. One night of sex saw to those needs. He saw no reason to share his life with a woman; it would only interfere with his plans. Being successful, rich and eternally single, *that* was what completed him. He didn't want anything more than that.

Swallowing back the emotion that started in the pit of his stomach, Bryce glanced down and read the red ink at the top of the pad. Jenna's handwriting was small and neat, flowing in a feminine way that did weird things to his gut.

Disgusted with his pansy-ass attitude, he picked up the notepad and read the title.

PROJECT BAD BOY:
Goodbye, Sexy Playboy.
Hello, Housewife Fantasy.

Trouble. That was what this was. First his weird thoughts about Jenna, and now her plan. God help him, he was going to be ruined.

There were two things in life that Jenna never could resist. Good food and Bryce Ryder.

Never had there been a more beautiful specimen of manhood than Bryce. He was so much more than the clichéd tall, dark and handsome. Of course he was tall, well over six feet. And he was dark, his hair a warm rich chocolate brown that was silky—not that she knew for certain. She'd never gotten close enough to run her fingers through his hair. But it looked silky, the way it shone in the light and slid through his fingers when he ruffled it while he was thinking. And his skin was that swarthy complexion that made him look tan or at the very least Italian. Next came the handsome. And, oh God, was Bryce handsome. With a killer dimple in his left cheek and hazel eyes, he left the ladies breathless with just a glance.

Jenna wasn't certain how many times she'd been robbed of breath and brain function after a smile from Bryce. Too often, she was afraid. And for too darn long.

She'd been in love—and lust—with Bryce since she was seventeen. Ten long years. Well, eleven in just three hours and thirty-nine minutes.

She'd met him on her birthday, in the school cafeteria, right after she'd dumped her tray of meat loaf and mac and cheese in his lap.

Instead of making her feel like the awkward geek she really was, he'd just laughed and dipped his finger in the meat. After licking it off his finger, he'd given her a killer smile. As if by the proverbial bolt of lightning, she'd been struck. It was love at first sight. Of course, Bryce hadn't been quite as smitten as her.

They'd become friends, and grown closer during their senior year at Bowden High. They had even managed to keep in contact, although sporadically, while she was at college and he was half the world away at a private French culinary school. A decade later, they were still friends.

That comment about them being only acquaintances had been

purely tactical. And the reason for the calculated maneuver was close at hand. In just under four hours, it was going to be her birthday. Her twenty-eighth birthday, to be precise. And she'd promised herself a gift: Bryce Ryder, wearing nothing but an imaginary red satin ribbon around that chiseled six-pack of his.

She'd told herself over and over as the days, the weeks, the months rolled by that she would not wait another ten years for Bryce to come around. One decade was long enough. As the lead hand on her parents' farm always liked to say, it was time to "do or die."

And now was the time. Oh, she knew it wasn't going to be easy. Bryce was careful with his heart. Chrissy had seen to that. After her betrayal, Bryce hadn't wanted anything more than casual sex. But all that was going to change. When Jenna was done with Bryce, he was going to want the happily ever after.

Even though he told himself he didn't want the tangle of a commitment, Jenna knew he secretly yearned for it. His own upbringing had sealed that desire. Raised by nannies, Bryce had never really known his parents or what it was like to be part of a family. That was, until he had met Jenna and started spending all his free time on her family's farm.

Bryce had craved the warmth of family. Had wanted that for himself—until that conniving Chrissy had ruined it all by trying to take everything Bryce had worked so hard for. Not only had the woman betrayed Bryce, but she'd made him believe that women couldn't be trusted, and that relationships weren't worth the effort. But that was soon going to change, once Bryce saw Jenna as something more than a best buddy.

Jenna smacked her lips together, ensuring coverage of the light pink gloss. She was so sick of being friend material. Tired of being seen as nothing but a safety net for when things got sticky.

Not that she was complaining. Any excuse to have Bryce in her company was fine with Jenna. The trouble was the damage it caused her heart when he left. When she saw him with his treat of the week, or the flavor of the month, that was when it got nasty. That was when she wanted to bash him over the head with her leather bag and scream at him, *"Why don't you see me?"*

But that would put a swift end to *any* sort of friendship she had with Bryce. So, she had bided her time, waiting for the opportune moment. And lo and behold, one had come along.

And it was Jenna to the rescue.

She was happy—no, ecstatic—to help Bryce. She knew he was a womanizer. Heck, he went through women like NASCAR drivers went through tires, but she also knew that the Bryce she had fallen in love with all those years ago was not a heartless cad. If he was, he never would have bothered to befriend an awkward, unfashionable girl.

No way was Bryce cruel. But he could have been. Bryce had been born rich. His father was loaded; he had even been the mayor of Lucan, the town where Jenna had gone to school. His mother was a wealthy socialite and a bigwig on the board of the local hospital. The Ryder name was hallowed in Lucan and Bryce had been the most popular guy in school. Even though Bryce had everything, he hadn't acted like a spoiled rich kid.

Now Jenna, on the other hand, had been as poor as Bryce was rich. She was rural, as the folks in Lucan liked to call the large farming community surrounding the town. And as a rural, she wore handmade clothes and hand-me-downs from her cousins. She did chores—around the house and the farm—and was frequently seen being driven to school in the cab of her father's cattle truck—usually with cattle still in it. The memory of that particular humiliation still had the power to make her want to cry.

Yep, Bryce could have been mean that day she'd tripped over her feet and plopped the meat loaf onto his lap. But he hadn't been.

Beyond the sexual attraction and her raging hormones for him, there was a healthy respect for Bryce. He was fun to be around and a good conversationalist. They had a lot of shared interests, and he made her laugh—sometimes at herself, and sometimes at him. He was a good man at heart, despite the way he ran through women. And deep down, she knew what he hungered for, even if he didn't.

When she had read the article in the gossip rag, she knew it for a trumped-up lie. She also knew it could cost him everything he loved. From that moment on, she had made herself a twofold plan. The first phase was to get Bryce out of hot water and back into the limelight, where the millions of housewives who devoured his books and sat riveted to his TV show would once again be clamoring for more of Bryce. The second, trickier part of her plan was to get Bryce to see her as someone other than his brainy friend.

Smacking her lips once more, Jenna fought the urge to reach into her purse and pull out all the expensive makeup she'd purchased. Smoky eyes . . . that was what she needed, she thought to herself as she checked her appearance in the mirror. And maybe some hair spray so she could tease her hair into fullness, into something a Victoria's

Secret model might wear. And she needed to learn how to pout. All the women Bryce dated pouted, Chrissy especially. Why men enjoyed the look was beyond Jenna. But there it was, pouting women did something to men's brains, and other parts as well.

It's best to start out as you mean to go on.

Her dad's favorite adage quietly ran through her thoughts. Jenna tucked away the dark gray palette of eye shadow and the tube of liquid eyeliner. She looked up from the marble vanity and back into the mirror. It was true, of course. She shouldn't make herself into something she wasn't, into something she really didn't want to be. It'd be awfully hard to commit to smoky eyes and teased hair for the next fifty years. Because fifty years at least was what she wanted with Bryce.

But first, she needed to set phase one of her plan into motion. She only hoped she could quit staring at Bryce like a sex-starved reject. Professional. That was what she needed to be. She needed to pretend that she was in her office, surrounded by her employees, heading a major marketing meeting. In that sphere, she ruled.

So it was phase one first; then she could move on to the much more exciting phase. That particular part of her plan included Bryce in her bed, doing all sorts of wicked, and probably illegal, things to her. But that couldn't happen before she properly showed Bryce that there was more to Jenna McCabe than what met the eye.

As much as she wanted Bryce for a birthday gift, Jenna knew it wasn't going to happen. At least not this year. One night of sex, while it would be mind-blowing, no doubt, wasn't what she was after.

With a deep breath, Jenna smoothed her slacks and turned to the side, scrutinizing her profile. She looked good. Although a few more bread sticks, and her little tummy bulge would become a balloon. She loved bread, and Bryce knew that. He also knew she loved pasta, so naturally he planned on serving it tonight.

When Bryce was serving up favorites, he was plotting. And when he was plotting, he was usually being very bad. Smiling into the mirror, Jenna brushed a few strands of hair away from her eye. One day she was going to be just as bad as Bryce. One day, they were going to be bad *together*.

With her game face on, she left the bathroom, fully prepared to launch Project Bad Boy!

Two

"This," Bryce fumed, slapping down the notepad, "is not going to work."

"Oooh, stuffed mushroom caps," Jenna squealed as Tyson set a small plate of hors d'oeuvres before her.

"Jenna," Bryce warned.

"What isn't going to work, Bryce?" she asked innocently before spearing a mushroom with her fork. Jenna smothered a loud groan as she tasted the first bite. Bryce made the best lobster-stuffed mushroom caps the world had ever seen. "God, they're good," she whispered, letting out a little moan as she bit into another one. "What's the secret ingredient that makes these so addicting?"

"Don't think to change the subject with flattery. And it's my fingers, by the way. I mix the filling and assemble it with my hands. Makes the lobster retain its buttery texture."

Jenna allowed her gaze to drop down to Bryce's elegant, artistic fingers. She imagined what those beautiful, skillful hands could do to a woman's body. Jenna could hardly bear the thought.

Schooling her libido *and* her appetite, Jenna reached for the white file folder she kept in her bag. "When was the last time you've had a rundown of your demographics?"

"The last time I had a book signing. Two hundred women, most with sniffling toddlers. I wound up with a cold for a month."

"You don't have to kiss the kids, you know."

"What else am I supposed to do when I'm presented with them in my face? To do anything else would be a slap in the face to these women. Besides, it was the dead of January and some of them had waited outside in the cold for more than two hours."

And he'd demanded that the bookstore open early and let them inside, or he would leave, refusing to sign. But Bryce wouldn't want her knowing that. He wanted to maintain his cool hauteur. He didn't want anyone to know he might have a soft spot or a vulnerable chink in his masculine armor.

Changing the direction of her thoughts, Jenna opened the file folder. "I have your stats for the past six months. Your highest rated show was the one entitled 'Simply Seduction.'"

He shrugged. "That was a fun show. I had good audience participation. There were lots of laughs, but the recipes were hardly over-the-top."

"Yes, but why was it different? It was just an ordinary Wednesday episode of *Heating It Up*."

"I don't know why it was such a hit. The recipes were easy enough, and the ingredients were nothing at all too exotic."

"That's it. The recipes were special but you didn't have to scour five specialty shops to get the ingredients. The local supermarket would have them all. That honeyed-fig recipe, the one where you serve them in pomegranate bowls? It's the number-one downloaded recipe from your Web site. And the reason? Because it's seductive and sophisticated, yet prepared in under ten minutes."

He grinned, his eyes flashing. "I love that recipe. And the added bonus is it's sexy as hell to watch someone eat it—especially if you're feeding it to her."

Jenna's mouth went dry. For a second she just stared at the man across the table, wishing she had the courage to climb on top of the table and hand-feed him a honeyed fig.

Not yet. Phase one first, then on to feeding each other.

"You see, that's why you're so popular with a specific demographic. The stats don't lie, Bryce. Eighty-five percent of your viewers are under the age of thirty-five. Ninety percent of those are married with families."

"And the other fifteen percent?"

"Everyone else."

He groaned and shoved his plate away. "I never intended to dominate the market in married females."

"I know you didn't, but your brand of cuisine is what they're looking for. Sophisticated for dinner parties and office get-togethers, yet easy and simple after dealing with the kids and work. That's what women need when they come home from work, or when they've spent the day elbow-deep in laundry and sticky handprints. Whether you want it or not, that seems to be your market. Now, if you want to go upscale—"

"You mean pretentious."

"Cuisine for aficionados."

"You mean, artsy crap that everyone oohs and ahhs over before stopping off at McDonald's for a Big Mac combo because the one-ounce piece of meat and two strings of green beans didn't cut it."

Jenna laughed. Bryce viewed things so much the way she did. She wondered if he even realized it.

"I won't change the way I cook, and I especially won't do it in order to please a group of self-important, puffed-up foodies. Haute couture and haute cuisine aren't me. I like jeans and T-shirts and full-bodied meals. The kind that make you feel satisfied, just like sex. In fact, the natural progression after eating one of my meals should be the bedroom. Lovemaking is a simple extension of the food. Or at least, in my mind, it should be."

Jenna's mouth was watering. So were other parts, she realized. Crossing her legs, she pressed her thighs together, trying to stop the vibrations in her clitoris, but the action only heightened it.

Business. Think business.

"Food for me has always been like having great sex. It should excite you and then fill you with peace after it's done. That's why you won't be finding two carrots and tofu surprise on my plates."

Food for me has always been like having great sex. Jenna hung on to the words, suspended by an image of being fed by Bryce. She imagined sharing a meal together like lovers, sitting side by side in an intimate booth. With Bryce, and a couple of glasses of excellent Chianti, she might be prevailed upon to really let loose and sit on his lap and make love to him in a celebration of food and steamy sex.

"Jenna?"

Shaking her head, she cleared the image of a naked Bryce feeding her something totally sinful. "See, that's why these women love you, Bryce. You tell them that cooking isn't a chore—it's a way to express love. And when the show has ended, these women feel *satisfied*. They feel as though you understand your love of food is tied up with loving them. That's the whole allure of you and your cooking."

He blinked, and Jenna blushed. She didn't mean to get so personal, but it was the truth. The women loved Bryce like men adored Nigella Lawson. Nigella was voluptuous, and she usually made little moaning sounds as she licked her fingers free of icing. The men ate her up and asked for seconds; even men who didn't know how to turn on an oven watched Nigella Lawson. It was a sexual, sensual experience. And it was the same for the women who adored Bryce. He was manly, sexy, and he spoke about food with an unabashed adoration. He never made low-fat this or fat-free that. He gave women permission to cook what they wanted and eat what they wanted. He made it known that a man wanted to share a meal with a woman like he wanted to share his body with her. A woman who loved good food loved good sex.

To Bryce, food and passion were symbiotic. And because of his views, and his virile, masculine earthiness, he was adored. But that cutting remark—the one the magazine had twisted around—had made his fans feel betrayed.

As if he read her mind, he sat back and studied her. "I get it now," he muttered. "These women . . . my fans," he said, clearly uncomfortable with the word. "They feel like I'm a fraud, saying one thing and doing another. I always talk about how wonderful it is for a man to come home to a house full of succulent aromas, made by the woman he loves, and it's true. But now they think I was just feeding them a line."

Jenna nodded and put down her file, wondering if Bryce had ever wanted that, to come home to a woman he loved cooking him dinner. God, she wanted to be that woman he came home to.

"This plan is going to help your fans see the real you, but it isn't going to happen overnight, Bryce. You have to be patient."

"I don't have time—"

"Like I said, if you're looking for instant relief for your present circumstances, then you can think about going more upscale. That part of society will adore you. Speaking as your PR and marketing adviser, it would be a windfall for you. You're young, rich and good-looking. All things that will make people want to get to know you. And the fact that there's a bit of scandal surrounding you won't hurt you, either. There's nothing celebrities love more than gossip about someone other than themselves. Your food, once they give you a chance, will speak for itself. That route is a win-win situation."

"And the other?" he asked, glancing up at her through his thick mocha-colored lashes.

"The other one is a bit riskier. It's a population that doesn't easily overlook being taken in and duped. You'll have to prove yourself, and it'll be a long row to hoe. It just depends on what you want."

He nodded and sat back in the booth, casting a glance at her marketing plan. "Frankly, I'm not looking for this thing to go away over time. I want it gone *now*. I've got some new projects in the works, and I can't afford any financial insecurity. I can't afford time or uncertainty. To be honest, I'll do whatever it takes to make certain it doesn't happen, and the quicker and quieter, the better."

Jenna tried to hide her disappointment. The Bryce she knew

would have told her flat out, no way. But maybe the man she had known had changed into this creature the tabloids loved to tattle about. Maybe he really was going to take the easy way and sell himself out for something he didn't want or believe in.

"Where are you going?" he asked, watching her pack up her bag.

"I've got a meeting tomorrow morning. A new client. I have to be up early, and I have notes to go over before bed tonight."

"Hey, Jenna, you can't bail now. I'm bringing out the main course," Tyson said behind her. "Spaghetti carbonara with prosciutto and freshly grated Parmesan cheese."

She smiled and passed him her half-eaten plate of mushroom caps.

"What, no good?" Tyson asked, glancing down at the plate. "I thought these were your favorites."

"Yeah, they are," she said, catching a glance at Bryce's dour expression. "Stomach's just a bit off tonight."

"Oh?" Tyson asked, looking at his brother.

"Yeah, but I'll be fine. Oh, and about the other day, when you called me." She saw Bryce sit up. His expression turned from dour to incredulous. "I do have an opening. I just need a list of your credentials."

"Oh, ah," Tyson colored. "You mean like—"

"Jobs," Bryce snapped. "You know, those things where you work and get paid for doing it."

Tyson shot his brother a lethal glare. "Shut up, Bryce." Then he turned his attention to her. "Truth is, Jen, I don't have much in the way of experience."

"Sure you do, Tyson. You've got a mountain of experience traveling the world and seeing the sights. Spending your trust fund's a full-time vocation for you."

It was Jenna's turn to glare at Bryce. "Don't worry about it, Tyson. Why don't you swing by tomorrow night after I'm done with work, and we'll talk about it? You remember how to get to my place?"

"Sure do." Tyson brightened. "I owe you, Jenna. Waiting tables doesn't turn my crank, if you know what I mean. Besides, the boss is a bit of dick."

Jenna bit back her grin. "Hey, it's the least I can do, especially since that client you directed to me took me on as head of their marketing campaign."

"Good deal. Hey, what about I pick you up and we go out for a bite to eat. You like Moroccan? I know this great place near your apartment."

"It's a date." Jenna picked up her bag and gazed down at Bryce, who couldn't have looked more shocked than if an alien spaceship had landed in the middle of his dining room. A perverse sense of glee slid over her. Maybe, he actually cared. Maybe he was . . . jealous?

"So, are you two done arranging your date?" Bryce asked irritably. "I'd like to remind you both that we're on my tab right now. And since I'm paying by the hour, get lost, Tyson."

"Don't worry about paying," Jenna returned. "This is really just the consultation phase. I don't charge for that, not until I get the job."

Bryce glowered at her. "Okay, then. Why don't you sit down and we'll get back to work and . . . consult?"

"I don't think so, Bryce. You need to think things through. I might not be what you need."

"So, you're just walking away?" A look of panic seemed to flicker in his eyes, but it cleared immediately.

"I'm not sure I'd be the right one. Think of what you want to do and let me know. You have my number."

And with that, she walked to the front of the restaurant, allowed the handsome maître d' to help her with her jacket before she made one hell of a magnificent, self-assured exit through the front door.

"What the hell was that about?" Bryce threw his napkin onto the table and followed Tyson into the kitchen.

"What was what about?"

"*Don't* screw around. I want to know what the fuck you think you're doing asking Jenna out to dinner."

"What do you think I'm doing?"

"You want the truth? I think you're trying to get yourself a job by getting into her pants."

"Yeah? Well, maybe you're wrong."

Bryce snorted. "Please. I know you. You're an operator."

Tyson wheeled on him. "Is it so damn hard for you to believe that maybe I want to get into Jenna's pants for no other reason than I find her incredibly sexy? Not all of us manipulate a woman with food."

"And what the hell is that supposed to mean?"

"Oh, c'mon. You did this tonight just because you're desperate to get Jenna to help you with your reputation. Not because you enjoy her company or the sight of her sitting across the table from you."

"Of course I enjoy Jenna's company. I always have. Besides, this conversation isn't about me," Bryce thundered, feeling a vein in his neck bulge and pulsate. "Back it up to the part where you said you wanted Jenna. That's what we're discussing."

Tyson gave Bryce his back and started stacking up plates, readying them to be washed. "I called her up, hoping for a date. She got the wrong impression that I was looking for a job. I was embarrassed, so I went along. But the truth is, I like her. I'd like to date her. And tomorrow is the perfect night."

Bryce narrowed his eyes. "Why?"

Tyson stared at him with a look of absolute astonishment. "Man, that's sad. But kind of expected. You're so self-absorbed these days with your head up your ass, it's a wonder you even come up for air."

"Tyson—" he growled.

"It's her birthday, Bryce. She's twenty-eight on May the eighth. That's tomorrow, if you don't know."

Bryce felt the blow to his chest. He'd forgotten. Completely. *Shit.*

"I mean to show her a good time," his brother went on as he loaded up the dishwasher. "She deserves it."

Bryce snapped to attention, his body balking, ready to fight. "Just what kind of a good time?"

"Whatever I can think up, and whatever she's willing to try," Tyson said with a lusty grin.

Red swam before Bryce's eyes, and before he knew it, he'd slammed Tyson up against the counter and got in his face. "She's not a plaything, Tyson. You got that?"

"Why are you so upset? You don't want her."

Yeah, but he didn't want Tyson having her, either. Or any other man, for that matter. *Oh, hell, no.* The thought of some other guy's paws all over her made him feel violent, and that was just stupid. He'd known her for ten years, and he'd never cared before. Hell, he'd even double-dated with her a time or two. He'd seen her with other guys. He'd even seen her kiss one beneath the mistletoe last Christmas, at the party he'd held at the restaurant.

Yeah, he'd seen it, and he hadn't liked his reaction. So he'd buried it and pretended he'd never seen the guy's hands go around her waist or her head dip back, allowing his kiss. He was so damn good at pretending that he'd forgotten the feeling of watching her with another. Until now, until Tyson made those feelings erupt like a volcano.

"I'm telling you right now, Tyson, break the date."

"Why?"

"Don't question me. Just do it."

"In case you haven't noticed, I'm not six anymore. I don't take orders from you. Especially about women I might be interested in dating."

"Jenna is off-limits."

"We'll see about that," Tyson muttered, turning once again to the dishes.

Bryce was about to wheel his brother around for another bout of fighting when his cell phone went off.

"Hello?" he snapped.

"Morning, Mary Sunshine. Man, I hope this isn't how you address your adoring customers." Trey. The eldest Ryder brother, and thankfully, the rational one.

"It's nearly ten p.m. here, and the morning is a hell of a way off."

"Well, it's morning here in London. Three a.m. to be precise."

"You just getting in?" Bryce asked, sending Tyson's back another glare.

"Yeah, couldn't resist a stroll through Regent's Park. The fog was beautiful, just hanging low over the grass and trees, and the moon's full—very atmospheric."

"Did you bring your camera?"

"Am I ever without it?"

Trey was a photographer—a famous photographer with an impressive portfolio. His specialty was people—stunning models to be precise—but his passion was moody landscapes.

"So, how did it go with Jenna?" Trey asked.

Bryce frowned, not wanting to relive that hour with Jenna. He wasn't in the right place to go down the strange path he'd started down earlier that evening. "Let's just say it wasn't as good as I'd hoped."

"And what were you hoping for?"

The question stopped him cold. Trey didn't need to know Bryce couldn't stop thinking of Jenna in a myriad of sexual positions.

"Bryce? What happened?"

"Nothing," he muttered, shaking his head. "I...ah...nothing. She came up with some lame plan. I can't believe she's actually gotten this far in business if this is the sort of idea she comes up with."

"What did she want you to do?"

Bryce pressed his eyes shut. "Oh, something about giving free lessons at local libraries and starting up a class for inner-city kids. And get this: She wants me to do women's clubs, like church clubs and parent-teacher councils at schools."

"Sounds like she wants to bring you some buzz, but a different type than what you've been getting."

"Yeah, well, cooking with blue-haired old ladies is not what I had in mind."

"Well, cooking with supermodels isn't going to get you back into the good graces of your fans."

"You've got it so damn good, Trey. You don't know what it's like."

"What, taking pictures of models?"

"Gorgeous, half-naked models," Bryce corrected him. "And dating those same models."

"Yeah, it's wonderful. I love putting up with their diva tantrums."

"I'm not feeling sorry for you," Bryce snapped.

"But you're feeling sorry for yourself?"

"No, I'm pissed off that I've spent a grand so far on a plan that I think will have me laughed at across the globe."

"I think she's hit on something."

"Yeah," Bryce drawled. "My total humiliation."

"Nah, Jenna wouldn't want you humiliated, little brother. She's not that kind of woman. What I think Jenna wants to do is rebuild your credibility."

"I've got plans to open two more restaurants, and my financial backers are waffling after this scandal. I just can't afford the time, Trey. I need a quick fix."

"I think I may have one—a quick fix, that is."

"And that is?"

"In my extensive experience with women, I've learned a few things."

"You don't have to brag."

"I'm not," Trey said with a long sigh. "It's just that I'm surrounded by women all day long. I know how their brains work. And what they hate the most is the thing that threatens them the most."

"And that is?"

"A perfect specimen. What you need, Bryce, is to be seen with your average, everyday girl. They don't want to see you with the types you usually go for, not after that slam at housewives. They don't want to see you with some tall, svelte runway model who doesn't eat. Being seen with someone nonthreatening is the first way to take the sting out of your comment. You know, get your fans to believe that you practice what you preach."

"I'm not going there, Trey. I don't do commitment. I especially don't do relationships that could threaten my restaurant."

"Not every woman is out for what you have, Bryce."

Bryce snorted. "Name me a woman who doesn't want to get her French-manicured nails into a pile of green. Look, I'm not parting with half my assets just to get my rep back."

"Man, Chrissy really did a number on you, didn't she?"

"I don't need your psychoanalysis. And why should I take your advice? When have you ever been in a relationship?"

"Well . . . I'll cut your tongue out if you ever repeat this, but it's not like I've never thought about it. I . . . there was a time—once— when I thought about it."

"Who was she?"

"Not important," Trey answered in his typically cool way. "Just know that I, too, have felt the lack of someone special in my life. For once I'd like to come home to someone instead of this empty flat. And what's more, I think you want it, too. You're just scared that you might find yourself another Chrissy."

Bryce was indignant. He was not scared, for God's sake. He was careful. Big difference. But he had to ask, "So where do you recommend I find this paragon of female virtue?"

There was a long pause, followed by a sigh. "I don't know, little brother. Maybe look around you. Maybe there's someone right in front of you."

What did Trey know? Bryce didn't need a nice, conventional relationship. What he needed was to go prowling for chicks. Then, he could pick out a suitable woman—one who didn't want anything more out of him than his bedroom talents—and screw his way to oblivion.

"Look, it's been great talking to you," Bryce muttered, checking the time on his watch, "but I gotta run. I've got a present to whip up."

"Oh yeah, for who?"

"Jenna. It's her birthday tomorrow."

"You baking a cake?"

"No, I'm thinking something else. Something with chocolate and caramel."

"Sounds good, if a bit decadent. I don't know one woman who would risk even looking at it, let alone tasting it."

"I hate that!" Bryce snapped. "I can't stand being around women who only pick at their meals, especially after I've gone to the trouble of cooking for them."

"I know. I usually eat while they watch me."

Bryce thought of the last time he had sat down and enjoyed a meal with a woman. An image of sharing fries with Jenna at the Lucan fall fair years ago came to mind. Jenna. Why was everything coming back to her tonight?

"Just realized you've been dating the same diet-crazy women that I have?" Trey asked.

"Yeah, I guess."

"That's pretty bad for a chef," Trey chuckled.

"Yeah, pretty bad. Look, I gotta bail."

"Hey, Bryce. Make sure you use your eyes, buddy. I know someone is right there, just waiting to be noticed. Just look around you, and you'll see her."

Three

"So, what'd he make?"

Jenna flicked through the TV channels while she cradled the phone against her shoulder and ear. "Mushroom caps, my favorite. Of course they were to die for. Everything Bryce makes is to die for. Unfortunately I didn't get to the main course, much less Bryce for dessert."

"Ooh, you sound horny," her sister said.

"Obviously. But I'm not going to ruin my brilliant plan by letting my needs get the better of me."

"Why don't you just jump him already? Maybe it'll be so damn good for him, he'll become obsessed with you."

"There's no way in hell Bryce is going to become obsessed with me, at least not yet, and not after the string of girlfriends I've seen him with. They all look like they've come from the Playboy Mansion, where I'm certain they honed many of their skills, if you know what I mean."

"Well, you read *Cosmo*, don't you?"

"*Cosmo* and actual hands-on experience are two different things.

So, no, I'm not going to have sex with him, even if he did offer, until I know I've got him ensnared—and what will get him that way is my brain. Right now Bryce is way too wary of women and relationships, so sleeping with him at this point would be a huge mistake. He'd never commit after a night of sex. There has to be more. I have to gain his trust and make him believe that I'm not out to hurt and destroy him."

"You sound...I don't know. Restless or something tonight, Jen."

Aiming the remote at the screen, Jenna tumbled through the channels for the third time. Usually her sister's phone calls made her feel so much better. Tonight it was the opposite. Sarah had just wound her up further.

"So, what did he think of the plan?"

"Hated it, as I suspected. You know, Sarah, I think I've finally come to understand something. The Bryce I fell in love with is long gone, replaced by this rich, social-climbing womanizer I don't know."

"Now, Jenna, c'mon. You actually believe that?"

"Yeah, I think I do."

"So, you're just going to give up?"

"I never said that."

"Yeah, right. I've heard that tone before. Look, does Bryce even know how you feel about him?"

"Well, he should," Jenna groaned.

"Have you ever given him any indication that you might be interested in more than just his friendship?"

Jenna paused. "No."

"And why not?" Sarah demanded.

"Because rejection is something that terrifies me. Especially coming from Bryce. And Chrissy, well, she's ruined him. He's not looking for forever, and that's what I want. Look, Sarah, I don't expect you to understand. I hardly understand it myself, but I do know this: I don't want to lose Bryce. I want him in my life, even if it's only as a friend."

"That's just plain avoidance, Jenna. You're using your friendship as a crutch. You know what I think? You should march over to the restaurant first thing tomorrow and lay it all on the line."

"Oh, right, like I can do that."

"See, you are a chicken."

"You should talk. I know your secrets, Sarah McCabe, and it's not like you're winning any prizes for bravery."

Her sister laughed. "Yeah, well, that's because I'm stuck here in Cowville. Now, maybe if I lived in the big city—"

"Oh, and there aren't any phones in Lucan? You couldn't call—"

"Nope. And besides, I called to talk about *your* sex life. You see, I'm living vicariously through you. I've been waiting all night for you to get home. Now spill. I want details."

"Let's talk about something else. How's Dad doing?"

"All right. But the next time I want details. Sheesh, even Emily gives me more than this."

"Yeah, but her stories are made-up." Jenna smiled as she thought of Emily's scandalous sex tales. How Jenna wished it was true for Em, that she had found some gorgeous hunk to bring her out of her shell, but the baby of the McCabe sisters was awkward and shy and possessed nerdy glasses, not to mention a severe lack of fashion sense. No, Emily was nowhere near man-magnet stuff.

"Poor Emily." Sarah sighed. "She needs to get out more and find herself a new job. The library obviously isn't doing anything for her social life. Now, as to Dad, he's doing better. The doctor gave him the all-clear to go back to work. The corn will be planted soon, and Ashton can't manage it all by himself. He's already overworked as it is."

"Dad needs to hire another hand. He's only ever had Ashton. He needs to realize he's getting older, and with his heart . . . well, he just needs to come up with a new plan."

"You try telling Dad that. You know how he is. Stubborn. This farm is his life, Jenna. He'll never give it up."

"But it's not producing, and its losses are eating away at Mom and Dad's life savings—what little they have."

"Ashton's been trying to steer him into new directions, but you know Dad. He won't hear of it."

"Don't tell them, but I had an appointment at the bank. I'm trying to get a second loan on my business so I can help out with the farm."

"That's sweet of you, Jen. I've started a second job, too, hoping to pull in a little cash to help out."

"Not at the Cadillac?"

"It's not that bad, and it's only a couple of shifts a week."

"Sarah, the Caddy is no place for you. My God, you must be getting groped and hit on every time you turn around."

"I can handle myself. Don't worry. And the crowd doesn't get too bad. They've got me working with Tanya, who as we both know is a little free with her lovin'. No one is hitting on me, not when Tanya's a sure bet. Don't worry about me, Jenna. But while we're talking about it, do you think you might hear soon about that loan? Because Ashton was telling me the other day that the loan officer from the bank was here, and he had a bunch of businessmen with him."

"I hope to hear in another week or so. Don't worry, Sarah. I'm not going to let the bank take the farm from Dad. I'll do anything to prevent that."

The buzzer to her apartment went off, scaring Jenna out of her skin.

"Is someone there?" Sarah asked.

"Yeah, the downstairs buzzer just went off. Just a sec."

Jenna carried the phone to the intercom, and pressed the TALK button. "Hello?"

"Hey," came the deep reply. "You didn't get any dessert tonight. Thought I'd bring some by."

"Oh, my God," Sarah squealed into the phone. "It's him."

Jenna released the TALK button and hissed into the phone. "*Shhh*, he'll hear you. Now be quiet, or I'll hang up." She pressed the button again. "It's kind of late, but sure, c'mon up."

"I cannot believe you just reminded him how late it is," Sarah said.

"Yeah, well, some of us have to get up early in the morning for work. And oh, God, I gotta go, Sarah. I'm in my nightgown. I can't let him in looking like this."

"Okay, but I want details tomorrow."

Jenna hung up the phone and made a beeline for her bedroom. She was almost there when she heard the pounding on her door. Too late.

She froze, a number of scenarios running through her mind, all of which involved leaving Bryce standing at her door while she prepared to wow him. Which would take far longer than the thirty seconds she had.

With a groan, she turned around and padded across the hardwood floor of her apartment. With a deep breath, she gathered her control and pulled the heavy chain from the lock, then turned the dead bolt. Opening the door, she cracked it just enough so she could peek around the corner.

She almost had heart failure right there on the spot. Standing before her was Bryce, wearing silver oven mitts holding a casserole dish covered with tin foil. She saw that his hazel eyes looked a touch more green in the light coming from the hall. That devilish dimple of his was out in full force as he smiled down at her.

"Hey," he said, his voice a deep rumble from his chest. "You gonna let me in?"

"I, um," she ran a self-conscious hand through her hair. "I was just heading off to bed. It's kind of late."

"Yeah. I know. Sorry about that." The green in his eyes seemed to fade. "I won't keep you. Let me just drop this off and I'll be out of your hair. It's getting too hot to hold."

Her gaze dropped to his hands and she noticed how he kept redistributing the weight of the casserole dish. He was likely getting scalded.

Every sane thought flew out of her head in that instant. The door was flung wide, and she was ushering him into her apartment, not thinking of how she was dressed.

He noticed the candles lit on her coffee table, and she redirected his attention to the galley kitchen ahead of him.

"Was I interrupting something?" he asked, his voice suddenly taking on a strange tone.

"No, why?"

"The candles? The fact that there are two glasses sitting on your coffee table."

"I often light candles, and what would two glasses signify?" she asked, slapping a hot pad onto the countertop.

"Oh, I don't know," he growled. "Maybe the fact that you were having a drink with a guest. Is that why you ditched me tonight, because you had another date?"

"Another date?" she asked, her eyeballs nearly popping out of her head.

His face seemed to grow a bit pale as he looked around. "Is he still here? Is that what you meant when you said you were going to bed?"

Jenna couldn't breathe. Was Bryce questioning her about her private life? She didn't know whether to be elated or ticked off at his gall. Where did he get off asking her such questions? The man who catted around with a different woman every night of the week.

"Is that why you're wearing *that*?"

Now it was Jenna's turn to go pasty. Oh, Lord, she'd forgotten what she was wearing. Suddenly, she wanted to cover her body with her arms, with anything, even the little white tea towel hanging from the handle of the oven would suffice.

"Where is he? Waiting for you in bed?"

The accusatory look in Bryce's eyes suddenly made her irrational. Oh, so it was perfectly normal, acceptable even, for him to get laid every night by a different woman, but she wasn't even allowed a date, let alone a sleepover.

That did it. Jenna plunged in. "There is no one here, if you must know. Not that it's any of your business, Bryce," she sneered, "but I frequently wear this sort of thing to bed. I like nice lingerie. Now, I think you better go, before we both say something we're going to regret later."

He reached for her arm, stopping her. "I'm sorry, Jenna. I had no right to question—"

"You're damn right you had no right to question me about my personal life. I don't pry into yours, so stay out of mine."

"Sorry," he whispered, rubbing his hand down her arm. "I'm just . . . I don't know what's wrong with me tonight."

"I don't know either," she snapped.

"Jenna," he said, turning her around to face him. "I just wanted to bring you something for your birthday. To let you know I was thinking of you."

"You completely forgot it was my birthday."

"No, I didn't."

"Yeah, you did. But I forgive you. You've had a lot on your mind."

"I don't want to fight, Jenna."

"Me neither."

His gaze drifted over her shoulder, toward the TV. "What were you watching?"

"Nothing much. There's a Brat Pack marathon. *The Breakfast Club* just finished, and I think *Pretty in Pink* is playing next."

"You loved *Pretty in Pink*," he said, smiling down at her. "I should know. We watched it together about a dozen times."

She'd told him she was in love with Blane, but really, she just liked to pretend that Bryce was Blane, and she was Molly Ringwald's character, Andie, and that kiss at the prom . . . that that would someday happen to her and Bryce.

"What do you say we have some dessert and watch the movie? For old times' sake," he added.

She noticed he hadn't taken his hand from her arm, and now his fingers were running along her skin in slow, lazy circles. "Okay," she said in a breathless rush. "Let me get the plates."

"I'll find the plates. You go and relax and get ready to be bowled over. I've outdone myself with this dessert."

"Okay," she said, smiling, liking the way her body had grown all soft and tingly. "I'll get a blanket and some drinks. I'll meet you at the couch."

As she walked away, she knew Bryce was watching her. She tried to remain confident, tried to think that maybe he actually liked the way she looked in the pink satin chemise. But she just wasn't sure. And it wasn't like she could look over her shoulder and see whether he looked turned on—or disgusted.

She also knew she shouldn't be sitting on the couch, entertaining

Bryce, wearing something like this. She should pull on her fleece pj bottoms, the ones with the moon and stars on them, and the baggiest sweatshirt she could find. But the inner vixen in her quickly nixed that train of thought.

She could do this. She would sit there in her chemise and try to believe that she looked sexy enough to turn Bryce on. Not that she would take it any further tonight, because that wasn't part of the plan. She couldn't just fall into Bryce's lap. She needed to show him that she wasn't the sort of woman he could beckon with just a flash of his dimple.

It wouldn't be easy, but she would have to ignore Bryce and how damn good he looked in his white T-shirt and snug-fitting jeans. She'd also have to ignore the wetness that had suddenly erupted between her thighs.

Bryce couldn't think. Hell, he couldn't breathe. Watching Jenna saunter away in that pretty little chemise was playing havoc with his synapses. He didn't even blink as he watched her walk away. The ecru-colored lace skimming just beneath the luscious curve of her cheeks commanded his attention, not to mention fueled his imagination.

She had the finest ass he'd ever seen. Full and round, begging to be cupped by his hand.

Shit! What was he thinking, cupping her ass? This was Jenna. Safe little Jenna. The friend he hadn't had any sexual thoughts about. Well, not since . . . Okay. He finally allowed the dirty truth to come up. There had been a few times when he'd awaken from a vivid dream, his sheets tangled and wet, his brain burning with images of him and Jenna.

But he'd always laughed it off. Always thought it absurd. He used to tell himself that the dreams were about Jenna because she was the only woman he really knew well. They were friends, had spent a lot of time together. Naturally she'd invade his dreams.

Pressing forward, he leaned over the counter and watched Jenna. Her profile was just as stunning as the back view. Her breasts were just as hot as her ass, and the way they bounced and moved as she reached for the blanket that lay across the back of the sofa had him groaning.

Man, he was hard. And completely fucking losing it.

Jenna was a friend. He wanted that friendship. Depended on it. No way was he going to toss a decade of friendship down the toilet because his subconscious all of a sudden decided to cough up a few instances of past wet dreams involving Jenna.

He couldn't imagine his life without Jenna in it. She had always been there, to talk to and hang with. He liked just calling her up for no reason and chatting. He liked how they laughed at the same things. If he couldn't have that anymore, if he ruined the relationship by making it all awkward and heavy with sexual shit, he didn't know what he'd do.

But what about when she finds Mr. Right, the insistent voice in his head asked. *How much do you think he's going to tolerate your phone calls and late-night visits?* Probably about as well as he tolerated the thought of Jenna wearing that skimpy nightie for another man—including Tyson.

God, he didn't even want to go there. His emotions and thoughts were all over the map tonight and he couldn't understand why. What was it about Jenna today? What was it about her walk, the way her ass moved, that had him wanting to risk their friendship by taking it into the bedroom? And what was it about her that suddenly had him thinking how damn nice it would be to always have this, this closeness with her?

The relationship word suddenly crept onto his radar and he panicked. Then, thank God, Jenna's voice squelched the thought before it could become a full-blown visual of a picket fence.

"Movie's starting," she called from the living room.

"I'm on it," he answered back, not moving, just watching as she sat on the couch and crossed her legs. They weren't overly long, but man, they were shapely. The kind that would feel really good and soft wrapped around him. The kind of shapely, womanly flesh he hadn't felt in all his other girlfriends.

He heard the Psychedelic Furs singing "Pretty in Pink," and he got his ass moving. Looking through the cupboards, he found two bowls and a couple of spoons, and tore into the still-steaming dessert.

Inhaling the aroma, he savored it, hoping to hell she liked it. This was an untested concoction he'd just created. And poor Jenna was the guinea pig.

Carrying the bowls, he hit the switch with his elbow, killing the light spilling from the kitchen. Candles glowed on the coffee table, and the light from the television screen made it bright enough for them to see.

"Mmm, what's this?" Jenna asked as she reached out for a bowl. "Smells delicious."

"Just something I cooked up in honor of your twenty-eighth birthday."

Jenna wrinkled her nose. "Let's not talk numbers tonight."

"Deal," he said, settling back against the leather sofa. "As long as that also includes my numbers and that plan of yours."

"Absolutely."

"God, it's been forever since I've seen this movie. Remember how you loved Blane?"

"Yeah," she said, blushing.

"I never got that, why you found him so hot. His hair really looked terrible in that prom scene."

Jenna laughed. "You always say that."

"Well, it did."

"I'm sure you had the hots for Molly Ringwald. All the guys did."

"I didn't."

"Oh, the blonde then, the one dancing around in her underwear?"

"Definitely not her. I liked Andie, actually. Not Molly. But the character of Andie."

Jenna shot him a sideways glance. "She was an outcast and kind of quirky, don't you think?"

"What's wrong with quirky?"

"Nothing." A strange expression flickered across her face before she picked up her spoon and motioned to the bowl. "So, what do we have here?"

"Oh, just a little white chocolate and cream, and caramel-filled chocolate squares, with some egg bread I had lying around. I suppose you'd call it chocolate-caramel bread pudding."

"I love bread pudding. I haven't had a pudding like this since I left home. Although I know my mom never made anything this decadent."

Bryce found himself grinning, filled with an absurd adolescent feeling of giddiness. He was always like this when someone waxed on about his cooking. He was even more giddy, he realized, when that someone was Jenna.

Jenna's mom was a phenomenal cook, and Bryce knew that to wow Jenna was a difficult task. She was clearly wowed now, though. She was closing her eyes, savoring the sweet smell wafting up from the bowl.

She dug into the custard mixture with her spoon and was about to raise it to her mouth when he wrapped his fingers around her wrist. "Wait." She looked at him, and all of a sudden his heart did this weird flopping thing.

"What?" she asked, her voice so soft and quiet and so very feminine.

"I . . ." He licked his lips and pressed closer to her. "I just wanted to say happy birthday." He bent to kiss her cheek, something he'd done numerous times in their friendship. But he couldn't bring himself to do it. Instead, he cupped her cheek and brought her forward, dragging his mouth against the curve of her ear and down lower to her jaw. God, she smelled good. And she felt good, so soft against his hand and mouth.

"Happy birthday," he said once more, kissing the corner of her mouth; then he pulled away, horrified by his actions and wondering what she was going to say.

But true to Jenna form, she saved his ego by not making a big deal out of his lost control. Instead she smiled and pointed at the bowl with the tip of her spoon. "So what do you call this?"

"It needs a name. If it's any good, that is."

She smiled and raised a spoonful to her lips. Catching his gaze, she slid a bit of the steaming pudding into her mouth. With a groan, she closed her eyes. "Good? Bryce, this is awesome. This is..." She blushed and looked away.

He put his bowl down on the coffee table and cupped her cheek. "Tell me what you were gonna say."

She wouldn't meet his gaze. Bryce saw some struggle waged in her eyes before she lifted her lashes and looked fully at him.

"This is so good, it could be sex on a plate."

His heart went into overdrive. Pressing closer, Bryce watched her take another bite. "Yeah?" he asked, his voice curiously hoarse.

"Yeah," she replied in a rush of breath.

Her breasts pushed against the pink satin, her nipples pressing against the bodice. He watched as a lace strap slid down her shoulder. He reached out, hooking his finger beneath it, knowing he should slide it back onto her shoulder, but wanting to lower it, wanting to expose her breast—*needing* to feel all that soft flesh in his hand.

Her breath seemed to hitch, and so did his. What was he doing? Hell, what was she thinking, looking up at him like that?

"Do you want a bite?" she asked, her voice a little shy and tremulous.

He swallowed—hard. His fingers were still beneath the strap of her chemise, still frozen, immobilized against her soft skin. They started to move then, to brush the soft downy skin of her upper arm. His body heated as he felt the first flush of her goose bumps erupt beneath his fingertips.

"I want to watch you eat," he said, feeling his erection harden even more.

She took another bite, which was laden with chocolate and caramel. He watched, his mouth dry as she spooned the delicacy into her mouth and closed her eyes in blissful surrender.

What would it be like to experience that sweetness as it coated her lips, her tongue? What would it be like to feed her and have her feed him, to taste that warm liquid chocolate as it dribbled its way over her breasts and belly?

Like a voyeur, he watched her eat, conscious of the way his body hardened and his lips parted as if he were eating each and every bite with her.

He wanted her spread on the table like a meal for him to devour at his leisure. He saw himself seated, Jenna spread atop the table, his tongue licking away the sweet rivers of chocolate as she moaned and begged him to *eat* other, more pleasurable parts of her body.

Her gaze locked with his, and she held out the silver spoon, which was overflowing with custard and chocolate. Unblinkingly, he sat forward and wrapped his fingers around her wrist. He put the dessert into his mouth, and didn't taste the rich chocolate or the sweet caramel—the only taste he had was that of desire. The sweet, heady elixir was swimming in his mouth.

"Well?" she asked.

This time, he heard the breathless pant of desire in her voice, saw the flicker of awakening in her eyes. He swallowed slowly, then holding her gaze, he brought his mouth to hers until his lips brushed her lower one.

"Taste me, Jenna."

Four

Slowly her tongue crept out, snaking along his lips, before darting away again. Bryce decided he couldn't wait after that. So he reached for her and kissed her: a warm openmouthed kiss, sinking his tongue inside, swirling it around, covering her with a kaleidoscope of flavors.

"Tell me what you taste."

"Creamy caramel and sweet bread. Rich chocolate. Man," she purred as his tongue swept across her lower lip. "Sin," she breathed raggedly as he lowered the strap of her chemise to reveal the crest of her breast.

"Bryce, isn't this...I mean, this is forbidden, right? Between friends?"

"Forbidden fruit is the best kind. And, Jenna, you're proving to be the most luscious fruit I've ever run across in my life."

Gently he tugged the bodice down over her breast. He cupped her in his palm, lifting her breast up to the candlelight, studying the golden glow of her skin in the light, the way the nipple darkened and budded even tighter for him. Lowering his head, he brushed his lips against the pebbled nipple.

Succulent. Luscious. There weren't enough words to describe how enticing Jenna was to his eyes.

"What do you taste, Bryce?" The shyness in her voice made him look up. She was shrinking away from him and his touch. But mixed with the shyness was desire.

She wanted this. Wanted it every bit as much as he did. He just needed to bring her back, bring her to that place where she wasn't afraid of what she was feeling.

"What do I taste?" he asked, taking the bowl from her. "I'm not sure. Let me try another bite."

Placing the bowl on the table alongside his, he put his finger in the pudding and brought it to her breast, covering her nipple with it. Then he cupped her and lowered his mouth to the chocolate-covered nipple that was making him salivate.

"Bryce?" she asked, as he hesitated above her.

"Just savoring, babe. Just taking it all in like a connoisseur should."

She relaxed against him. Finally he gave in and licked her nipple, taking the chocolate off in one thorough swoop of his tongue.

She gasped and arched beneath him, brushing her lower body against his. He pushed back, making her feel his cock. Her little moan, and the way her body seemed designed to cradle him, excited him. Damn, she was made right. Made perfectly for the kind of sex he wanted.

*   *   *

Bryce reached for the hem of her chemise and Jenna felt her body melt. She should really not be doing this. Knew that there would be embarrassing regrets tomorrow morning, not to mention the destruction of her plan.

How was she supposed to tell her body to shut down, to stop feeling the delicate touch of Bryce's hands, to stop wanting to be filled with the massive cock he kept brushing against the apex of her thighs? She was soaked. Her arousal had seeped onto the fly of Bryce's jeans. He knew how wet she was. He no doubt felt it—that was why he was pressing against her more insistently.

She could lie, could tell herself all sorts of things about why she shouldn't be doing this. But one thing she couldn't do was make her body reject Bryce. Her body wanted his so much, so badly, that her hips started slowly undulating, rising up to meet his denim-covered groin as they began to grind into each other.

"You're so hot, baby," Bryce said to her as she felt the lace hem slide up over her thighs. That voice, and those sexy words, made her drenched in one flush. And he knew, because he slowly circled her with the tip of his erection, soaking up her wetness with the front of his jeans.

"How hot do you want to get, Jenna?"

She couldn't answer. She just gulped as she felt his hands brush the undersides of her breasts as the chemise rode up over her chest.

"How hot in here do you want it to be?"

On a scale of one to ten? Try a hundred. But she was robbed of speech when the chemise was pulled over her head and she was lying beneath Bryce, wearing nothing but pink lace panties.

He eased away from her and straddled her hips with his thighs. Jenna held out her arms, wanting him back against her. But he shook his head while he trailed his hands along her body, feeling every curve and indentation. Every imperfection that Jenna had hoped to hide.

"How hot, Jenna?"

"Hot," she finally answered. "As hot as you can make me."

His hand snaked into the waistband of her panties. He brushed his fingers down the middle of her, parting her. She nodded, letting her thighs fall apart, giving him more access. His fingers worked magic on her. She was wet and slick and ready for him.

Never had she gotten this wet, this fast. But then, never had she been with someone like Bryce. Someone she loved.

Bryce was leaning over her, covering her nose and lips with tiny kisses as he worked his hand between her folds, while the impressive size of his erection continued to press into her belly through his jeans. If she wasn't paralyzed with passion, she would have reached out and touched him, but she couldn't move.

"Damn, Jenna, you feel good beneath me."

She writhed as he put another finger inside her and slowed his rhythm. She protested and bucked up against him, telling him without words that she wanted more of him, wanted his touch harder, deeper.

"I can make you hotter," he said darkly. "I want you scalding, Jenna. I want you combustible."

Oh, she was close to combusting. Another stroke or two and she'd be there. But he suddenly cooled, depriving her of the flames.

"What?" she asked, but he caught her mouth and kissed her.

She could hardly believe it, not after ten years, but they were finally making out on her couch. And Holy Mother of God, Bryce Ryder could kiss!

He was slow and lazy with his kisses, but masterful. His tongue and fingers were thrusting forward and back, in and out, mimicking sex, winding her up so tight until she was rubbing her pussy against his hand while clutching his hair. More . . . she had to have more.

Finally he tore his mouth from hers and pulled his T-shirt over his head. He didn't give her a chance to look at him, but moved downward, nipping at her breast and belly. He had her panties pulled off and thrown aside in a flash, leaving Jenna exposed.

"You like this, Jenna?" he asked as he nuzzled her inner thigh. "You like a man's mouth on you?"

"I . . . I . . ." She couldn't talk, just kept panting in anticipation. "I don't know."

He made a strange choking sound, before she felt the warmth of his tongue trailing up her leg. "I promise you, Jenna," he said, looking up from the vee of her body, "you're gonna love *my* mouth on you."

And then he parted her wide and set his mouth to her, tasting her, drawing his tongue down and up before pulling her clitoris between his lips.

She was burning with every lash of his tongue, combusting with the sight of Bryce's beautiful dark head between her thighs, his shoulders glistening in the glow of the candles, the strong muscles rolling over his back and shoulders as his mouth moved teasingly along her pussy.

Before she knew what was happening she was shaking and crying out, and most definitely having a meltdown of biblical proportions. And the whole time, Bryce watched her as his mouth kept working on her, adding to the intimacy and the incredible pleasure of her orgasm.

As the world splintered, and her every thought began to shatter, Jenna realized that this was a birthday dream come true. She only hoped that when she awoke, Bryce would really be there, and not her proud and sturdy vibrator.

Sliding up her body with his sweat-slicked chest, Bryce reached for her hand. "Sit up, baby. I want to see you."

He sat back against the plush cushions and immediately unzipped the fly of his faded jeans. No briefs or boxers, for Bryce—just commando. Jenna nearly died right there. How would she ever forget that first glimpse of Bryce?

He was thick and long, the head of his penis glistening with precum. She licked her lips, suddenly wanting to taste him, but he reached for her, surprising her with his strength and swiftness. She was not a willowy little thing, and yet she found herself astride him with an ease that baffled her.

"That's it, Jenna." He cupped her breasts and brushed his thumbs along her sensitive nipples. "Sit right down in front of me and let me see all of you."

Instinctively she moved against him as she grabbed on to his muscled biceps. Her thumb brushed over the tribal tattoo that curled around his arm and he moaned as she stroked him. His gaze suddenly left her face and fixed on her hand. He watched the way she brushed her fingers along the muscle and black ink. When his gaze finally landed back on her face, his eyes were dark with passion.

"Your hand looks so good on me. And fuck, it feels so good to be touched like that."

Her legs went weak and suddenly her mound was rubbing on his cock. He hissed, gritting his teeth before reaching for her bottom with one hand. With a firm grip, he pushed her down so her sex was rubbing him more intimately.

While she found her rhythm, Bryce nuzzled the cleft of her breasts.

"That's it, Jenna. Now put me inside you," he commanded. "I want to watch you riding my cock."

He threw his head back and watched her through the veil of his dark lashes. He was breathing hard, and his chiseled six-pack quivered with his every breath. She saw the sheen of perspiration coating his skin, saw a trickle of sweat run between his pecs. God, he was beautiful like this.

"C'mon, Jenna," he pleaded as he ran his big palms up her thighs to her hips, where he held her tightly. "Sit down on me and let me fill you up. I can make this so good for you. Show me how hot you are for me."

This was really happening! She was having hot, spontaneous sex with the man of her dreams—and on her birthday, too.

"Condom?"

Their gazes collided and the world skidded to a startlingly grinding halt for Bryce.

Condom?

Shit, he hadn't brought condoms. Why the hell did she think he would? He was coming to visit her, not out whoring at a club. A realization that in itself really should have sent him running.

But the thought of being denied this moment with Jenna nearly killed him. There was nothing in the world he wanted right now more than to be inside Jenna's body, watching her ride him to completion. She was going to look so sexy riding his cock, her big breasts bouncing. And he was going to watch her, every second of her body grinding on his.

"Bryce?" she asked, pulling away from him.

He couldn't have that. She wasn't leaving him, not before he got inside her.

"I don't have one, Jen. I...I didn't plan for...that's not to say..."

"I know what you mean. Maybe we should cool things down."

She tried to get off his lap, but he held her there, his fingers digging into her thighs.

"Don't move."

Shifting his hips, he reached into his back pocket for his wallet. Jesus, he hoped he had one in there. He found a foil square behind his credit cards and pulled it free, showing it to her, wondering what she thought. Her gaze dropped down to his hand.

"No backing out now, Jenna."

And he meant it. It was more than just a touch of fate that had him carrying around that condom. Tossing aside his wallet, he opened the packet, slid the condom on his aching erection and reached for her.

"I want this more than anything else in the world. Tell me you want this, Jenna. Tell me you want *me*."

"I want you, Bryce," she said on a gasp as she slid down onto his cock. She was tight. And warm. And . . . *perfect*.

She felt so right, like she'd been made to fit him. Better than any other woman had ever felt to him.

"Look at me, Jenna," he whispered as he cupped her face, tilting it up to his. When her gaze was on him, he couldn't help but take his thumbs and caress her flushed cheeks. She certainly didn't look average now. She looked like a sex kitten, and he was eating her up. He wondered how he had never been struck stupid by her beautiful eyes or her full lips. He wondered how he could have missed this lush, beautiful body that made love to him like the most skilled concubine.

Maybe he had noticed, but refused to see it. Because . . . He didn't want to think of "because." He only wanted to think of making sweet love to Jenna.

As she followed his lead, she moved on him, her breasts bouncing, her hair swinging. For long minutes he sat back and just watched her, marveling at her body and its sensuous, undulating moves.

Damn, she looked perfect on him, fucking him slowly.

But then he got restless. He wanted to go deeper. So he grabbed her hips and thrust forward, filling her, making her cry out.

That cry was the sweetest sound he ever heard. She was begging for him, pleading like no woman ever had. And he wanted her to have him—all of him.

Parting her sex, he stroked her clitoris with the tip of his forefinger. She moaned and twisted, but he held her in place with one hand on her hip as he penetrated her deep and slow. Over and over he stroked her clit, finding the rhythm she liked, and soon she was riding him hard and wanton, just as he hoped she would.

When she took her breasts in her hands and started working them, Bryce nearly came undone. The sex kitten was a tigress, and he was growing addicted.

It should have been a dangerous admission, but he was too enthralled with the sight of Jenna, with her hands full of her perfect breasts, to realize it.

With two more deep hard stabs, his release was upon him. He didn't bother to pull out of her warm body like he did with all the other women he'd been with. Even with a condom he hadn't wanted to risk getting them pregnant. But with Jenna he couldn't bear it, couldn't stand to think of being separated from her during his climax. As he felt cum shoot up his shaft, he clutched the back of Jenna's head and brought her mouth down to his as he spilled inside the condom while he was sheathed in her tight pussy.

"Oh my God, Bryce. That was hot."

"Hot?" he drawled, circling her ear with his tongue. "Sweetheart, I'm just getting warmed up."

Five

Strategic retreat. That was what was needed now.

Holy shit! She'd actually done it. Had sex with Bryce. Twice! The memories were enough to make her thighs clench and her clitoris tingle.

Never had sex been so damn good. Although she shouldn't be surprised. This was Bryce, after all, and clearly, he was a very gifted man. A man who knew his way around a woman's body just as well as his gourmet kitchen. And what he had cooked up inside her was better than the most decadent chocolate dessert Jenna had ever had.

Through the early-morning light streaming through her window, Jenna once more turned her head on the pillow to watch Bryce sleeping. She blinked. Then blinked again, half wondering if this was just a wild dream, and when she opened her eyes once more, he'd be gone.

Her lashes flickered, and she raised her lids. He was still there, one arm thrown above his head, the other lying across his naked torso. The sheets were all tangled, wrapped around his lean waist and long, well-muscled thighs.

She watched him for a long time, studying the gentle rise and fall of his chest, listening to the soft breath whisper past his slightly parted lips. His longish dark hair was rumpled, falling down across his brow and over his eye. His chin was sprinkled with dark scruff, which Jenna found very sexy.

All in all, Bryce Ryder wasn't hard to wake up to. But Jenna knew that was all going to change when the day began. Morning afters were never her strong suit. Not that she had had many of them. But the ones she'd experienced had been awkward murmurings followed by her stealing the sheet from the bed to hide her nudity as she ran to the shower. This morning, she realized, was going to be the same. Only this morning she wasn't waking up beside one of her past boyfriends, who had only barely satisfied her. This morning it was Bryce, her best friend. The friend who had made her explode like a firecracker. And damn it, she didn't know how the hell she was going to look him in the face, much less what she was going to say to him.

It wasn't like she was an expert at casual sex. Maybe if she were, she wouldn't be stressing right now, trying to think of something sultry yet blasé to say to him when he woke up. Somehow, everything sounded too needy, too desperate. Bryce would be on edge this morning, terrified she was going to think that there was something between them—something permanent. And while she wanted that, she knew Bryce wasn't yet there. So she decided that honesty was not the best policy this morning. "I love you and want to have your babies," was definitely going to send him packing.

With a sigh, Jenna glanced at the clock, and saw she had only ten minutes before the alarm was set to go off. Being the coward she was, she slid the alarm button off and slowly inched her way to the edge of the mattress.

Waking up to see regret shining in Bryce's beautiful hazel eyes was something she didn't care to stick around for. Last night was gone. Now it was morning. A new day. And God only knew what the day was going to entail. Probably some nasty high drama between them, followed by her crying in her office at work, too ashamed to show her face. Or worse, maybe Bryce would act like nothing happened. Maybe he'd use that infuriating nonchalance he had mastered over the years to make it seem like it was no biggie, that last night's bone-melting sex had been nothing more than a meaningless fuck. And that would kill her.

She'd made love to Bryce, and his encouragement and praise as she had done so had given her a sexual self-confidence her other lovers never had. So for Bryce to brush off what had happened between them would be a death blow to the memory she was clutching tight to her chest.

Jenna glanced at Bryce once more as she slowly stood up, avoiding the squeaky part of the mattress. Yeah. It was going to be more than awkward this morning, coming face-to-face for the first time after she'd screamed his name and scratched her nails down his back.

Stupid. Stupid. Stupid. She should never have gone through with it. Should never have compromised her friendship, or her plan, like this. But what was done was done. She couldn't take it back, didn't want to take it back.

Jenna took in the rumpled bed sheets and the thick down duvet that Bryce had thrown onto the floor as he had crawled on the bed before covering her with his hard naked body. She remembered what they'd done when they had fallen into bed, and how damn sexy Bryce had looked, looming over her, thrusting into her slow and hard.

Look at me, baby, I want to see your face as I fill you with my cock. I want to see how much you want it.

Jenna shivered, a whole body tremble, as she recalled the velvety darkness of his voice, the way the dirty words skimmed along her flesh and heated her blood. Oh yeah, she'd liked how wicked his dirty talk made her feel, how much it turned her on.

He'd taken his time, learning what she liked, what made her hips rise to meet his and her head toss back on a moan. He touched her, not only with his cock, but his hands, his mouth, covering every inch of her body, leaving no patch of skin untouched, unkissed. He'd waited until she was trembling and begging before giving her another mind-shattering orgasm.

In that moment, as she'd cried out and clutched him, she could have sworn that Bryce had made love to her. That it hadn't been just an empty physical act. The look in his eyes as he watched her come was like nothing she'd ever seen before. Then it simply vanished, and he looked away and rolled off her. But he hadn't left the bed, leaving her wondering what had happened. He'd simply gathered her up in his arms and tucked her head beneath his chin.

He'd yawned, a fake one, and pretended to go to sleep. That was when the worries about the morning had begun to take shape in her mind. She began to fear that maybe the sex on the couch and the magic in the bed had been pure insanity and pent-up lust on Jenna's side and mere physical need on Bryce's.

And that was why, this morning, Jenna couldn't face Bryce. Her feelings were out of control, and completely controlled was what she needed to be. So, chickenshit or not, she crept quietly out of the room after gathering up her clothes for the day, and headed for the shower.

The morning after wasn't going to happen this time. She could be dressed and out of here in half an hour. Lots of time before Bryce and his regrets woke up.

"Answer the fucking phone." Bryce growled.

On the fifth ring, voice mail clicked on. "This is Jenna McCabe of Global Marketing. Please leave a message and I'll get back to you as soon as I can."

Bryce cleared his throat as he waited for the long beep. This was the third fucking message he'd left. Christ, he was looking desperate. But what the fuck? Why wouldn't she pick up? She *always* took his calls.

The beep sounded and he cleared his throat once more, trying for charming, not desperate. "Hi. Me again. Just...ah...well, just checking to see if...ah...yeah..." He kind of laughed, to hide a groan. He sounded like a moron. "So, now that I've put out, are you dissing me?" he asked, trying to sound playful.

"I made breakfast. I can swing by the office and maybe we can eat it together. I don't want to waste your groceries or anything. Give me a call."

He hung up and threw his cell phone onto Jenna's couch. Well, wasn't that smooth? Fucking brilliant. He sounded like an adolescent after his first lay, but hell, he had no experience with this. He never made the "after sex" calls. Those were placed by his lovers, cajoling and whining and bribing him to return their calls. And he'd mostly ignored them. But Jenna? What the hell did she think, he was going to walk out on her before she woke up? Maybe she did, and she wanted to beat him to it.

Maybe, the evil voice in his head whispered, *she does this with all the guys she's been with. Or worse, maybe she's really not that into you. Maybe you were just a body to get it on with.*

The sizzling from the nearby griddle drew his attention, and mercifully pulled him out of his black thoughts. Picking up the spatula, he started flipping the pancakes he'd made, trying not to think about how much of an idiot he'd been. Had he actually believed she was just in the shower?

Of course he had, because he never could have believed that Jenna was a screw-and-cruise kind of girl. So naturally he thought Jenna had been in the shower, taking a few extra minutes in the hot water to work out those stiff muscles she likely had after their hot and sweaty sex last night. So, while she was showering and getting ready for work, and because he didn't have an appointment till ten that morning, he'd decided to go to the kitchen and surprise her with a birthday breakfast. As he worked, he kept an eye on the closed bathroom door, waiting for it to fly open, catching a quick flash of Jenna, all flushed and wet, wrapped in a thick white towel.

Twenty minutes later, he'd found himself standing in the middle of the bathroom realizing she'd left him alone in the apartment without so much as a note in lipstick on the bathroom mirror.

He'd been stunned and oddly hurt.

The pancakes were finished, and he piled them high on a plate before slipping them into the warm oven. Reaching for the bowl, he scooped more batter onto the griddle while trying to think about anything other than Jenna. No such luck. He couldn't stop thinking about her, or how damn good they'd been together. Two full-blown orgasms and he still wanted more.

Spending the night in bed with her had been a slice of heaven he never knew existed. He'd slept like the proverbial baby, and that was saying something, because since the fiasco with *Celebrity Gossip* he hadn't slept for more than two hours at a time. Mostly, he spent the nights pacing the floors of his condo, worrying about how he was going to dig himself out of the shit pile. But last night. Man, last night had been so great. Cathartic. And when he awoke that morning, he'd reached for her, hoping to feel more of her gorgeous ass filling his hand, waking her up as he made slow love to her as the sun crept up above the clouds. But instead of soft flesh, his hand had come into contact with nothing but the cool white sheet.

Now here he was, making breakfast and wondering what the hell he'd done. Maybe she hadn't enjoyed herself quite as much as he thought—hoped—she had. Maybe she was afraid. Mornings after could be such a bitch, and granted, this one was going to be a touch awkward, but nothing they couldn't have handled.

Maybe she just doesn't want to be bothered with you.

And wasn't that a bit of rotten karma. Because this was the way he'd pretty much treated all the women in his life. At least *he* usually said goodbye.

Cleaning up, he soaked the bowls and silverware in hot soapy water, all the while trying to grapple with his current predicament. Did he truly believe that Jenna was that casual about who she took to bed?

She did have a box of condoms in her bedside table drawer, he reminded himself. He'd been surprised, but pleased, too, especially because he'd wanted to get inside her again, and that box of condoms had given him full license to make love to her on the bed. Maybe that was evidence enough that she made a habit of taking guys to bed.

He'd always assumed she had a lover or two, but in truth, he hadn't ever allowed his thoughts to travel down that murky path. Whenever he thought of Jenna getting it on with other guys he'd stop, reminding himself that she was a friend, and that she wasn't his type.

In reality, he didn't really know what type she was. Was she the clingy sort who thought one night of sex was a declaration of commitment, or was she a love 'em and leave 'em type?

Two days ago Bryce would have laughed off that thought about Jenna. No way would he have said sweet little country girl Jenna would take sex as casually as he did. But this morning, being one of the loved and lefts, he was starting to wonder—and worry.

And the worrying part was scaring the hell out of him. Why should he worry? He should be counting his lucky stars and getting the hell out of her apartment before she returned. With another woman, he would have said a prayer of thanks to the big guy upstairs and closed the door behind himself without another thought. But not with Jenna. He couldn't bring himself to be so cavalier.

This morning he was feeling something he'd never felt before with all the other women he'd been with. The feeling was nearly indescribable. It had no name. It was just an ache. A yearning. A longing for more . . . and that more was not just sex, although he most definitely wanted more sex with Jenna. It was something else. Something he had never ached for before.

A future that consisted of more than just mindless sex with a different woman each night.

Knowing what he had to do, he left the dishes in the sink. He still had two hours before he needed to meet with the investors about the two new restaurants he was planning to open. That was plenty of time to get a change of clothes, stop off at the restaurant and check in on things, then head over to the office where Jenna worked.

Whether she liked it or not, Jenna McCabe was having company for breakfast. She'd just have to deal with the reality of their morning after. The reality that she wasn't getting rid of him that quick or that easy.

Six

"**M**iss McCabe?"

"Just a sec," Jenna said to her sister as another light rap on her office door interrupted her yet again. "Yes, Jessica?" she called impatiently. "I'm on the phone."

"I know. I'm sorry to disturb you, but your visitor, well, he's most determined. He says he's not leaving."

"Hold on, Sarah," Jenna said in exasperation, then rested the receiver on her desk before crossing the short distance to the door. When she opened it, her young and inexperienced secretary was grimacing.

"He told me to tell you that he has no plans for the day and that he'll sit here all . . . umm . . ." Jessica glanced over her shoulder to the reception area, which was hidden by frosted glass.

"Sit here all what?"

Jessica swallowed hard. "He said, 'Tell her to get her ass out here, or I'll sit here all fucking day and be a general pain in everyone's ass.'" Jess leaned in. "Should I call security?"

"Want me to deal with him?" Rachel Warner asked as she came

out of the copy room. "I had a peek, and *whew*," she said, fanning herself, "I could do with someone like him after that loser I took home from the bar last night."

The last person Jenna wanted "dealing" with Bryce was the man-eating Rachel. Gorgeous and tall, and built like a supermodel, Rachel was everything Bryce liked in his women, and if Rachel wasn't such a shark with advertising, Jenna would have fired her on the spot for looking yet again in the direction of the reception area.

"Look, tell him I'm in a meeting. A conference call," Jenna clarified.

Both Jess and Rachel looked at her as if she were insane. "He has something for you," Jess began, "and it smells reeeally good."

Jenna strove for composure and tried to shake off the feeling she was acting like a stupid adolescent. Now was not the time for this. Her morning had already gone down the crapper. First the irate phone call from her new client in Milan, then Bryce's messages on her cell. Messages that she just didn't know how the hell to deal with.

"Look, I'll send Mr. Lover out the door, and Jess will make sure you look nice and busy, okay, honey?" Rachel asked.

Jenna gritted her teeth at the teasing she heard from Rachel. "Fine," she muttered before swinging around on her heel and slamming her office door shut. Exhaling a big breath, she flopped down into her chair and picked up the phone. Sarah was laughing on the other end of the line.

"Oh, my God, you are in so deep, Jen. I can't believe you."

"Okay, if all you're going to do is laugh at me, then I'm hanging up. I've already had a shit day, and we're only two hours into it."

Sarah sobered. "Sorry, sis. I just couldn't help it. This is so unlike you. I mean, you're lying to Bryce."

"I'm engineering a reprieve, that's all. It's not lying. I *am* on the phone, with you."

"Jenna—"

"I just need some time, okay," she snapped, pressing her eyes shut. Where the hell was her Advil? Shit, by the time five o'clock rolled around, she was going to go through half the bottle. She could tell. It was going to be one of *those* days.

"Why are you so scared, Jenna?" Sarah asked.

"Why do you think, Sarah? Because I screwed up, that's why. I mean, I slept with Bryce, for crying out loud. The first time, on the couch, I suppose we could write off as a moment of madness, but the second time? Sarah, we knew what we were doing. And I just can't . . . I can't figure out what to do."

"Try letting him into your office for starters," Sarah said sarcastically. "He's there, isn't he? It's not like he's blowing you off."

"Really? And how do you know that? I'm sure Bryce has no problem telling women right to their faces not to get any ideas about their future just because they've slept together. The man has balls of steel."

"What if he's not blowing you off?"

"I'm sure he is, but even if he's not, even if he wants to continue this . . . this sex thing, it won't last, Sarah. And man, that's got me panicking, you know? I'm scared, because my heart's engaged. I don't want to lose him. I'd rather have him as a friend than nothing at all. Sex with him is only going to pull me in deeper, and when he cuts bait and runs, I'm going to be left totally annihilated."

Sarah sighed. "I have a feeling that Bryce cares for you, and as more than just friends. After last night, I'm sure he's put the puzzle together and realized what everyone has known for years: that the two of you belong together."

"Yeah, right. *Everyone* knows that."

"Of course everyone knows that," Sarah said indignantly. "Even that stupid older brother of his realizes the two of you were made for each other."

"Not Trey?" No one but her sisters knew of her love for Bryce.

"Oh yes, even Mr. Hoity-Toity High-Fashion Photographer who thinks his shit doesn't stink knows that the only woman who is right for his brother is you."

The door clicked open and Jenna looked up to see Rachel sliding through the small opening. She was holding two plates.

"Look, I really do have to run, Sarah. I'll call you tonight."

"Don't give up," Sarah whispered into the phone. "Just tell him what's in your heart.

Jenna hung up the phone and motioned to the vacant chair in front of her desk.

"Thanks," Rachel said with a smile before handing her a plate. "Now, are you really going to blow off a guy who makes you breakfast *and* delivers it to you at work?"

Jenna felt her heart twist in her chest as she looked down at the steaming circles. "Cookie-dough pancakes with chocolate chips," Rachel said around a mouthful. "It'll put ten pounds on our hips, but oh my God . . . it's heaven."

"Bryce is a great chef."

"Tell me about it. I eat at his restaurant at least once a week. Mostly for his food, but the occasional glimpse of that tight ass does wonders, too."

Rachel swirled her fork in a puddle of syrup, and Jenna felt venomous that any woman could eat something like that without gaining any weight. Jenna watched Rachel shove another pile of syrup-laden pancakes into her mouth. "Man, that body is hot. The guy should be in an ad for Levi's."

Jenna smiled. Oh, yeah, Bryce had a fabulous butt, in and out of jeans. There was no denying that nothing was sexier than Bryce in a pair of faded jeans and a tight-fitting T-shirt.

"So, what's the deal, boss?" Rachel asked. "It's cool if you don't want to talk about it. Just thought I'd offer a little girlie advice. You seem . . . on edge." Her dark eyes flashed up through a fringe of long lashes—mostly fake but long nevertheless.

Jenna studied Rachel, from the expensive Jimmy Choo heels to the cashmere skirt and silk blouse. Rachel was the epitome of style and sex appeal. She was *Sex and the City* while Jenna felt like Daisy Duke without the hot bod, just the backwater manners of a woman who had almost zero experience with men.

"Look, if you want my opinion," Rachel said as she licked her fork clean, "you're in a great position. Mr. Sexy Chef is hot for you. You should have seen his face when he realized that you were not coming out of the office. He couldn't believe you weren't skipping your way over to him. A guy like that thinks he can snap his fingers and have anyone with breasts salivating over him."

"Yeah, but the truth is, Bryce pretty much *can* have whoever he wants."

"Really? He couldn't have you this morning, could he? And you should have seen his face, honey. Oh my God, if looks could kill, your office door would have exploded and Sexy Chef might just have choked you."

"Bryce wouldn't do that."

"You're missing the point, honey."

"What's the point, Rachel?"

"The point is, keep him off balance and you'll have him eating out of our hand. Make him work for you. Play the femme fatale and he'll become obsessed."

"He has had it very easy with women," Jenna said out loud before she thought better of it.

"Exactly. Turn the tables on him. Be the playgirl to his playboy and then you'll see how determined he is. He'll never let you go. The object denied becomes so much more desired."

Jenna's eyes lit up. "That's exactly right, Rachel. I'll be as untouchable as he was all these years."

"But don't forgo the sex," Rachel said with a wave of her hand. "No use suffering unnecessarily. Take the sex but leave out the emotional stuff. Think like a playboy, not a woman looking for a wedding band, and you'll have him trailing after you like a puppy."

Jenna sat back in her chair and studied Rachel. "And this is going to work? You're sure? Because, in truth, I am looking for the wedding band."

"It'll work. I was looking for a five-million-dollar account last week, and I landed it, didn't I?" Rachel said with a smile that was all vixen. "Money, marriage, it's all the same thing. Good luck, honey. Remember, your goal is in sight. You're just taking a tiny detour before you get to it."

The door closed behind Rachel. Jenna sat staring at it for a long time before she smiled. A perfect plan. Act all blasé about sex. Pretend that she was in it for pleasure, that she really didn't mind if they were an item. Casual sex. That was what she needed to play up. Nothing to make Bryce nervous. No "c" word—at least not yet. Once he was in love with her, then they could talk commitment.

And if that never happens? the doubting voice in her head asked. Well, she'd deal with that when or if it happened. No sense worrying about it now. She couldn't allow those little fears about Bryce and their future to settle in. She'd find out if he was the settling-down type at the end of the road. Besides, she hadn't yet worked her magic on him.

Smiling to herself, Jenna picked up her plate of pancakes and dove in. Oh, they were good. The only way they'd taste better was if she was in bed, sharing them with Bryce.

One day they would, she told herself. One day soon she'd be licking syrup from every part of his body, especially, she thought with a smile, that big gorgeous cock of his.

"Is there something wrong, Mr. Ryder?"

Bryce flipped his cell shut. No fucking message. "Ah, no. Just expecting a call, that's all."

Mr. Greenwood, CEO and chief lending officer of Greenwood Financial, arched one thick graying brow. "Your portfolio is in excellent shape, Mr. Ryder. Impressive that you've paid off that loan and managed to buy your restaurant outright while still tucking away a sizable sum."

"Well, I still live in an old condo in a cheaper part of the city, and I keep my expenses down."

"I can see that," Mr. Greenwood said with a haughty sneer.

OK, so the jeans were not one of his better ideas, but shit, he'd nearly been late for this very important meeting. If only Jenna would have come out of her office, he wouldn't have wasted nearly an hour. As it was, he hadn't even gotten to his restaurant. Hell, he'd only arrived at Greenwood with three minutes to spare. Finding a parking spot downtown at midmorning was bad enough, but riding the elevator up to the twenty-fourth floor when it stopped at every damn floor was worse. He'd been out of breath when Mr. Greenwood's secretary had seated him in the office.

But what should his clothes matter? He had financial security and a prospering four-star restaurant. His portfolio and skills in the kitchen should speak for him, not his clothes.

"Mr. Ryder," Greenwood began as he sat back in his chair while drumming an expensive fountain pen on a mouse pad, "I will be honest with you. Based on your finances, you should have no trouble securing this loan. Indeed, my partners and I were rather pleased when you approached us to help back you in your latest endeavor. However, the talk, the gossip and the general black cloud looming over you are really rather worrisome. It is not only your skills and financial security we must take into account, but also your reputation. Without a good reputation, a chef has nothing. And your reputation, Mr. Ryder, has been sullied to the point of damage."

Bryce's hands curled into fists. *Yeah, tell me about it.*

"I'm fixing that, Mr. Greenwood," he said, instead. "I've hired Jenna McCabe from Global Marketing to help me with the damage control."

"Jenna McCabe," Greenwood said with some surprise. "I've heard of her. Quite good, if a little green in the business."

"Green perhaps," Bryce said, trying to sound polite, when all he felt was indignant at the slight, "but a brilliant mind. She's already come up with a plan we'll be launching into action."

Where the hell had that come from? Jenna's plan was absurd, but hell, he was drowning here. He needed to say something.

"I'll be frank, Mr. Ryder. Greenwood Financial is in the business of making money. We aren't quite certain we can do that with you. Your restaurant, which only two months ago had a one-month wait list, is now virtually wait-free. Your television show has dropped from number one in its slot to third. The housewives, Mr. Ryder, have tuned you out, and turned on Dr. Phil. I'm sure you'll see that you are not a wise investment choice for Greenwood Financial."

"With all due respect, Mr. Greenwood, I'm working on it. I have two perfect pieces of coastal property and I know I can make a success of the restaurants. I have great ideas and innovative cuisine. What I need is someone to give me a chance."

"Your father, have you approached him?"

Bryce would rather have his nuts shaved off than ask his old man for anything, especially business advice or, God above, money.

"We have a difference of opinion, sir, about what makes money and what is a waste of money."

"Ah." Greenwood's smirk said he knew what the difference was. Bryce's father would buy anything and turn it into a shopping plaza with cheap chain stores and fast-food joints, not a gourmet restaurant. "I know your father. Lance Ryder is a sound judge of investments. His purchase of the Bargain City chain was pure brilliance."

Really? Ask the people whose downtowns became ghost towns after the discount Bargain City stores took up valuable land. Bryce would bet his restaurant that most of those towns would love to have his father's head on a pitchfork. But Greenwood, like his father, was old school. They didn't give a shit who they ran over to make their buck. But getting into it with old Greenwood wasn't going to help his cause. The kind of backing Bryce needed could only come from an institution the size of Greenwood Financial, so there was no point in riling the old guy. It was best just to swallow his opinions and play stupid.

"Perhaps, Mr. Ryder, you might wish to discuss things further with your father. I'm certain that with his years in business he would have much wisdom to impart."

Not fucking likely. "I'll take it under consideration."

"Have you ever thought of purchasing land that is more . . . reasonably priced and perhaps a little closer to home, Mr. Ryder?"

He thought of the oceanfront property he was going to turn into his next restaurant. Goddamn, he wanted it. Could taste it, the salt air, he wanted it so much.

"I know of a fifty-acre parcel coming up for foreclosure, not too far from here. There is another buyer interested—"

"No, thanks." Bryce wanted the ocean view, one facing the Pacific, the other the Atlantic. There would be no giving in on that.

"Very well, Mr. Ryder. One month. Turn your image around in four weeks, and Greenwood Financial will back you."

Standing, Bryce shook Greenwood's hand.

"And next time, Mr. Ryder, have enough self-respect to wear a suit. It's all about the image, you know. Four weeks. Remember that. Get that reputation of yours cleaned up and we'll be happy to back you."

Bryce nodded and whispered, "Fuck you," under his breath before letting himself out of Greenwood's office. Ten minutes later, he was in his Jag, the top down, driving to his restaurant.

Four weeks? How the hell was he going to turn his rep around in four goddamn weeks? Even if he did follow through with Jenna's plan, which he still had no intention of doing, it would take months before they saw any results. He didn't have months. He had weeks. And damn it, he was starting to worry—seriously worry about how he was going to do this.

His cell rang, and he jumped, nearly swerving off the road. Damn, he was wired tight, and it was all thanks to Jenna McCabe, who was doing a fucking number on his head. First with her plan, and then with her sexy body and that hotter-than-hell self-confidence he was suddenly going crazy for.

"Hey, little brother." It was Trey, but Bryce could hardly hear him. "Thought I'd check in to see how dessert went last night."

Bryce struggled to hear Trey through the static. The signal was bad and the call was dropped. Thankfully Bryce had just pulled up in front of his restaurant. He'd call Trey back, gather a few things, then head back to Jenna's apartment. There was no way in hell he was letting her off the hook that easily.

And man, she was going to pay for making him crazed. All he could think about was when he could get inside her again. When all he *should* have been thinking about was his four-week deadline.

"Hey, Bryce." Tyson was moving around the restaurant, placing crisp linens on the tables.

"Hey," he grunted in return. He was at the swing door of the kitchen when he stopped and looked back over his shoulder. "Tyson," he called, waiting for his brother to glance over.

"Yeah?"

"That date you have tonight, with Jenna?"

"What about it?"

"If you don't cancel it, there's going to be some serious fucking problems between us—you got that?" The little shit had the audacity to laugh. "I'm not kidding, Ty. Ditch the date or find yourself in traction."

"That's telling," his sous chef laughed from behind the hanging pots and pans that were suspended from the ceiling.

"Can it," Bryce snapped back. "Listen, the kitchen is yours tonight."

Mark peeked between two copper saucepans. "You're shitting me, right? I've been your sous chef for nearly five years and you've never left me alone."

"Don't remind me. Just . . . don't screw up."

Mark saluted him. "Aye, Captain. I won't let you down. We still going with the tilapia for the special tonight?"

"Yeah. And make that citrus sauce of yours. I like that combination. And find a nice white wine pairing, too. Something mild, maybe a tad on the sweet side in case the fish is a bit fishy-tasting. And if you need me, I'll be on my cell."

"And what are you cooking tonight?" Mark asked with a leer. "Something hot and spicy?"

"Steaks. Big, juicy, thick ones."

"All that red meat," Mark said with a shake of his head. "That'll give you some staying power."

For the first time that day, Bryce grinned. *Oh yeah.* He was going to wine, dine, and definitely sixty-nine tonight. He was going to give Jenna McCabe one hell of a birthday gift. And damn it, she was going to wake up beside him the next morning, even if he had to tie her down.

And that image, of Jenna tied down and him having his way with her, was never far from his thoughts for the rest of the day.

Seven

'm fucked.

Trey stared at the subject line of Bryce's e-mail and chuckled. "You got it bad, little brother," he said, reading the e-mail for the second time. "Real bad."

> So we share an incredible night of sex, and then she leaves me. Can you believe it? She just fucking walks out the door without even so much as a "Pick your clothes off the floor and lock the door when you leave"??

Why was Jenna playing hard to get? Something was definitely a bit off there. Maybe she's just protecting her heart, because God knew, Bryce was a heartbreaker.

Trey knew Jenna loved his brother. The only person on the face of the earth who didn't know was Bryce.

Idiot.

For almost as long as Trey had known Jenna, he'd known that she was in love with Bryce. And, Trey also knew, if Bryce wasn't such a chickenshit, he'd admit that he loved her back. But Bryce was screwed up. Bad breakups would do that to a guy. Trey stayed clear of anything more than one-night stands, but this went beyond bad for Bryce. It clouded everything he saw, including Jenna. Which wasn't good. Because Trey wanted Bryce to be happy. And Jenna was the key to that happiness. But pushing Bryce and playing matchmaker could only backfire.

Trey was going to have to be careful that his gentle nudge didn't send them both into hot water.

> And to make matters worse, Greenwood told me today that he won't back me unless I get my rep back. And the bastard is only giving me four weeks. FOUR WEEKS. How the hell is that supposed to work?

Trey had an idea, but Bryce would surely resist. Sitting back in his chair, Trey hit REPLY, and added another bit to Bryce's already cryptic subject line. *I'm fucked* became:

> I'm fucked but can be saved by Project Jenna McCabe.

Yeah, Trey liked the sound of that, and it wasn't something that Bryce was going to sense was a setup.

> Hey, little brother, why not use this to your advantage? I mean, I told you that you need to be seen with a plain Jane. Well, Jenna fits the bill. She's hardly "hot girlfriend" material. She's exactly the type you need to be seen with to win back your fans. And just think—

while you're with her, you can have all the sex you want. When your
rep's back and the sex is boring, you can drop her. See, no cooking
with blue-haired old ladies or working with kids, and all the sex you
want. I mean, four weeks is a tight deadline, even for you. So go
with someone you already know. Jenna's perfect for your needs.

The e-mail, Trey admitted, was pretty underhanded and more
than a bit mean, but it was the way it had to be. Bryce would dig his
heels in if he thought Trey was suggesting anything other than a
casual affair. If he could just get Bryce to give Jenna a chance, though,
to spend some time with her, he would realize how good they were
together.

Trey could even send one of his photographer buddies to snap
their pics and get the images circulating in a few magazines. That was
a good step toward shedding Bryce's playboy image. His fans would
see Bryce with a regular woman, not one who was stick-thin like his
other lovers, and definitely not as threatening. Jenna was a country
girl, and all those housewives who worked so hard would feel that
Jenna was a kindred spirit once they saw her arm in arm with Bryce.

It was a win-win plan if he could get Bryce to go along with it.
Except for one clinker. That nosy, tight-ass sister of Jenna's. If she
found out about the plan, it'd be ruined. Especially if she discovered
that Trey had called Jenna a plain Jane and that he'd basically shoved
Bryce into using her to get his reputation back.

Knowing what he needed to do, he picked up his phone, not even
wanting to contemplate how he was able to dial the number from
memory.

While it rang, his gaze strayed to the stack of black-and-white photographs that were on his desk. He picked through them, looking for his favorite. He stared at the beautiful face, gave in to temptation and traced the lips of the woman. The camera loved her, there was no denying.

On the fifth ring, a breathless feminine voice answered, jarring him out of his thoughts.

"Hello?"

"Sarah, it's Trey."

There was a moment of silence, followed by an aggrieved sounding sigh. "What do you want?"

"The same thing you do, Jenna and Bryce together—forever."

"Talk," she said, perking up. "I'm listening."

Jenna fumbled with her keys in the lock while she spoke to her colleague James. "Gabriella was cursing a blue streak this morning when I talked to her. She was completely unglued, threatening to sue us for breach of contract. We've got to do something about that botched presentation for the ad campaign. The Giancomo design account is huge for us. We can't ignore her concerns."

James held his hand out for her key. "The concept was my mistake. I'll rectify it. In fact, I've already started on it. But maybe the hallway in your apartment building isn't the place to discuss business."

"I know," Jenna said, flushing as she tried to put the key in the lock once more. "It's just . . . I don't want to lose this account. It's important to me."

"I swear, I'll clean up the fallout from my bad judgment, but first, give me the keys and let me open the door for you. Obviously you're too emotional right now."

"I'm not emo—"

Her words died as the lock on the other side clicked and the door opened.

Jenna's jaw dropped at the same time she heard James' breath catch. *Oh. My. God.* Bryce was standing there, shirtless, wearing a pair of sexier-than-hell faded jeans that were frayed around the waist.

She saw James glance up at the number on her door. 24. Yep, right apartment. Jenna swallowed convulsively, struggling for the words, trying to find that inner vixen who could casually breeze in and pretend like they hadn't had sex last night.

"Hi, babe, you're home early."

Jenna caught the incredulous look on James' face as Bryce greeted her and pulled her into the apartment. He would have slammed the door in James' face, too, if James hadn't put out his hand, stopping it with his palm.

"Come on in, James," she said, trying to act like having a half-naked man in her apartment was no big deal. "We can go over those files and your new ideas for the campaign before dinner."

"Dinner?" Bryce asked as he cast a dark look between her and James.

"Yeah, Tyson canceled," she said, throwing him an "I know you had something to do with that" look. "So I invited James out for a business supper. I thought we'd eat at Cravings."

Direct hit. Bryce's gaze turned venomous at the mention of her eating at his precious restaurant with another man.

"Well, your *business* dinner will have to wait till tomorrow night, because I've already got dinner on. I made a pitcher of peach bellinis. Why don't you get comfortable and I'll bring you one while we're waiting for dinner to cook?"

What the hell was this? Bryce was acting like he had every right to be in her apartment. Hell, he was acting like he had every right to *her*. Like he was her boyfriend, for crying out loud.

A little thrill shot through her at the thought. It was kind of nice, seeing his dark expression as he stared James down. But then Jenna got a little perturbed.

Just who did he think he was? He could make claims on her, but she wasn't allowed the same luxury? She almost snorted knowing what Bryce's response would be if she ever dared to question him about his dinner dates. And frankly, the thought really pissed her off.

"Hey, it's no problem with me, Jenna," James said very gallantly, obviously sensing the turbulent undercurrents in the room. "We can do dinner tomorrow night, or I can pick you up early in the morning and we can go out for breakfast and talk."

She saw Bryce's eyes grow black and the tiniest thrill of victory washed over her, whisking away her earlier peevishness. Could Bryce be feeling jealous of James? She shouldn't be savoring the emotion, and certainly didn't want to put James in the middle of anything, but the knowledge that Bryce might be a little threatened was the sweetest thing she'd ever felt.

And it was about damn time, too. She had always been the one to feel envious, seeing Bryce with his women. So this novelty was something she was going to savor, even though she knew it wasn't very kind to her coworker.

"I have an idea. Why don't you stay for supper, James?" Jenna asked.

Bryce's head snapped in her direction so fast she heard the bones in his neck crack. She smiled and kicked off her heels. "Bryce always cooks more than enough. Don't you?"

Bryce's mouth moved, but no words came out.

James was suddenly looking highly uncomfortable. "Well, that is...," James said after he cleared his throat. "Well, just as long as we're not having seafood. I'm highly allergic."

"Aw, that's too bad, Jimmy," Bryce drawled.

"That's James."

"Right, Jimmy. Well, that's a bitch because I am dishing up seafood."

"Oh, these steaks look so good," Jenna purred as she lifted the lid of the indoor grill, inhaling the succulent aromas of the rib eyes sizzling. She hid her smile as Bryce shot her a lethal glare.

"All right, steaks," James said, smiling as he tossed his suit jacket onto the sofa. "I was feeling like steak. Hey, Jen, why don't you slip into something more comfortable and I'll pour you a drink while Chef Fred here fixes dinner."

"Bryce," he snarled through bared teeth.

"Whatever," James said with a smirk.

Oh, boy. What had she started? Jenna was almost afraid to leave the two of them alone. Not that she and James had anything going on. But still, Bryce didn't know that.

James rolled up his shirtsleeves and flopped onto her couch. Bryce glared at him, then stalked into her galley kitchen. She watched the way he prowled toward her from beneath the veil of her lashes. He pressed up behind her and pushed his button fly into her skirt, finding the cleft of her bottom while he pretended he was reaching for a spatula from the container in front of her.

"Get rid of him. Unless, of course, you want him to watch me take you on the table. Or maybe right here, like this. You think Jimmy might like it, watching me take you standing up? To be truthful, I'm more than ready for that. *Fucking ready,*" he whispered harshly against her ear. "So tell me, Jenna, you wanna give Jimbo a show he'll never forget?"

Her knees went weak, and her hand trembled the slightest bit as she lowered the lid to the grill. Oh man, just the thought of being taken by Bryce again was more than she could bear.

"Too bad you left so damn early this morning, babe," he murmured, as his seductive lips nuzzled her nape. "I would have liked to watch you get dressed. This tight little skirt fits your ass like a second skin. I bet all the men in your office couldn't keep their eyes on their work today. I know I wouldn't have been able to. But then, if I'd seen what you were wearing, I wouldn't have let you leave. Guess it's lucky you left before I woke up, after all."

There was something in his words besides a compliment. Hurt perhaps? But why would he be hurt that she'd left before he was awake?

Jenna felt his breath on her neck as he leaned closer to her. His palm slid down her hip, to the hem of her skirt, and then beneath it.

"What are you wearing under this skirt, Jenna? Is it as sexy as what you were wearing last night when you greeted me at the door?"

The warmth of his hand permeated the silk of her stockings, and she didn't breathe, *couldn't* breathe, as he slowly slid his palm up to the lace tops. He sucked in his breath and pressed even closer into her until she could feel his naked chest, the heat of it, burning through her thin blouse.

His fingertip slid along the lace, until it came to the little bow at the end of her garter. He circled his erection deeper against her, almost grinding up against her as he slipped his finger beneath the elastic strap, stretching it, then letting it snap against her thigh. The sting of the strap aroused her, and the way he smoothed away that little tingle made her wet, aching for more.

"Garter belt and stockings," he murmured. "You're a naughty little girl, wearing something like this to work. And all this time I thought you were a good girl. Tell me, baby, is it black and racy, or is it white and virginal?"

She looked up, stealing a peek around the corner of the wall, to where James was going through a stack of papers.

"Don't look at him," Bryce growled as his hand wrapped around her thigh. "Don't you dare let those beautiful eyes rest on him, not when it's me you want." His palm found her ass, and he rubbed her back and forth with his warm hand, his fingers trailing along the lace edging of her panties. He found the wetness through the silk and rubbed it with his fingertips. "I'm dying to see your ass in these panties, Jenna. All I need to need to know is are they black or white?"

"Pink and black," she said breathlessly.

His breath hitched again. "Good and bad, huh, Jenna? Well, baby, that's all I want to see you wearing as I lay you out on that table and feast on you. What a hot dish you'll be, spread out for me. I want you to keep the stockings and garters on. And the panties," he whispered against her neck. "I'll just shove those aside while I taste that pussy of yours. You want that, Jenna, me going down on you?"

Please, please, please, she nearly begged out loud before she stopped herself. Bryce always had it so easy with women. And now he expected her to be just as easy a conquest as the others. She'd gone from ticked off to melting in a span of four minutes. Giving in to what he wanted would be too telling. He'd know that he could manipulate her with sex. That she was ruled by her body and her need for him.

Make him work for it. Be the playgirl to his playboy. Rachel's words came back to Jenna, and she straightened, pulling his hand out from beneath her skirt.

"I'm not sure what you thought last night was about," she murmured, channeling her inner Rachel as she turned around and faced him, "but I think you should know that I'm not looking for anything . . . steady."

"What?"

"A casual bit of sex, that's good, but I'm not looking for anything more than that."

"Excuse me?"

His frown was something truly frightening. Jenna didn't think she'd ever seen Bryce looking so fearsome and she was kind of confused by his anger. "Last night, it was fun and everything, but . . . you know . . . ," she said, trailing off.

"Hey, Jenna, I got the file opened. You ready to talk shop yet?" James asked.

"Be right there," she called to James before looking once more at Bryce. "Last night was nice. But I think we both know that doing that again would be a mistake. We're better as friends."

Nice? Last night was *nice?*

What the fuck?

Bryce fought the urge to stalk into Jenna's living room and haul her up from the couch and show her just how nice fucking her could be.

Jesus, he was losing it. What the hell was going on here? Everything he had ever thought, ever known, about Jenna McCabe had suddenly been turned upside down in less than twenty-four hours.

Bryce glanced into the living room and saw that Jenna had sat down on the couch next to what's-his-face and was sipping away at a drink that dickhead had made for her.

Bryce felt his mouth turn into a snarl. Every sip was a fricking invitation to sex, and Jimbo wasn't missing a beat. When James' gaze strayed to the little gap between the buttons on Jenna's blouse, Bryce wanted to hurl himself onto the couch and drag the asshole to the ground.

Going over files, his ass. James was here to go over something totally different, mainly Jenna's curvy body.

And Jenna looked . . . what? Receptive?

Fuming at the stove, Bryce watched the two of them together. James was everything Bryce was not. From the artfully coiffed tips of his hair—which, Bryce thought savagely, were frosted—to the toes of his expensive Italian leather loafers, James was the very image of a young, successful businessman. A fucking glossy-magazine image for the metrosexual man women seemed to adore these days.

Hell, even his nails were perfectly manicured, and Bryce would bet his left nut that James had a layer of clear coat on his buffed nail beds.

Did Jenna really go in for this guy? *She did last year at the Christmas party*, the merciless voice in his head reminded him.

How could he forget James beneath the mistletoe, bending Jenna back and Frenching her by the coat check.

Bryce had followed them, wanting to know the reason Jenna was leaving the party so early. And man, he wished he hadn't. Because now all he could see was James' perfect hands roaming up Jenna's sides, resting beneath the curve of her tits as he slipped his tongue into Jenna's mouth. He felt much the same way now, watching James and Jenna together. Were these two an item? Or was James just a casual fling she invited over from time to time?

Was I just a fling?

The thought crushed Bryce. Had he been the only one affected by last night? Did Jenna scream for James just as easily as she had for him?

The thought literally made him sick.

Bryce glanced once more at Jenna. Felt his guts churn as well as something in his chest. Something he didn't want to think about. It was too soon to examine any feelings he might or might not have. Certainly, he couldn't think about such things today, not when he was feeling so out of control—uncharacteristically out of control.

The only thing he knew for certain was he wasn't allowing Jenna to just brush him aside. No fucking way. Not after last night. Not after she'd turned his perfectly ordered world upside down. And if she had thoughts of getting it on with both of them, she was sadly mistaken. Because Bryce didn't share, and he sure as hell wasn't sharing Jenna McCabe, especially after just discovering how tasty a morsel she truly was.

So, if she wanted what's-his-face to stay for supper, then fine by him. It was easier for Bryce to monitor pretty boy's intentions that way, anyway. But there was a part of Bryce that hoped the dickhead would choke on his steak. And he would *not* be the one to administer CPR.

Lifting the lid to the grill, he flipped the steaks and checked on the potatoes. Both were nearly done, so he turned to the heads of garlic he had on the cutting board, and started chopping, taking out his frustrations on the knife and the tender roasted garlic flesh. If he wasn't careful, he'd chop off his fingers. He really should be thinking about what he was doing, concentrating on the razor-sharp knife in his hand. But all he could think about was Jenna and the pretty boy sitting beside her, leering down her blouse.

Bryce was a rough-and-tumble type of guy. He was as comfortable working on his Jag as he was in a kitchen. Maybe he could shave a bit more, and get his hair cut, but there was a part of him that secretly wanted Jenna to like his rough edges. He wanted her to desire the man that he was, not secretly yearn for someone he didn't want to be. He could never be like dickhead. Get his hair frosted? Never. And a fucking manicure? Not in this lifetime.

You've got mail.

The sound of his computer made Bryce jump. He narrowly missed slicing off the tip of his finger. He'd forgotten that he had been in the middle of writing some business e-mails about the oceanfront properties while he waited for Jenna to come home. Now, needing a reprieve, he wiped his hands on the towel and went to the island, where his laptop rested on the countertop.

About fucking time, he fumed. Trey had finally responded to the e-mail that Bryce should most definitely not have sent that morning after leaving Greenwood's office.

I'm fucked but can be saved by Project Jenna McCabe.

Hmm, this sounded interesting. Bryce scanned his brother's e-mail.

Not "hot girlfriend" material? Bryce grunted. If Trey had seen Jenna in that skimpy nightie last night, he'd quickly change his tune. Jenna could be one fucking hot girlfriend.

Bryce suddenly scowled. He hadn't had a girlfriend since Chrissy, and the term made the hair on his nape stand up to full height. Yet he couldn't help but let the thought sneak into his brain. What kind of girlfriend would Jenna make? She'd always been so warm and caring. And Jesus, he'd always had so much fun with her. She laughed and made him laugh. And the sex. Trey was saying he could have all the sex he wanted. Could make Jenna as hot as he wanted, as frequently as he wanted, *and* get his reputation back.

Now he was grinning. Trey knew exactly what words would put a smile on his face. Trey's language was harsh, but Bryce let it go. He didn't have time to correct his brother's assumptions about Jenna, and frankly, he was too riled up to send off a reply. The words wouldn't come, only the thought of having more of Jenna.

And not just to save his reputation. To explore . . . whatever this was between them. He saw himself cooking her dinner and maybe going for long walks, a Saturday afternoon of shopping and maybe the art gallery. Maybe they could even take the weekend and drive down to Lucan. He loved his hometown and the McCabe farm, where he'd always felt welcome and part of the family. Hell, maybe he could get Jenna to climb up the rickety old stairs to the hayloft in the barn, where he could get her naked.

Yeah, Trey was right. Spend time with Jenna. That's all he could think of.

He hit REPLY.

You're a fucking genius. Consider Project McCabe launched.

He hit SEND as he glanced out into the living room. James was still looking at the cleavage spilling out of Jenna's blouse, while Jenna, completely oblivious to James' ogling, pored through the manila file folder.

He'd teach the bastard to lust after Jenna.

Bryce pulled the fridge door open and reached into the bowl of ice, pulling out a bag of shrimp. He then turned to the griddle and opened the lid.

"Shit," he cursed, loud enough so that both James and Jenna could hear him in the next room.

Jenna jumped out of her seat. "What is it?"

"Sorry, there, Jimbo, I seem to have cross-contaminated everything with this shrimp juice. Fucking bag is leaking like a sieve."

Dickhead glared at him. "Did he or didn't he?" was written all over his face.

He hadn't, of course, but his adversary didn't need to know. *Law of the jungle, buddy,* Bryce thought smugly. *Kill or be killed.*

Pretty boy wasn't taking any chances. "Pick you up in the morning," James said to Jenna as he reached for his suit jacket.

Don't fucking bet on it.

The door closed behind James. Jenna was standing there with her arms crossed over her chest. The things he was going to do with those tits . . .

She glared at him and he threw the shrimp bag back into the fridge, then reached over and shut off the oven burners and the grill. The food would keep warm.

"Dinner will be ready in a bit. Let's start on the appetizers."

He pulled the pitcher of peach bellini from the fridge.

"What are the appetizers?" she asked, taking a step back.

"I thought I'd start with you on the table. That should whet my appetite for the main course. Hop on up, Ms. McCabe. You're about to get eaten by a very hungry man who's in the mood for peach-drizzled pussy."

Eight

Bryce set the iced pitcher on top of her glossy mahogany dining table. With a glance he disrobed her, telling her without words what he wanted from her.

"I think we need to discuss things," Jenna mumbled, trying to regain control of the situation.

"What's there to discuss, Jenna? I want you out of those clothes and on that table. Legs spread, pussy waiting."

God, Bryce had a dirty mouth and she loved it, couldn't believe how aroused she got when he talked like this. Who knew that side of her lurked beneath her good-girl veneer? Maybe it was just because this talk was Bryce—the true him—the rough-around-the-edges guy that she'd always adored.

But she had to get her brain back on track. "And what about what I want, Bryce?"

"I promise you, Jenna," he said in a sexy drawl that curled her toes, "I'll give you everything you want, and more, too."

He looked so hot as he came toward her, a slow, assured prowl that made her pussy ache. She wanted him inside her. She wanted more of his words, wanted, too, to know what effect she was having on him.

"Bryce, just because last night . . . we got a bit carried away—"

"Last night was the hottest night of my life, Jenna, and frankly I want more. All day I've been imagining what your breasts would look like cradling my cock. I promised myself, as I sat in your waiting room, that by tonight I'd make that vision a reality. You ever taken a cock between those beautiful breasts, Jenna?"

With each one of his measured steps, her skin felt stretched. Butterflies began to flutter and circle madly in her belly. He was standing before her now, his faded jeans tented with a formidable erection. Swallowing thickly, she found she could barely breathe, could barely take her eyes off his cock, imagining what it would feel like to take him in her hand and run her tongue up the long length of him.

"Take your blouse off, Jenna, then the skirt. Show me that hot body of yours."

"Bryce, this is . . ." She licked her lips, trying to get the words out, trying to pretend that what she was going to say was what she truly believed. "You know this is just about sex, right? I mean, this is just . . . you know . . ."

"Fucking?" he asked, his eyes darkening. His fingers had slipped to the top button of his jeans. He was opening the fly, pulling it down slowly, letting the denim part over his thick cock. "Take your blouse off, Jenna. Now."

"This is going to get all weird between us," she muttered as she managed to undo the buttons of her blouse. When she tossed it to the floor, she watched Bryce's expression turn from desire to full-blown lust.

Her body nearly went up in flames.

"Jesus, you're gorgeous. Your tits are perfect, Jenna. I *love* your tits."

"Bryce—"

"Yeah," he murmured as he caught his finger beneath the black strap of her lacy bra, "I know. This is just sex. No commitments, no demands on either side. I got it."

She didn't know whether to be disappointed that he was OK with it or happy she was going to have sex again with Bryce.

The strap slid down her arm, the cup lowered, baring the crest of her breast. "The skirt now, Jenna."

Reaching behind her waist, she undid the button, then the zipper, and let the skirt skim along her hips. She was wearing a pair of black lacy boy shorts with pink lace ruffles and a matching garter belt.

"Now *that's* too sexy to take off."

He reached for her, a bit rough as he gathered her close to him, letting her feel his erection, which had been freed from his jeans as he ground it into her belly. His hands were everywhere, sliding up her thigh only to cup her bottom. His kiss was hungry, his tongue commanding as it filled her mouth.

She met him, inch for inch, and he groaned in her mouth as he pushed her back against the wall and reached for her hands. Holding them high above her head, he arched her back, forcing her breasts up to his mouth. "You're so hot like this, Jenna."

She moaned as he took a nipple between his lips and sucked.

"Then take me here, right now."

"Not yet."

Pulling her by the hand, he brought her to the table. His smile was sinful. Wicked. And the dimple in his cheek completely adorable. She was blushing, she knew. She could feel the heat in her cheeks, and that heat only grew as she watched him lower himself into a chair and spread his legs wide, capturing her knees with his thighs. She watched as the thick bundle of muscles in his belly flinched and constricted. His cock was hard, heavily veined and lying on his belly, nearly hitting his belly button.

"Sit down, baby, right on top of me." He reached for her hips and helped her to straddle his thighs. His hands went around to her butt and he traced the curve of her ass through the pink and black lace panties.

"Why don't you give me a lap dance? Let me feel that hot pussy."

Jenna closed her eyes and let her head fall to the side as his skilled, smooth fingers found their way beneath the lace hem of her panties. When his fingers started rubbing her, her hips responded, and she started grinding and moving on his lap. His gaze drifted lower, resting for a few seconds on her breasts, which were spilling out of the demi cups, then lower, to her waist, then her silk-covered pussy, which was sliding along his jeans as if she were a world-class stripper.

"I want to see your tits jutting out of that bra, Jenna. Show me. Tease me."

In a sexy dance, she reached for her breasts and slowly freed them from the cups. Jenna couldn't believe how brazen she was being. Never would she have done such a thing with her other lovers, but there was something about Bryce that brought out the vixen in her. Somehow he had seduced it out of her, let her know that it was okay. That was the secret of getting down and dirty with Bryce. He wanted her like this, and he gave her the confidence to experiment with some of her secret fantasies.

His fingers were now in her panties, and before Jenna knew what he was doing, he was pulling the silk and lace to the side, baring her pussy, which she knew was drenched with arousal. Before she could feel shy, Bryce reached for her hand and put her finger in the pitcher of bellinis; then it was on her sex. The cold was a shock, at first jarring, then soothing against the heat coming out of her core. When Bryce brought her hand to his mouth, sucking off the remainder of the peach puree, Jenna moaned, loud and long.

Without any further encouragement, she sank her hand back in the pitcher. She spread her thighs, to allow Bryce to watch her part her pink lips. Her middle finger, coated with icy puree, filled her hot core. Her eyes closed in bliss at the sensation.

Her clit was hard and erect. Another few strokes and she'd be shaking on his lap.

"You're gonna come, aren't you?" he growled. "Well, not yet, Jenna. Not until I've got my mouth all over you and you're screaming my name."

He lifted her up from his lap and placed her on top of the table so that her ass was on the edge, and she was opened to him while she continued to pleasure herself and her aching clitoris.

"Lie back and put your feet on my shoulders."

She did as he asked. He brushed her hand aside, then filled her with his fingers. He found the rigid little spot at the back of her vagina, and her eyes went wide. Oh God, no man had ever found her G-spot before. She couldn't hide the moan of ecstasy as he tapped the spot; then curled his fingers forward in her pussy.

"Deeper," she cried in a dark, husky voice as Bryce expertly worked her G-spot. When he leaned over her and captured a nipple between his teeth and tugged, she groaned. "Oh, God, yes, Bryce! *Yes!*"

All of a sudden, he was pouring the peach puree between the valley of her breasts, over her turgid nipples to her belly, and then down over her pussy.

It was so cold it made her nipples stand at full attention. Bryce flicked them with his thumbs, sending her pussy clutching and contracting. The sensation was like nothing she had ever felt before. It was a pain, so icy cold against her heated flesh, but soon gave way to the most erotic pleasure she'd ever felt as it melted over her warm skin and trickled down her body.

Jenna lay back on the table, her back arched, her hands thrown high above her head, her thighs splayed wide. Bryce tore at her panties, shoving them aside, and then his mouth was on her, sucking, lapping at the peach that had warmed and liquefied. Feeling wanton, Jenna rubbed the peach juice all over her breasts, making them glisten. She pulled at her nipples, making them harder.

True to his word, he'd made her wait until his mouth was all over her before she climaxed. It was earth-shattering and she rode it out hard, her hand fisted in his hair, and his teeth gently pulling at her swollen, tender lips.

There was a tear of foil. Then a second later, Bryce was embedded fully inside her, filling her hard, holding her arms up above her head as he loomed over her, thrusting into her like a madman.

Thrusting and retreating, he reached for her hips, pressing his fingers into her hips so that he could grip her and bring her down as he thrust his cock upward, filling her with his entire length. And still she gasped and moaned, begging for more, needing more. His finger searched for her clitoris, and he flicked it, making her arch and scream.

"That's it, baby. Scream my name."

Her second orgasm was just out of reach. A few more strokes and it would be there. But he pulled out and brought her up from the table.

"Turn over," he said, smiling wickedly. "I want to take you from behind."

Her eyes went wide. She'd never been taken that way, never felt comfortable enough with her other lovers to be so exposed. But Bryce didn't give her any time to let her worries take root.

He turned her over, his hand covering her ass as he positioned her before him and tilted her hips back.

"Bryce!" Jenna heard the arousal and need in her voice as Bryce thrust into her. His breathing was harsh, and she looked over her shoulder and saw that his gaze was fixed on his cock entering her. In that second she knew she'd never see anything as sexy as Bryce taking her like that.

His hands fell lower on her hips and he showed her how to rotate them, giving them both more pleasure. Soon she was lowering her body to the table, taking gratuitous joy in the way her hard nipples brushed against the polished wood. She imagined that he was beneath her and she was rubbing her nipples against his lips, and he was teasing her with the hard tip of his tongue, and she smiled secretly at the image of tormenting Bryce.

She could become addicted to this. Sex with Bryce was more potent than any drug.

"You ready, Jen? You ready to come with me?"

She nodded. His expression hardened into a fierce scowl as he came deep inside her. And then, while he was still inside, he cupped her breasts and fondled them softly as he kissed her neck in fluttering sweeps.

"That was one hell of an appetizer," she said as she came back to herself.

He grinned. "Let's say we move to the bedroom for the main course."

The night air was warm, far too warm for early May, but the humid breeze blowing in through her bedroom window felt perfect as it ruffled through her white curtains before caressing her skin in a sultry, fluttery caress.

Shivering as her body responded to the breeze, she felt Bryce press closer to her, spooning up against her.

"Cold, babe?" he asked, throwing his heavy thigh over her legs and gathering her up closer to his warm body. With a sigh, she allowed herself the pleasure of Bryce's body fitting around hers. His arms were strong, cocooning her in steel and heat. She liked the way his forearm nestled between the cleft of her breasts, and the way his skin smelled—a touch spicy from his cologne, as well as very male from the thin layer of sweat caused by their torrid romp in bed. Yes, she loved the way he smelled, but what she loved more was the fact that his musky scent coated her body as well.

Cuddling with him like this, spooned close together while Bryce idly toyed with the ends of her hair, was something worth savoring. It was almost as if . . . Jenna bit back the thought and instead cast her gaze out the window, to the dark sky and the smattering of stars that dotted the horizon.

She mustn't read too much into this closeness they were now sharing. Just because she was falling deeper and deeper into love didn't mean Bryce was.

What he'd done to her on that table with his mouth and hands . . . Good Lord, she couldn't bring herself to think of that, or how damn hard it had been to keep from crying out *I love you*. She'd only just stopped herself in time by biting her lip and allowing herself to totally give her body up to Bryce.

But while she had been crazed with lust and devoured by passion, Jenna couldn't conceal the fact that Bryce had been all too happy to accept her terms. Hot, sweaty, anywhere sex without entanglements. If she hadn't been so crazed with lust, she might have felt sick at just how quickly Bryce had jumped at the chance to have all the sex he wanted with her, and no commitments.

Jenna closed her eyes when she felt Bryce's soft, pliant mouth move along the column of her neck. He was hard again. She could feel his cock thickening against her bottom. His palm, so warm and soft, was gliding up her thighs, moving between them until he cupped her sex.

This was what she wanted, wasn't it? This was the perfect execution of her plan, the "play the playgirl" scheme. And it had worked, hadn't it? She'd secured Bryce's sexual interest. But the glow of victory had suddenly faded.

"Damn, you were incredible, Jenna," Bryce murmured as he nuzzled her earlobe while he brushed the head of his erection across her butt. "I had no idea you were such a hellcat in the sack." His chuckle was deep and sexy. "For that matter, who knew I would come like a hand grenade? God, it was explosive. I've *never* felt that before. I think I went blind for a second or two."

Warmth tingled through her veins at Bryce's compliment. She had been wild, but so had he. And the way her body seemed to come alive with his touch, the way it opened, like the petals of a rose, was sheer beauty. He had such command of her body, her mind. God help her, Bryce Ryder owned her body and soul.

"What about some supper?" he asked as he took a nip of her neck. His hand had slid down to her belly, where her stomach rumbled none too discreetly. "The steaks are probably ruined but I could cook the shrimp. We could eat it in bed while we watch a movie. Then," he said around a yawn, "we could take a shower, slip into bed, make love and fall asleep."

Make love? Every pore of her being was heating up, just replaying what she'd heard. Had Bryce made love to her? Was he already feeling a closeness to her that he hadn't felt with his other lovers? Was she already special to him? Something more than just an easy and convenient lay?

Play the playgirl.

Rachel's mantra suddenly filled Jenna's head. She needed to keep to the plan, even though her heart wasn't fully in it. Jenna wasn't the type to play games, but sexual games were something Bryce excelled at. If she were going to have any sort of chance with him at all, she needed to be as aloof and as untouchable as he'd always been. The object denied was always more desirable.

"Actually," she said, as she turned to peer up at him, "I really do have those files to go over. Tomorrow morning my client is calling from Milan, and I need to have some sort of plan put together."

"So we'll skip the movie, and we'll eat in bed while we look over the files?"

"No, really, I can't do that."

He blinked, and Jenna saw something that looked like skepticism shine in his hazel eyes.

"Little Jenna McCabe, playing hard to get?" he asked in a teasing, seductive voice, but Jenna heard the disbelief he was trying so hard to disguise. "C'mon, Jen, you know you want me to stay the night."

God, yes. Stay the night. Stay forever.

No. She had to be strong. If she gave in now, he would quickly lose interest.

Jenna sat up and held the sheet to her breasts while she searched the floor for something to put on.

"I know you'll find this hard to believe, but I haven't been putting my life on hold, waiting around for the day you decide to grace me with your renowned bedroom skills."

"Hey," he said, brushing her hair over her shoulder. "What's wrong?"

"Nothing that about three hours of work won't cure."

"I know something that will be a far better cure for what ails you than work," he said teasingly, reaching for the sheet. "Why don't you lie back and see just how much I can relax you?"

Something in Jenna suddenly snapped. She didn't know where the anger came from, but she let it out. "Maybe all your other women had nothing better to do than allow themselves to be enthralled by the pleasure of your company and cock, but I have a life. And a business."

His mouth dropped open, and Jenna saw his eyes suddenly grow dark. This was what came of being chased by women.

Jenna was suddenly seeing a side of Bryce she never had. The self-ish, egotistical side. The side that liked to call the shots. He liked control, and relationships were about give and take. Bryce was selfish.

But not in bed, a little voice reminded her. He was the most generous lover she'd ever had.

That's not enough, she argued back. Jenna had told herself that the forever after would come in time, but the longer she looked at Bryce, the more she began to believe that he was incapable of a real relation-ship.

"OK, I get the point," he grumbled as he got up off the bed and reached for his jeans. "You don't need me hanging around, distracting you."

"It's not like I can't focus on anything else when you're near, you know," she snapped, shooting his muscled back and tight ass a glare.

Pulling his jeans over his hips, he turned to face her as he buttoned up the fly. "Okay, so what is it then? What's with kicking me out of your bed when I know damn well you enjoyed what I did to you in it?"

Self-preservation.

The word snuck into her thoughts before she could stop it. She could tell herself it was part of the plan to play the vixen to his playboy, but that wasn't the whole truth. In reality, having Bryce spend the night, holding her, sleeping beside her, was . . . too much. To wake up beside him would be a taste of what it would be like if he loved her. And Jenna couldn't stand to have just a taste.

He was studying her, she realized, and she turned away, still wrapped in the sheet. It was the only thing protecting her right now.

"So, this is what you truly want? Just some sex on the side when you're feeling like it?" He cursed, dragging his hands through his hair. "I never figured you for that kind of girl, Jenna."

She stiffened at the innuendo she heard in his voice, but steeled herself against the tumultuous feelings it produced. "There's a lot about me you don't know."

"Bullshit. You've always been an open book to me, and you always will."

"People change."

"So, do you have plans for the weekend?" he asked in what could only be described as a snarl.

She cast a glare his way. "No."

"No? You and Jimmy not getting together to hit the files?" he taunted. "He seems like such an eager employee. I'm sure you'd have no problems convincing him to spend the weekend with you."

"James is my employee."

"Yeah, with fringe benefits. Last time I saw Jimbo, he had his tongue down your throat. Don't tell me he's just business, Jenna. I got eyes."

She gasped in outrage. "What are you talking about?"

He glared at her as he smoothed his hands through his rumpled hair. "My Christmas party last year? You two were practically fucking in the cloak room."

"We were not," she cried, sounding all screechy and guilty.

"*Please.* I saw the two of you. I saw where Jimmy liked to keep his hands, which were either plastered on your ass or your tits all night long."

"We . . . we kissed," she fumbled, flustered that Bryce knew of her brief flirtation with James. "It wasn't anything."

"Oh, really?"

"James and I are associates, nothing more. When we meet, it's business."

"And I'm certain that it's all in the name of work, of course. Because you don't need another fuck buddy, do you? That's where I come in."

"Bryce—"

"And I plan on being the best damn buddy you could imagine. So, no plans? Good. Since tomorrow is Friday," he mumbled as he shoved his T-shirt over his head, "we could do dinner and maybe a movie. Or maybe hit a nightclub if you want."

"I—I don't think so, Bryce. It sounds like a date, and we've agreed we're not dating. Let's leave things as we first intended."

The woman standing before him looked like Jenna, a delightfully rumpled, passion-ravaged Jenna. But the words didn't belong to her.

"Look, Bryce. There's no need to do dinners and movies. People will just think that there's something going on between us."

"And there isn't?" His voice was flat.

"Well, sex," she said, shrugging. "Good sex. But that's all."

Something in his gut fell to his feet. This wasn't the real Jenna talking. The real Jenna wouldn't offer her body without any commitment. The real Jenna wouldn't want sex without emotion. She'd want the romance. The relationship. This was the woman who watched that rain-drenched kiss scene from *The Notebook* over and over, until even he had it memorized. This was the woman he'd teased after finding her piles of romance novels hidden in the hayloft. This woman, the one standing before him, couldn't possibly want just the sex. Could she?

"I know that's what we agreed," he said slowly, "but I thought maybe . . ." His heart was pounding in his chest. God, was he really going to say it? That he wanted more than just a romp in her bed? That he wanted that kiss in the rain and everything that went with it? And he wanted it with Jenna. With the sweet, shy girl he'd known for so long. He staggered back a step with the shock of what he was admitting to himself.

But she was done waiting for him to speak.

"The sex *is* good," she said as she dropped the sheet and pulled on a pink satin robe. "But both of us know that these sorts of things die out as quickly as they flare up. Why make people think there's more to this than there is?"

For the briefest of seconds, time felt suspended as they looked at each other.

"So you're really okay with this?" Bryce said. "You don't want anything more?"

"I've told you—"

"Let's hear it. For the record."

"No, I don't want anything more."

Rage and hurt like nothing he'd ever experienced before sliced through him. "Thanks for the fuck," he spit out. "When I feel like getting laid again, I'll know who to call."

He couldn't stay another minute. He didn't want to see her standing there in her pink robe and kiss-swollen lips and her rumpled hair. He didn't want to see the bed where they'd shared their bodies.

He didn't want to see this Jenna. Christ, he was really beginning to hate the woman standing before him. How could what they had experienced mean nothing more to her than just fucking?

He knew fucking. Had done it hundreds of times. And what they'd done was the furthest thing from just an empty screw.

In a flash he was at the door, reaching for his car keys on the shelf of Jenna's entertainment cabinet. As he grabbed the keys, he knocked down a silver frame. He picked it up, meaning to set it back in place, until he saw what the picture was.

He couldn't help but smile—a sad smile—as he looked down at the picture of him and Jenna sitting in the hayloft of her father's barn. They'd just come from the pond, and his hair was long and wet, clinging around his neck. Jenna was wearing a white T-shirt that clung to her bathing suit.

They were sitting side by side, Jenna's arms around his neck and his around her waist. They were smiling, their heads tilted so that they were touching each other. He'd been wearing nylon swimming shorts, and had been horrified by the hard-on that had sprung up between them as he felt her breasts, big even then, press up against his chest. He'd been afraid of Jenna knowing. But she had just smiled, her own sweet smile, and kind of melted into him.

This was the Jenna he had always known. The longer he stared down at the picture, the more he asked himself if any of the old Jenna resided in the woman he'd just left in the bedroom.

When he closed the apartment door, he was still staring at the picture he'd taken. As he looked at Jenna—looked at them together—he realized that he needed to know what remained of the old Jenna. Because, he admitted to himself, that was who he wanted.

The real Jenna McCabe.

The hellcat he'd been doing these past two days was a turn-on—there was no doubt about it. But had the hellcat eaten his kitten?

Shaking his head, he tossed the picture onto the passenger seat of his Jag. He couldn't stop staring at the image of him and Jenna together.

"What the fuck do you want?" he asked himself.

It took a long while before he could bring himself to admit the truth. But it finally arrived, in a headache-inspiring moment.

What he wanted was Jenna, all of her. The soft, vulnerable friend Jenna, who always brought out the tender side of him, and the sex bomb, who could wring an orgasm out of him like no other woman ever had. Was it possible to have them both? Or was the friend gone forever, replaced by this woman who was willing to share her body and nothing else?

There was only one way to find out. They were going to have to go back. To those days when he'd had so much fun with Jenna. When life had been a pleasure. Not a headache.

Putting the gearshift in drive, he pulled out of his parking spot and out of the garage. It was dark, the stars obstructed by heavy clouds. He smiled, remembering how the stars had looked from the hayloft. When he and Jenna had lain there for hours, just staring up at the sky, talking about their dreams. He wanted those days back.

Nine

The Italian language had never been Jenna's forte. If only she had her Italian phrase finder and dictionary handy.

Yeah, like that was going to help her. The way Gabriella Giancomo was rolling through her tirade, Jenna would never be able to keep up. She heard a bunch of rolled r's, could almost imagine the fashion designer's hand flinging around her head as her voice reached a shattering crescendo.

Jenna picked out the words *incasinato, merda* and *stronzo* before Gabriella could take a breath. Screwed-up, shit and jerk. Well, that made things easy. Gabriella was screaming about the terrible ad concept James had done.

Another string of strong words, followed by the sound of a hand slapping against wood, thundered through the speaker phone as James slid a piece of paper across the desk.

I think that's Italian for I'll get you and your little dog, too!

Jenna shot him a warning glare, but smiled, too. Wasn't that the truth? Gabby was going to ruin Jenna and her company if they didn't do something.

"Parli piu lentamente, per favore, Gabriella," Jenna said in terrible Italian.

"I will not speak slower!" came the hissed reply. "I am mad, *arrabiato-a!*"

"I understand, Gabriella. I'm angry as well."

That seemed to calm the wind in her sails. "I thought you would be good designer for this line. You're a woman. You understand. But you send a stupid man who thought it was good to put a nightgown over a chair and call it a masterpiece."

Jenna grimaced as she recalled the proofs of the ads and cross-promo concept. There was no denying that James had missed the mark—by a football field.

"I want beautiful, full women to wear my clothes. That is what the line is all about, no? There is no other couture house doing lingerie and beautiful clothes for real women. It is all my idea. And it is good idea. The world thinks these women don't want to feel beautiful and sexy? That they don't have dreams of having some *bello uomo* love them? Desire them? And this shitty presentation tells me you could not find one beautiful, full woman in the whole world and a sexy man who wants to be with her in a picture."

"You're absolutely right. Part of the reason I jumped at the opportunity to market Duchess Lingerie was the chance to work up something beautiful for the women out there over a size fourteen."

"So why you no work on this ad campaign yourself?" Gabriella shot back.

That was the hardest question of all. Probably because she'd been devoting her brainpower to Bryce's dilemma. She'd come up with his plan and not the one for the Duchess account. And now Bryce wasn't even going to do any of the things she thought he should, and Global Marketing was going to lose a huge account. An account that Jenna sorely wanted to have. Lingerie and pretty things were near and dear to her heart. And while she was a size fourteen and could normally find those pretty things in regular department stores, her sister couldn't. Even though she loved lingerie and sexy stuff just as much as Jenna did.

Jenna had seen the marketing campaign as a chance to break down the walls of stereotyped beauty. She'd had a million ideas floating around in her head to get women breaking down the door of their local Duchess retail outlet just to buy themselves a pair of pretty panties to wear beneath their jeans.

In her heart, she knew this line, if marketed right, could be so successful and rewarding.

"Gabriella, I swear to you, if you would give me one more chance, I will make this ad campaign into something magical. One more chance."

"One more," Gabby said. "And I want sexy men."

"Done. *Bello uomos*, I promise." Jenna shot James a relieved expression. "What are you doing on Monday? I'd like to come to Milan and show you a few things I'm thinking of for the marketing campaign."

"Come Saturday," she ordered. "I leave for Greece on Monday—for vacation."

Shit, that was tomorrow. Jenna checked the clock. It was eleven a.m.

Plenty of time to run like mad around the city preparing for a hare-brained trip to Italy the next morning.

"Well? You come?"

"Of course, tomorrow is great. I'll book a flight right now. Just let me get the details from you."

When she was done writing everything down, Jenna shut off the button for the speaker phone and collapsed against the chair. "Well, at least we still have the account. I don't know how much money we're going to make since this last-minute airfare to Italy is going to bite into profits big-time."

"You did what needed to be done, Jenna. And I accept the blame. I should have consulted you first about my ideas. I just don't get the female psyche when clothing size is involved."

"Most men don't. That's why I blame myself for passing this job on to you. I shouldn't have. I know what women are looking for. I have a sister who is plus-sized. She's beautiful and so sexy, but shopping with her makes me want to cry. It's difficult but not impossible to find trendy clothes. But pretty lingerie? That *is* impossible. She always leaves those stores feeling ugly and bad about herself."

"Well, you'll get the job done, Jenna. And you know what? I know it's going to be the best campaign we've ever done. Your heart's in it, and that's what is going to make it such a huge success. From now on, I'm sticking with things I know, and women's lingerie isn't one of them."

"Don't beat yourself up over this one, James. You brought in that neat little company that makes Italian leather shoes. It was a nice profit for the company, and one account I wouldn't have landed without your savvy."

James stood up and stretched. "Thanks, Jenna. I felt like a real ass when I screwed up. I'll get the flight and hotel logistics worked out. I'll leave the hunky male model to you."

"Geez, thanks. That's so good of you. Because you know, I can find one of those anywhere."

They both laughed, then sobered. Together they said, "Rachel."

"Oh God," Jenna groaned. "We're beginning to think alike."

"Scary, huh? Maybe it's time we relooked at that idea of me becoming a partner. I got the money, Jenna. And I'd love to be a partner with you."

Jenna thought of the loan she was waiting to hear about. Any day she should know about the extra cash for her parents. She didn't want James getting embroiled in that. Plus, she liked running her own business, being her own boss, making Global Marketing a success on her own.

James was watching her, an expectant expression on his face, so Jenna said, "Maybe when I get back from Italy."

"Okay," he said. "I'll send Rachel in and get your flight organized."

Jenna barely had time to assimilate everything she had to do before going to Milan the next day when Rachel breezed through her office door.

"You wanted me?"

"I did. What's the name of that supermodel from Rome who's so hot these days—the one with the pouty lips and the six-pack like granite?"

"Eduardo." Rachel replied. "I think he's with the Palissier Agency. Why?"

"I need a stud to pose for an ad, and I'd prefer that he be Italian."

"To please Diva Giancomo?"

"Something like that. Plus, I think women kind of gravitate to the dark, swarthy type of guy. I want this campaign to be all about fantasy, but not so out there that it's beyond the realm of the possible. I want the chemistry between the two models to be palpable. And I think Italian guys go for the more buxom, curvy type."

"He'd be perfect."

"Great. You think you can set something up for me? It's such short notice, but I was thinking maybe something tomorrow or early Sunday."

"I'll try."

"You might want to remind him that the account is Duchess Lingerie, and the designer is the daughter of Italy's very own Carlo Giancomo. A good job with this could mean work for him with one of the most influential couture fashion houses."

"Oooh, a little bribery. Love it. I'll get right on it."

Jenna was just picking up the phone to call her sister when Rachel stopped at the door and looked over her shoulder. "Hey, speaking of hot men, how goes it with your sexy chef?"

Jenna groaned. She'd done remarkably well not thinking about Bryce all morning. Of course, when you had an irate client screaming obscenities in Italian at you, you tended to forget a lot of things, including your own name. But now that she was reminded of Bryce, she started to feel sick to her stomach. Last night had been such a bad scene. Over and over, she had tried to search for clues, to see if there was any hidden meaning or any nuances of feeling she could decipher in his angry words.

Thanks for the fuck. Those words curdled her blood. He'd said it as though he were spitting out poison. She'd felt the puncture of them go straight to her heart.

"Well, we seem to be having lots of sex," she finally said.

"Hey, you go, girl! Good for you. It's fun, isn't it, just having sex and not worrying about anything other than getting off?"

"Uh, yeah, it's great."

"So, is he panting after you?"

"Not really. He was pissed that I made him leave last night."

"Oooh, did you really? That was a good move, Jenna. He'll be snapping you up tonight and chaining you to the bed. Good work. See, I told you this was what you needed to do. You've got him ensnared. He'll be coming around tonight again for more."

Rachel shot her a wink and closed the door, leaving Jenna alone. No, he wasn't panting after *her*. Just the sex. *I'll know who to call the next time I want to get laid.*

That pretty much said it all.

The intercom buzzed, and Jenna's secretary thankfully interrupted her black thoughts. "Your sister is on the line, Miss McCabe. Are you taking calls?"

"Thanks. Send her through, Jessica."

The phone rang and Jenna picked it up on the first ring. "Sarah?"

"Hey, big sister."

That always made Jenna smile. Jenna was barely even a year older than Sarah. A fact they both liked to tease their mother about.

"So, what's new? Got a shiny princess cut on your finger yet?"

Jenna snorted and leaned back in her office chair. Kicking off her heels, she put her feet on top of her desk and wiggled her sore toes. "Right."

"What, are you holding out for a bigger rock?"

"Hardly. We're not quite there yet, Sarah."

"No? Where exactly are you, Jen?"

"Still at the 'no strings hot sex' stage of my new plan."

"What new plan?"

"I've decided that what Bryce needs is what he's been dishing out to all the women in his life—just sex and nothing else."

"Do you really think that's wise? I mean, you don't want him to get the wrong impression about what you're really looking for."

"I know what I'm doing, Sarah."

"What's happened to change your plans?"

"Nothing. I just think it's a better way to manage Bryce. I'm going to make myself unattainable, and he's going to chase me."

"And then what?"

"He's going to become obsessed, of course. God, Sarah, aren't you listening to me?"

"I'm trying to follow your reasoning, but personally, I think it's going to lead to disaster. You don't want him obsessed with the notion of getting it on with you. You want him passionate about *you*—the person you are."

"He will in time, but sex is the way to snag his attention in the beginning."

There was long a pause before Sarah said, "I think this is the most dim-witted idea you've ever had."

Jenna felt her eyes bug out. Sarah was always her champion. They were more than sisters—they were friends. How could her sister not understand that Jenna had been reduced to this because of Bryce's skittishness about relationships?

"You wanna know what else I think?"

Jenna closed her eyes. "Not really, but I know that won't matter to you."

"Nope. It won't. What I think is, you're not giving Bryce a real chance. I think you're afraid of failure, so you're setting yourself up with this stupid idea so that you won't have to admit you want more than his seduction skills. I think you're afraid to let Bryce get to know the *real* you."

Jenna dropped her legs from the desk and jumped up from her chair. "Just what exactly does that mean?"

"Exactly what I said. You must really think Bryce is an asshole to offer him such a deal. And what do you think Bryce thinks of his best friend now, offering him unlimited sex without having to give anything in return but his renowned nine inches?"

Ten at least, but who was counting?

"You know, I don't even think Bryce will go along with this."

"Well, guess what. He's totally on board," Jenna snapped.

"Really? I...I can't believe this. Maybe from Bryce. But you? Never. What about your pride, Jenna?"

The insinuation hung heavy between them, stopping Jenna cold. No, she was right, damn it. This was the way to deal with Bryce. Sarah was wrong.

"Look, Sarah, for the last time, butt out. What I'm doing is right for me. I'm trying to make this relationship work, but in a way that I can survive with my heart still intact if it doesn't work out."

"Just putting out isn't going to bring him close to you, you know. You need to remind him of why you're so good together, why you're such good friends, and how, good friends or not, you've got good chemistry, in and out of bed."

"Fine. You've said your piece. Now let it go."

"What about coming back to Lucan with Bryce? At least for old times' sake. You guys could get really close here, where it all started. I know Bryce has always considered those times to be some of the best he's ever had. And, you know, next week is the long weekend. Monday is the planting festival. Bryce would love that—it's all about food and stuff. You used to always go together."

"Oh yeah, right. Like I really want to be spotted with Bryce there. The whole town turns out for the planting festival. And who told you that he considered those times at the farm some of the best he's ever had?"

There was long pause on the phone before Sarah spoke. "No one."

"Well, it doesn't matter. I'm not coming home to Lucan with or without Bryce. I'm leaving the country for the weekend, and by the time I get back, I'll be knee-deep in work."

"Pardon me?"

"I have to fly to Milan. I have a client there who needs immediate attention."

"Ooh, Italy. You're bringing Bryce, right?"

"No. Why would I? It's not like we're exclusive. We're screwing each other, Sarah. We don't need to keep tabs on each other every second of the day."

"But you are telling Bryce you're leaving the country?"

"I don't see why I need to."

Sarah sounded incredulous. "You would have before, when you weren't putting out. You'd think now that you're sharing your bodies, you'd give him the consideration of knowing you're leaving. He might be worried."

"He won't be. And our deal is no strings. No emotional entanglements. Calling him with the details of my life is not going to interest him. It's only going to irritate him. He might think I'm looking for him to tell me he's going to miss me or something. Besides, we didn't part on good terms last night. I doubt he cares what I'm doing. He's only interested in the next fuck."

Jenna's voice broke as she said the hated words. Tears clouded her eyes, but she blinked them back.

"Oh, Jenna, I'm sor—"

"Save it, Sarah. I know what I'm doing. I'm going to Milan and Bryce can stew and sulk, or he can forget me. Doesn't matter."

"It does matter, Jenna. It matters a lot to you."

"Look, I'm done talking about this. Grab a pen and paper and I'll give you some information. I'm only staying a night or two at the most."

A tear trickled down her cheek and Jenna swiped it away. She could do this. Playgirls didn't cry. Only awkward, lovestruck girls bawled like babies when the men of their dreams were out of their reach.

Sarah shut the lid of her cell phone in stunned disbelief. What the hell had happened to her sister in the past twenty-four hours?

Sarah replayed their entire conversation, still not believing that it was Jenna who had said those things. This behavior just wasn't like her. And this behavior, Sarah feared, was going to cost her sister the guy she wanted above all others.

Knowing what she was going to have to do, she flicked the pink lid open and hit the speed dial. The British double ring echoed in her ear.

"Hello?"

Sarah took a deep breath. "Trey?"

"Yes?"

"It's Sarah."

"I'm sorry. I can't hear you. Just give me a minute."

Background noise drowned out Trey's voice. She could hear laughter, both male and female, as well as some sexy blues-type music in the background. Oh great, Mr. Stuck-Up was at some highbrow gala, even though it was only four in the afternoon over in London.

Suddenly she heard his muted voice, followed by the velvety sounds of a woman's husky voice. "Hurry back. I'll be waiting for you."

Sarah rolled her eyes, wondering which stunningly beautiful and frightfully skinny supermodel was whispering in his ear. Like she gave a shit, she told herself, even as she skimmed a hand down her hip. Hips that were not in supermodel shape, but that had attracted many a guy, nonetheless.

"Okay, I'm back. Can you hear me?"

"Yes," she said, turning her back on a guy standing beside her. "I'm not sure if you heard me before, but this is Sarah. Sarah McCabe."

"I know what Sarah," came the deep reply. "I know your voice."

Silence. Mr. Highbrow knew her just by her voice? No way. He must have caller ID.

"Sarah, where are you?"

"Work."

"Since when does La Belle Boudoir play Guns n' Roses?"

"It's La Belle Salon, and I'm not there. I'm at my second job."

"Sounds like a bar."

"It is."

"Not the Cadillac?"

"The only bar in Lucan," she said, much too peevishly. She could just see him on the other end of the line, sneering in disgust. Mr. Stuck-Up would never find himself in an establishment like the Caddy. His type of watering hole was some fancy martini bar, not a beer house with rock music and peanut shells on the floor. The man would probably break out in hives the minute his five-hundred-dollar Italian leather shoes hit the floor.

"Sarah, do you really think you should be working at the Caddy? I mean, it's a pretty rough clientele. The pay can't be worth it."

"Well, six-figure jobs are a little scarce here in Cowville, if you know what I mean. Besides, the fringe benefits aren't bad at all, and I'm not just talking about the tips, either. There's something to be said for these blue-collar boys and their rough hands."

She smiled to herself. *There. Put that in your pipe and smoke it.* There was dead silence on the other end and Sarah took perverse pleasure in robbing Mr. Highbrow of speech.

"You ever thought of getting out of Cowville," he asked. "Or do you like the thought of shackling yourself to one of those redneck idiots in Lucan?"

"There's nothing wrong with being married."

"Those fools will you give you nothing but heartache and babies."

"I happen to like babies. I want at least four, you know. And I've already had heartache, and it wasn't at the hands of one of the Caddy's rednecks."

"Sarah—"

"Look, I know what you think of me and what I want in life, and I don't really care."

"Really? I bet you a grand you don't know what the fuck I'm thinking now."

Yeah, she knew—that he wished he could find something to gag her with. But what Tight Ass was thinking wasn't important here. Mr. Highbrow had a way of making her feel as insignificant as a pesky, irritating bug. But she would not be baited. Not today. Today she had bigger issues.

"Look, as much as I enjoy tossing around insults, that's not why I'm calling you."

"No? Maybe you just like the sound of my voice."

"In your dreams," she groaned. "Look, something is up with Jenna, Trey."

"What?"

"For some reason my sister has decided to act like a total moron where your brother is concerned."

"How so?"

"She's pretending she wants just sex and nothing else. She's ruining everything, including our plan for their happily ever after. I mean, they're both out for only sex now—that wasn't what we thought was going to happen."

"Well, I never thought Jenna would offer Bryce carte blanche with her body."

"I know. She's done this weird personality switch, like she's trying to be all city girl and stuff. Do you know, she actually turned Bryce down when he asked her out to dinner and a movie?"

"Not good." Trey sighed into the phone receiver. "I wonder why she's blowing him off. That's so unlike Jenna."

"I'm worried, Trey. What if Bryce thinks that he's getting a good deal with Jenna—I mean, he's not even having to work at the sex part. He might see this as a way of getting his rep back with little effort. And with Jenna just in it for the sex, and turning down dates, Bryce is never going to have the opportunity to see Jenna for the person she really is."

"I need to talk to my brother."

"Like pronto, because Jenna for sure is losing it. Let's hope Bryce is saner."

"I'll do what I can. You want this—right, Sarah? Me and you working together."

Sarah hesitated, letting those words wash over her in a way she didn't care to think about.

"Sarah?"

"Yeah, sure, this is what we want, for Bryce and Jenna to be together."

"Okay, then, so that means you and I have to work together and keep each other informed of our siblings' intentions toward each other."

"Then I should probably tell you that Jenna is planning to leave on a flight late tonight for Milan. She's making an emergency trip to one of her clients who's decided to have a meltdown."

"Milan? On such short notice?"

"I think part of the haste has to do with your brother. She doesn't want to be in the city this weekend. She wants to show Bryce that she's not sitting around waiting for him. It's all part of her stupid plan to play the playgirl. If you ask me, it's just going to make Bryce mad."

"Mad? He'll go ballistic. Shit," Trey snapped. "She wasn't even going to tell him she was leaving?"

"Nope. It's so not Jenna. I just don't know what's gotten into her."

"Did she give you any other details?"

"I have her hotel information. You want it?"

"Yeah, let me grab a pen."

"Trey?" The woman's voice drifted again in from the background. "Darling, are you in here?"

"Just a sec, Mandy."

Mandy. She knew the woman now, all six feet of her, five of them long coltlike legs. *Bitch.* "Why don't I just e-mail you with it? It sounds like you're busy," she snapped.

"Okay, then."

Well, that was easy. The bastard almost sounded relieved. "Yeah, well, talk to ya later."

"Sarah—"

She didn't let him finish. With a click she closed her phone. One sidelong glance at the bar and she was staring at the stunning picture of Mandy gracing the cover of the latest *Cosmo.* No doubt Mandy had been photographed by Trey. After all, he was the most sought-after photographer in the fashion world. Goddamn Tanya for bringing in that magazine.

The redneck seated at the bar grinned at her, then pointed at the magazine. "She's a hottie," he said around a mouthful of cheeseburger.

"If you ask me, she needs a sandwich."

The man gaped at Sarah as she walked around the bar with a trayful of beers.

Damn Mandy for being perfect, and damn Trey for liking that sort of unattainable beauty. He was such a cold asshole—always had been. So different from both of his brothers.

"Hey, hot stuff," Ashton called as she walked past his booth. "What's shaking, besides that gorgeous ass of yours?"

Sarah stopped and turned around. Ashton, her dad's one and

only employee, always had a way of making her feel like a sex goddess. "Hey, Ash. Have you ordered yet?"

"Nah, I was waiting for you. Wanted to see if you were on the menu today."

Normally she didn't consider this sort of thing, but her pride for some reason was stinging. Trey. He always made her feel this way—worthless.

"So, beautiful, what's the lunch special?"

"If you ask nicely, it could be me."

Aston flashed her his killer smile. "Pretty please, with you and a cherry on top."

Sarah pressed in and whispered, "On top of where?"

"Wherever you want me to find it, beautiful."

Winking, she whispered. "I think the lunch special is me in the bathroom in about five."

"Oh, good. My favorite."

Sarah shot him a flirty smile over her shoulder. Mandy she might not be, but she managed to get the guys just fine. Heck, Ashton was already following her. And oh, look, he had an impressive hard-on.

Lunch break today was going to be anything but boring.

Ten

Jenna heaved a huge sigh of relief. Gabriella had liked the new concept for Duchess Lingerie that she had presented, and even seemed enthusiastic about helping pick the location of the shoots and the magazines they wanted to target. All seemed to be back on course, and Jenna couldn't have felt more relieved.

The conference with Gabby had been a success, but clearly she could not say the same about this meeting with the supermodel Eduardo.

They'd been talking for nearly half an hour. And a couple of espressos and ricotta-filled cannolis later, they were still no closer to a deal. And Jenna so desperately needed to close this deal.

When she took a second cannoli—she was starved from the long flight—the hunk looked at her like she was an alien. His gaze skimmed over her figure for a third time and she wondered if he didn't approve of her taking another pastry. Bryce, on the hand, wouldn't have batted an eye. He loved to be around people who loved food as much as he did. And Jenna really loved food—and Bryce, damn him.

Biting into the rich custardy filling, Jenna realized she really needed to stop thinking about Bryce and focus on the matters at hand.

"So this is an ad with big women. Could be lucrative. Who is the woman?"

Jenna popped the last bite of pastry into her mouth and brushed the crumbs from her hands. As she chewed she looked at the handsome god and couldn't deny that with his face and body, he could drive up sales of lingerie. Too bad his attitude sucked. He was a little too sulky for her tastes, but then it wasn't her preferences she was worried about. What mattered was what the women who would buy Duchess Lingerie would desire. Jenna had a feeling that this guy's looks would satisfy even the pickiest woman's palate.

"I'm not certain who we'll be using. We're still searching through portfolios."

"But she'll be big?"

Jenna gritted her teeth. "Voluptuous."

Eduardo shrugged in deference. "But beautiful, yes?"

"Very."

"And what is in it for me?"

"A chance to work for Giancomo Designs."

He held up a perfectly manicured hand. "The daughter of the house of Giancomo. Not the same thing."

"The beloved *only* daughter of Giancomo," Jenna reminded him, "and a protégé of her papa. Trust me, if you make Gabriella happy, and her undies sell like hotcakes, Don Giancomo will make you the star of his runway."

Eduardo seemed to take that little tidbit into consideration.

"I leave tomorrow, but you have my number. Give it some thought. This is a good opportunity for you, and I won't lie: It's a fabulous opportunity for Duchess Lingerie."

Nodding, he stood to his full height. He was tall but not as tall as Bryce. Why couldn't she stop thinking about him? She blamed it on fatigue and lack of food.

"Thank you for meeting with me on such short notice. I really do appreciate it."

"Thank you for the invitation to pose. I'll do it, but I'd like to have input into the woman who will pose with me. Chemistry is very important for making something like this believable. If you want a sexy ad, I'll need to be attracted."

Surprise set her back. "Even with a plus-sized model?"

"I'm Italian." He smiled. "I love women with curvy bodies. And I like blondes, if you're interested in my preferences."

Jenna swallowed hard as he looked down at her. He reached for her hand and brought her knuckles to his mouth for a kiss. "No ring?" he asked as his gaze slipped down to her ring finger.

Jenna felt herself flush. He pulled her a bit closer and kissed one cheek, then the other one before whispering in her ear, "Perhaps we might talk some more. My apartment is only a few blocks from here."

Jenna's first impulse was shock. Then a little thrill shot through her. Wow. Eduardo was a hot fashion model who was obviously interested in her. Her confidence shot up, but then her blood cooled as an image of Bryce came into focus. Eduardo was hot, but Lord, oh Lord, Bryce was hotter.

And she missed him. Even though she was still steaming from their fight the other night.

"I'm sorry. I can't. I really should go."

"Previous commitment?" he asked silkily. "Perhaps later this evening, for dinner."

"The *bella signorina* will be busy *all* night."

Jenna fought the urge to faint. No way, she could not be hearing Bryce's deep velvety voice. She took a steadying breath . . . and smelled him. He was standing right behind her. Here. In Milan.

Eduardo's hand still held hers while Jenna did a little half turn to look over her shoulder. There was no denying it was Bryce. There was also no disputing that Bryce was way more gorgeous than the man holding her hand. One look at Bryce with a five-o'clock shadow was enough to make her thighs quiver.

Oh God, what was she supposed to do now?

The color from Jenna's face drained to a pasty white and Bryce felt immense pleasure at the sight. What the hell was she thinking letting this guy put his hands and lips on her?

"Do you know this man?"

"Oh, she knows me," Bryce growled. His response left no room for misinterpretation. The man knew just how well acquainted Jenna and he were, and if he was too stupid to hear it in the words, then he would definitely pick up on it from the way Bryce glared at him as he pulled Jenna's hand from the Italian stud's grip.

"Ah, the previous commitment, I assume."

"Yeah."

"I will be in touch soon. I like your offer," he said to Jenna, before flashing Bryce an enigmatic smile.

And just what the hell was that supposed to mean? Had Jenna offered this guy the same deal he'd gotten?

Oh hell, no! Over his dead body.

Mr. Tall, Dark and Handsome left the table and Bryce finally turned his attention to Jenna, who was staring at him as if she couldn't quite believe what she was seeing.

"I love Italy. You should have told me you were coming. I would have kept you company on the flight."

"What are you doing here?" she snapped, finally collecting herself.

"Coming after you. And just in time, too. That guy was about to devour you whole."

"*That guy* is business," she said mutinously, her beautiful blue-green eyes turning a shade darker. And that pissed him off.

"Oh, the same kind of business I am?"

"What is it to you?"

"It's a whole lot to me, Jenna. That's what I've been trying to tell you, but you won't listen."

"Let go of me," she grumbled, trying to shake off his hold.

"Hell, no. I've flown all the way here, and it wasn't for you to dis me."

"Yeah, I know. It was for sex."

Bryce felt his skin stretch tight over his jaw. He didn't know if it was jet lag or the remnants of his anger at seeing Jenna with another man that had him seeing red, but that comment sent him over the edge.

"Well, that was our agreement, wasn't it? Anytime, anywhere, no-strings sex."

Her gaze narrowed. "You spent money on airfare and took time away from your beloved restaurant just for sex?"

"Hey, I told you the next time I felt like getting laid, I'd let you know. So, consider this your notification."

She gaped at him, and he pulled her by the hand toward the side-walk and a small car that was idling. This was not the way he had imagined greeting Jenna in Milan. When he'd closed his eyes and dozed off during the flight, he had imagined a somewhat more wel-coming Jenna. He also hadn't imagined himself being such a jerk. Why had he said such a thing?

Because he was still seething from finding Jenna—*his* Jenna—being kissed by another man. Bryce didn't care that it was really only a chaste kiss, not to mention the national way of saying hello or good-bye. Formality and tradition could go to hell for all he cared—he didn't want anyone groping Jenna.

"Get in," he said more gruffly than he'd intended, and she balked. She folded her arms across her chest and glared at him as he held the door of the little economy compact open for her.

"And where are we going?" Jenna asked.

"Where do you want to go?"

"Take me back to my hotel. Please," she added as an afterthought before she slipped into the car. Bryce watched the way her skirt rode up her thigh. He couldn't wait to get his hand up it and feel the smooth creamy expanse of skin.

When he climbed into the driver's seat he was aware of Jenna's eyes on him. When he reached for the gearshift and put the car into first, he glanced over at her and saw that she was still watching him.

She looked damn gorgeous in her fashionable business attire. Her hair was pulled up, exposing her neck and the cleavage spilling from her blouse. His gaze dropped to the exposed part of her thigh and he gripped the gearshift to avoid touching her.

Stepping on the gas, he refocused. Surely he could keep his libido in check for the hour or so it was going to take to get to Tuscany. But the urge to see if she still belonged to him was strong.

Jesus. Did Jenna want him even half as much as he wanted her? On the flight over, Bryce had done a lot of thinking. He'd come to conclusions that he'd refused to even think about these past years.

Somehow chasing Jenna halfway around the world had made him face the facts. No way would he run after a woman for sex, no matter how hot it was. He'd dropped everything, even his restaurant, to go after her.

So, the truth, while not surprising, had come swift and hard. He wanted more than sex. He wanted Jenna. For always.

"How do you know which way to go when I haven't even told you where I'm staying?"

"I've already been to your hotel. Your luggage is in the back."

"What?"

She swiveled in her seat, exposing more thigh, and he felt his jeans grow tight. He really needed to keep his eyes on the road, but that patch of creamy skin was playing havoc with his concentration. All he could think of was tonguing it—making little circles on that soft skin with the tip of his tongue until he got closer to the apex of her thighs. Then tonguing something completely different.

"Bryce?"

Lifting his gaze from her lap, he looked into her face. No help there. She was so beautiful. He wanted to pull her hair down and let it tumble around her shoulders. Then he wanted to put her seat back, strip her bare and climb on top of her and fill her with one hard thrust.

"How did you even know I was here?"

"That's the thing, Jenna. Don't ever think to do this again, because you should know I'll just be right behind you." She blinked as if she couldn't understand what he was saying. His hand left the shifter and landed on that sexy patch of skin. "How could you think I wouldn't want to know where you'd gone? How could you think I wouldn't be worried for your safety?"

She snorted and looked away, directing her gaze to the buildings of Milan. "Please. You were never worried before we started sleeping together."

He squeezed her leg until she looked at him. "Why do you think I called you every night?"

"Habit?"

He was growing angry at her nonchalant attitude. "No! To make sure you got home from work okay."

"Oh, because the country girl is too stupid to spot danger in the big city—is that it?"

Bryce turned off the main street that led out of Milan and into a narrow alley between two office buildings. He put the car in park, then turned to glare at Jenna.

"Why are you being so fucking pigheaded?" he snapped. "I've never thought that way about you and quit insinuating that I do. I called you every night because I did want to make sure you were okay, but mostly I called you because I needed to hear your voice before I went to sleep."

She didn't answer. Just blinked and stared at him as though she thought he'd lost his mind. He touched her hair, pulled out the clip that was holding it up, and watched the strawberry blond strands slide to her shoulders.

"I've always needed to hear your voice at the end of the day. You're my calm, Jenna. I would have gone out of my mind if I hadn't known where you were. Thank God your sister realized that and called my brother. Trey is the one who told me where you were going."

"And you came here for me?"

"Yeah, I did."

"Why?"

"We're going to Tuscany. I have an old farmhouse there."

"You do?" Her beautiful eyes were big as saucers. "I had no idea."

"I actually just bought it. I wanted you to see it."

"Bryce, I really do have business to tend to."

"I know. But you can do that from the house."

Bryce put the car in reverse and pulled out of the alley. He was back on the main road and heading out of the city toward the countryside.

"Why are you really doing this?"

Why did she have to be so stubborn? Bryce thought. "Why do you think?"

She shrugged. "You must have the urge to get your freak on in Italy."

He groaned in frustration. "Why do you have to be so unpleasant?"

She had the decency to look abashed. "I'm sorry. I'm jet-lagged, and I just have so much to do...."

"Why don't you lie back and sleep for a little bit?" he muttered. "It won't take long to get to San Gimignano. Then we can talk."

Nodding, Jenna closed her eyes. "You know, Bryce," she said sleepily, "I didn't think it was part of the deal that we would have to tell each other our plans for every minute of our lives."

"Yeah, well, you bargained with the wrong man, Jenna. Because I want to know where you are every second of the day."

"But—"

"Go to sleep," he interrupted. "Unless, of course, you want me to pull over and get my freak on."

She closed her eyes. Bryce had never been more disappointed.

Jenna awoke slowly and blinked. The sun was hanging low in the azure sky. Fingers of orange and hot pink streaked across the horizon, making the clouds a kaleidoscope of pastels.

In the distance, row after row of grape vines and olive trees dotted the hills. Sun-warmed houses in the color of terra-cotta rose out

of green fields. Cypress trees lined the narrow, rambling road they were
now traveling.

"We're almost there," Bryce said as she stirred and sat up. "That's
San Gimignano, where the house is. It's a medieval town dating from
the thirteenth century. Has the best piazza in Northern Italy. At least
I think so. Piazza del Duomo has a fabulous market where you can
buy anything. I love going for the fresh produce and meat. I think you'll
like it. And I know a great place for gelato. It's right in the piazza."

Jenna could hardly take it all in. First Bryce was here in Italy, and
now he was whisking her away to Tuscany to his house, for God's
sake? When the hell had Bryce bought a house, and why hadn't he
told her?

Maybe he hadn't wanted her to know about it. Maybe he liked
coming here with other women. Oh God, how many others had he
brought here?

"Here we go. You can see the house on top of the hill. It's small,
but the view is outstanding."

"When did you buy it?" she asked, not bothering to add *and why*.

"Last year. You remember our nanny, Maria? Well, it was her
family's place. When she left us, she came back to Italy and lived
there. She died last year and the family couldn't keep it. They con-
tacted me and asked if I would be interested in purchasing it. I jumped
at the chance."

"Oh." She could just imagine how many other things Bryce jumped
when he was here.

"Tuscany is Italy's breadbasket. Since I'm a chef, it's a dream to
visit. And owning a piece of its land is surreal."

Yeah, and so was this.

"Here we are," he said, with obvious pride in his voice. "It's not much, but it's cozy. And like I said, it's got a great view of an estate vineyard out the back."

Bryce pulled the car up to a small farmhouse made of the same stone as the other houses she had seen. It was old, rustic and utterly charming.

Bryce was already out of the car and coming around to her door. He helped her out, but didn't let go of her hand. "So what do you think, Jen? You like it?"

"It's great."

And it really was. Suddenly Jenna felt a little sick. Had Bryce done this before, brought women here?

All those business trips, she reminded herself. Had they really been business, or had he lied to her and come to Italy with some gorgeous blonde for a few days of romance?

"I pay a local to watch the place for me. I called her before I came so that the inside would be ready for us."

Her. That was all Jenna heard. A woman. No doubt an exotic Italian beauty who doubled as Bryce's lover.

"You want to go in?"

Not really. But then she was in the middle of nowhere and she wasn't sure how she'd get back to Milan. And the prospect of sleeping in the hatchback wasn't appealing, either.

"Jenna?"

"Yeah, let's go in."

He held her hand as they walked up the path. He opened the door with his key and ushered her through. Jenna knew her mouth was hanging open as she looked around. The house was small, but it was warm and beautiful and looked like something out of a magazine.

"Estella decorated for me. What do you think?"

That she hated Estella, but that was hardly fair to the woman. Besides, it wasn't like she was going to admit it to Bryce. She was in this for the sex, and nothing else, as far as he knew. No need to blow her cover by getting all jealous. Even though she was feeling like she could scratch Estella's eyes out and string Bryce up by his balls.

"It's great," she replied as she set her purse on the tile countertop. She saw that Estella had placed a bowl of fresh fruit and a loaf of crusty bread on the counter. To the right, a bottle of red wine was sitting atop a handwritten note. Too bad her Italian sucked. Then again, maybe she really didn't want to know what the note said.

"I'll be right back," Bryce said. "I'm just going to grab the suitcases."

Jenna didn't say anything. What could she say? Nothing that was in her heart—that was for sure.

Bryce was back in what felt like two seconds. Far too soon for Jenna to have come up with a plan to get her emotions in check. If she didn't want Bryce to bail, she needed to get rid of these clingy, jealous feelings that were ruling her.

"Are you hungry?" he asked. She noticed he made a beeline for the letter.

Jenna turned her back, not wanting to see Bryce read Estella's letter. She was hungry. But not for food. Just for Bryce. And not just Bryce's body, either. She was hungry for his affection. For his love.

"No, I'm okay."

"Really? Because Estella says she's put some cheese and prosciutto in the fridge."

"No, really, I'm not hungry."

"Then do you want to get cleaned up and go into town?"

What? So he could meet Estella? God, she really needed to get a grip, for crying out loud.

He came around the counter and reached for her, wrapping his arm around her waist. "I know this is strange, but I hope you're as excited as I am to be here. I've been wanting to tell you about this place, but with the magazine fallout and all that, I got sidetracked."

"You don't owe me any explanations, Bryce. What you do with your life isn't my concern."

Something flashed in his eyes. Was it—hurt? "I brought you here because I wanted to spend time with you. No work. No family. You wouldn't allow me to take you on a date, so I decided this was the best way to get you alone."

"I have a lot of work to do, Bryce."

"One night, Jenna? You can't leave work to be with me for one night?"

When had Bryce ever asked that of her? Never.

"I just want it to be like it was, Jenna. When it was just the two of us hanging out. I want to take you to the piazza and show you around. I want to have dinner with you and talk, share things. Don't you want that? Don't you want more than just sex?"

Yes, she wanted to scream, but then what would he do? Would he regret his rash words? Would he think that she'd read too much into them? One night of talking didn't mean he wanted to marry her.

She was spared answering him by the ring of her phone. She moved to her purse, but Bryce beat her to it. He slammed his palm down on the leather bag, covering it.

"Who the hell is calling you? It can't be anyone from home."

"Why not? I stopped and got that little chip you need to make and place international calls."

"Always business," he snapped. "You ever think of anything other than business?"

"Bryce, I really need to see who's calling. It might be important."

He dragged his hand through his hair. "Obviously more important than this."

Jenna reached into her purse and retrieved her phone. "It's James," she said, turning her back. "I'll only be a minute."

"Jenna—" Bryce tried, but then stopped. "Whatever. I'm going to shower. Then I'm going to the piazza. You can stay or you can spend all fucking night talking to James. I don't care anymore."

She flipped the phone open.

"Hey, sunshine, how'd you make out today?" James asked.

Jenna watched as Bryce stripped out of his T-shirt. The muscles in his back rippled beneath his bronzed skin. Her mouth actually began to water. She wanted to touch him. To feel him. But most of all, she just wanted to be held by him.

These last few days had left her emotionally raw.

"Jenna?"

"Ah, it was good, James."

"Not a good time to talk?"

"Not really."

"Okay, just wanted to check on you and make sure you're okay. We'll catch up Tuesday morning when you get back to work."

"Okay. And, James, thanks for calling."

"No problem."

Jenna clicked her phone shut and stared at the bathroom door, which Bryce had slammed shut. He was acting strange. First flying here, and then this, this desire to spend time with her out of the sack. What did it mean?

If he were any other guy, she'd know what to think. That Bryce was looking for more than just some casual fling. But this was Bryce, after all. He was a commitment-phobe. He couldn't possibly want what she wanted. At least not yet.

The doorbell rang, and Jenna went to get it. When she opened it, she looked down to see a little old lady standing there with a basket.

"Signorina Jenna?" she asked in a heavily accented voice.

"*Si?*"

"Signor Bryce asked for this."

Jenna took the basket from the lady and tried to peer into it, but it was covered by a cloth. "*Grazie,*" she said, trying her limited Italian.

"*Mi chiamo Estella.*"

"You're Estella?" Jenna gasped.

"*Si?*" the woman replied.

Jenna reached out and grabbed her hand. "It's so very nice to meet you."

The woman's eyes widened and she smiled, as if she knew of Jenna's relief. "It is very good also to meet you at last."

"At last?"

The woman smiled, and then turned away. "Signor Bryce speak of you all the time. It is good to finally meet his *bella signorina*," she said again. Bryce had talked about her? Really? Jenna was suddenly giddy at the thought.

As the woman disappeared down the cobbled sidewalk, Jenna tore the cloth from the basket and peered in. It was filled with chocolates. Ooh, and chocolate-covered cherries in syrup—her favorite.

Bryce Ryder truly was a god, she thought as she looked once more at the bathroom door. Now she just needed to figure out how to capture him.

Eleven

Watching Bryce in the shower was something Jenna knew she shouldn't be doing, but she couldn't seem to draw herself away. She'd only meant to sneak a peek, but with a view like this, who wouldn't want to stay?

God, he was beautiful, with the water rushing down over his naked, glistening muscles, then running in rivulets down his chiseled six-pack. Hungry for him, she let her gaze follow a particular stream of water as it trickled down his perfect torso, down the fine black hair on his belly, which she wanted to trace with her tongue. Down lower to where his hands cradled his thick shaft.

Sex with Bryce in a steaming shower had always been a favorite fantasy of hers, but there was no way she could ever have imagined just how beautiful he looked totally naked and glistening wet.

Look away, the modest voice inside her screamed. But the vixen lurking inside her lured her on. Besides, it wasn't like he knew what she was doing. He probably thought she was still on the phone with James. Man, he'd been pissed when she'd taken the call. And the little thrill of euphoria that shot through her blood was still swimming inside her.

He'd been so possessive today. He'd said he wanted to spend time with her, alone in a rustic farmhouse, tucked away in the vine-covered fields of Tuscany. She'd been mesmerized, buoyed by the thought that he might actually want more from her than sex.

Thank God, her cell had gone off. One minute more and she would have been lost. Would have risked everything and told him how much she loved him. How badly she wanted to make a life with him.

But what did Bryce want?

The sound of the water changed. It was harder, pulsing, and it drew Jenna's attention away from her thoughts. Bryce was reaching up, angling the showerhead down toward his groin, letting the hard spray hit the head of his cock as he stood in the open ceramic tile shower, gloriously naked, just asking to be watched. And the way his fingers were traveling up and down his shaft, a slow, teasing glide up one side, then down the other, kept her rooted to her spot, all thoughts and questions about Bryce's feelings replaced by lust.

Bryce was already impressively aroused, but she watched him grow ever thicker and longer as he gently—teasingly—trailed his fingers along his engorged shaft. His eyes suddenly closed, his lips parting a fraction as the hard spray pelted his cock.

Wild horses couldn't drag her away from the erotic sight of Bryce in the shower, masturbating.

Jenna watched as he lifted his face to the warm spray of water. His eyes were still closed and he swallowed hard, his Adam's apple bobbing up and down. His neck suddenly arched back and his biceps seemed taut, the ink of his tattoo stretched. With a quick glance downward, she discovered the reason. His fist was now enclosed around his cock and he was driving it up and down, pumping himself as the water continued its pulsing beat where his hand and cock were joined.

Sexy as hell. She'd never seen anyone as sexy as Bryce. And if she had any sense at all, she'd strip down naked and join him in the shower, throwing herself at him, not caring about her heart or what motives were driving him.

But this stolen moment, watching him touch himself, was too much temptation. She might never have this opportunity again, so Jenna watched him masturbate, all the while wondering what it'd feel like to be taken by Bryce in the shower.

He was working himself harder, his fisted hand sliding up his long length. With a quick flick of his wrist, he rubbed the swollen head, then changed direction, stroking downward. His right hand came up and cupped his sack, kneading in time to the way he was fisting his cock.

With a groan that was so erotic it made Jenna tremble, he turned toward her, his back to the wall, his head thrown back against the tiles.

How primal he looked, his biceps bulging, his stomach muscles quivering. And his cock. Oh God, his cock looked so good in his hand.

"Jenna," he suddenly moaned, and she froze, unable even to blink. Had he seen her watching him from behind the cracked door? Had he finally realized that she'd invaded his privacy and was watching this very intimate personal moment?

"Ah, yeah," he moaned again as he stroked himself. "Jenna," he whispered again, his teeth clenching. "Christ, I wish this was you jacking me off."

Oh God! Was Bryce fantasizing about her?

"Here it comes, baby."

He was! Jenna nearly came right there, right as Bryce did. His seed shot out of the head of his cock and onto his hand, then he rubbed it along his shaft. Jenna heard him whisper her name once more. And that was it! Her clit was vibrating against the silk of her panties, which were soaked. One swipe of her finger against the wet silk was all she needed to begin shaking.

The water shut off, and Jenna quickly rose from her knees. Her legs were still shaking as she made her way to the bedroom. Flinging open the suitcase, she pulled out a white gauzy sundress and hurried to dress before Bryce could enter the room and find her still needy from watching him.

Her damn legs were still shaking a half hour later as they headed out the door toward the piazza for supper.

Damn Bryce, he was as addictive as a drug, and she was fast becoming a junkie.

They walked hand in hand around the piazza, taking in the sights and smells of Tuscany. Jenna was amazed by the beauty and history—Bryce knew she would love it. They made a plan to come back in the morning for the market.

He loved that idea. Shopping with Jenna for food was something he'd always enjoyed. Knowing that food was going to be shared between them at a picnic was even better. He had all kinds of plans for that picnic formulating in his mind.

After their stroll, they dined alfresco at the piazza. Bryce was starved, but the lure of sharing a glass of Chianti and a plate of pasta was too much of an enticement. So he ordered a meal *per uno*—for one—and they shared it. He fed her from his fork, picking out the tender pieces of chicken and the finest strands of spinach. He'd picked a rich and creamy Florentine sauce, knowing the delicate flavors of roasted garlic and white wine would be something that Jenna would enjoy. And enjoy it, she did. And he loved every minute of feeding it to her, and kissing her in between bites. He also loved the way she responded, the way her fingers traveled up his thigh as they sat close together, kissing and eating from the same fork, drinking from the same glass.

It was the most romantic meal he ever had. And he hadn't even been the one to cook it for her.

Bryce wasn't the only one smitten with Jenna. The guy at the next table kept staring at her. The waiter was also taken with her, sending her smiles and coy looks. At the end of the meal, he brought her a lemon gelato—on the house.

"*Grazie*," she said, her face lighting up as the waiter handed her the cone.

Bryce cast a glance at the next table. The guy was still there, nursing a glass of vino—still watching Jenna.

Bryce took Jenna's hand. "Let's go for a walk. I'll show you some of the medieval towers. They look spectacular in the moonlight."

"Okay," she said, licking the gelato. "But first give me a second. I want to enjoy this."

Bryce cast a glance around and saw that the Italian stud was still seated at his table. He'd slid down into his chair, his legs spread like he couldn't hold them together, like his dick had grown so huge inside his designer pants that it made it impossible for him to do anything but stroke his cock. And Mother of God, didn't he do just that? He took his hand and slipped it beneath the table until it rested on his groin; then he began rubbing himself over the silk flap of his pants.

Bryce looked at Jenna. She didn't seem to notice the guy as she licked her gelato in the most scandalous, most insinuating way, while the Italian stud eye-fucked her.

Total understanding hit him. The jerk was getting a blow job by proxy.

With a flick of her tongue, the gelato glistened against her lips. A lick, and it was gone, followed by a low, sexy moan. Another lick— this one a bit slower, a bit longer, a bit more enticing. As her tongue came away, it was pointed, and she used that sexy little point to stroke her top lip.

The scene was right out of his dirtiest, raunchiest triple-X fantasies.

Throwing some money down on the table, Bryce grabbed Jenna's hand and pulled her to her feet. "Time to go on that walk," he said. He was not going to be a jerk, he kept repeating to himself. But by the time they'd left the piazza, he was completely beyond rational thought. All he knew was that Jenna was damn gorgeous in that white sundress, sexy sling-back heels and a glowing complexion that was tinted the color of peaches. He had to have her, and damn if he didn't know just the place.

He guided her down a dark alley between the Piazza del Duomo and Piazza della Cisterna.

He pressed her up against the brick wall, caught her surprised expression as her soft breasts pressed tight up against him. He was molding into her so close that he could feel the heat of her pussy warming his thighs.

"Have another lick," he commanded while his hands went to work beneath her gauzy sundress. His fingers instantly met with the warm, smooth skin of her supple thighs.

"Why?"

"Because I want the same show you were giving that stud."

"What stud?" she asked between licks, and he heard himself growl at the sight.

"The one rubbing his dick while he watched you lick that thing. Now I want to watch, but this time, I want you to do it for me— just me."

"I think you're getting far too much enjoyment from watching me eat this gelato."

"It's a fetish," he whispered as he looked down into her upturned face. The lemon gelato was millimeters from her lips, and his palms were still sliding up her thighs, working toward the apex, where he knew he'd find soft, damp skin covered in lace.

"Since when did eating an ice-cream cone become erotic?"

"Since I began having masturbation fantasies of you."

"You've had . . . fantasies about me?"

She gulped, and he watched the sensual way her throat moved up and down. He thought about her swallowing him. He hid his groan of need with his words. "Maybe one or two," he admitted. *Maybe hundreds*, he silently acknowledged.

"About me eating an ice cream?"

"Yeah, well, that image is kind of seared in my brain."

"What image?"

"One day by the pond when you ate your cone like a porn star, sucking, licking, drawing it into your mouth. I had a hard-on so big I was afraid it was going to climb out of my shorts."

Her beautiful eyes flashed, and she looked up at him through her lashes. It was a shy look, and it shook Bryce to the core. This was the Jenna he wanted to see. Part kitten, part lioness.

She held his gaze while she flicked her tongue out, slowly licking at the gelato that was running down the sides of the cone. "Really?"

"Yeah, really."

"What were you thinking, watching me eat my ice cream?"

"Same thing as I am now."

"And what would that be?"

"How I'd give anything for that cone to be my dick and your tongue circling my shaft."

Her eyes flared and she smiled before making tiny circles at the top of the cone. "Like this?"

"Fuck, yeah. Just like that," he groaned. His heavy cock was pressed against her belly. He dropped his head, letting his lips rest against her temple as he watched her.

"Now swallow." He placed his fingertip on her throat and felt the velvety slide of her skin beneath his finger. He wanted to do this when she was swallowing him and drinking him down.

Not caring that someone might catch them, Bryce lowered his mouth to the gelato and dragged his tongue through it, just as if he were licking her pussy.

Restless, his hands started the upward slide once again for the lace panties that shielded her pussy from him.

Together they licked at the cone, their tongues growing closer with every flick, until they touched and rubbed, and Jenna tossed the cone aside, letting it splatter on the cobblestones before reaching for his hair and tugging him closer.

The kiss was explosive. Fuck, he couldn't kiss her hard enough, deep enough. He was ravenous for her, tearing at her sundress, pulling on the delicate straps until he had them down over her shoulders and her bodice pulled to her waist and her tits out, totally exposed.

She broke the kiss, panting. He couldn't stand not touching her. Filling his hands with both breasts, he watched the expression of pleasure cross her face. Unable to resist the temptation he pressed forward, nuzzling the valley of scented skin. Her nipple was inches from his mouth and he flicked it with the tip of his tongue, first in short flicks, then in slow, sexy circles. His cock grew to massive proportions, and he drove it against her belly as he sucked her nipple into his mouth.

She was panting now, writhing against him, wrapping her leg around his calf so she could ride her pussy against his thigh. He was about to pull her panties down and slam into her when he felt her hand slide down between their molded bodies. Her palm flattened against the fly of his jeans, and he closed his eyes allowing himself the pleasure of imagining her hand surrounding him, pumping his thick shaft slowly until he couldn't stand the torture.

The little kitten knew what he wanted. She tore open the buttons of his fly, freeing his cock into her palm. Oh hell, yeah, this was what he wanted.

He felt his cock stiffen, felt a change in his lower body, and instinctively he moved his hips away from her. She followed him, wanting more, but he knew somehow that if he let her continue touching him, the moment would be over. And Bryce knew he was nowhere near done exploring her body. In fact, he knew he would never be done with Jenna.

And then, like a vision, she began a slow slide down the wall. He watched her as he braced one flattened palm against the still-warm bricks; then with his free hand, he took his cock in his hand and slowly began to pump himself.

She watched him with rapt attention and that only made him hotter. "You like watching me jack off, Jenna?"

Her gaze flashed up to his. "Yes. I watched you today, in the shower."

He closed his eyes, remembering the way he'd cradled his balls in his hand and stroked himself so hard that he'd come in a massive explosion. "I know," he finally admitted. And that was why he'd come so damn hard. He'd known she was there, watching him masturbate. He'd heard her, her breathing harsh with arousal. He'd seen her glide her hand over her breasts in growing excitement. As he'd come, he'd seen her hand sneak beneath her skirt as she touched herself, and he'd gone off, wishing she had come into the shower with him so he could have taken her from behind.

"You were so beautiful," she said, reaching out to stroke her finger down his engorged shaft. "And watching you like that, all primal and male, was such a turn-on."

Shit, so was this. He was literally going to explode at any second. Already, a white pearl glistened at the slit of his head. She brushed it with her thumb, then brought it to her mouth. As she licked it away, his breathing stopped.

She looked up at him, her finger still in her mouth, the head of his cock inches from her lips.

He circled her shining mouth with the tip of his cock. She looked so damn gorgeous kneeling on the ground before him, her tits free of her dress and jutting out at him with swollen, needy nipples.

"Suck me off. Right here."

She grabbed his dick, sucking him deep into her hot mouth. "Shit," he hissed as he thrust forward, filling her mouth further with his cock, "you look so damn hot going down on me."

He'd never really done much talking with his other lovers. But there was something about Jenna that freed his tongue. He could be himself with her. He was hard and rough around the edges. But Jenna didn't seem to mind. She liked his dirty mouth. And Jenna getting off with dirty talk ramped him up so hard that every orgasm he had with her nearly killed him.

"Yeah, Jenna," he heard himself growl. "Like that, baby. Yeah, looks so good," he groaned as she circled her tongue around his shaft.

He heard voices, the words unintelligible. Footsteps came closer, then laughter—a man's and a woman's—echoed off the tall stone wall. But Jenna didn't stop. Instead she reached for him, pulling him closer like she didn't want to let go. And he didn't want her to, either.

"Turn you on, that we might have an audience? If that guy could see how good you are at blowing me . . ." He stopped talking. He had to concentrate. His cock was filling, getting thicker. She was having a hard time taking him in, he was so big.

"Oh, fuck, Jenna. I'm gonna come, babe. Let me—"

But she wouldn't let him. She clung to him, sucking him into her perfect mouth, drinking him dry until he could barely stand. Two fingers found their way to her throat and he placed them there, against her hot skin, and felt her swallow him. He pumped into her, giving her more. He felt her, swallowing, taking him inside her, and cried out loud and long—her name.

As she nuzzled her face against his thigh, he felt her smile. His hands were clenched in her hair and he was breathing hard. Damn, she'd blinded him with that orgasm.

And he was still hard.

He helped her to stand, brushed her hand away from his cock. Out of the corner of his eye, he saw the guy from the restaurant standing at the mouth of the alley. *Let him watch*, Bryce thought. He was so out of control now that he knew he was going to have Jenna—right here. He wrapped a hand around her neck, drawing her gaze down as he took his cock in his hand and resumed control. He brushed his dick along her soft white gown, which was glowing in the moonlight, wishing it was her belly he was caressing with the head.

"I want you, Jenna. Now."

* * *

Bryce's gaze skimmed the length of her, and Jenna closed her eyes when she felt his fingers encase her throat, then slowly slide down her neck. Jenna knew she was breathing too fast, too hard, but she was excited beyond what she had ever thought possible. He was master over her body, knowing instinctively how to please her, how to pleasure her body and feed her imagination.

"You ever been watched, baby, as you take a cock?"

Jenna shook her head. Never. But suddenly she knew *he* was watching her. The guy Bryce had told her about from the piazza.

She could feel the heat of his gaze traveling along her body. She was in a shaft of moonlight, and knew that the silver glow gave a luminescence to her body. Her breasts were bare, heavy, silhouetted in moonlight and shadow. He could see everything. What did he think of her, of them in the alley, and what they were doing?

With a smile she tossed back her head and raised her arms to lift the hair away from her neck. The position pushed her breasts forward, making her back arch so that she appeared to be flagrantly offering herself to Bryce. She listened to the harshness of his breathing as she leaned back, giving him a full view of her naked torso. She writhed and moaned, stroking her hands along her body, sensitizing her already-heightened flesh. Bryce's hands were sliding up her hips and over to her waist, where they rested on her ribs. She felt his gaze burning her nipples, and knew then that both Bryce and the stranger were watching the sway and bounce of her breasts.

"Touch my pussy, Bryce," she said as she cupped her breast.

Bryce obeyed her command. Jenna had to cover her mouth with her hand to stifle the moan that threatened to escape her. Slowly, he filled her, first with one finger and then two, plunging and retreating until she was nearly gasping.

Her head snapped to the right and Jenna saw that the stranger was indeed staring, his gaze sliding over her body. In that second, when she met his gaze through the darkness, she felt like the most wicked, most beautiful woman in the world.

With slow, sensual purpose, she ran her palm down over one breast, then down her belly to her sex, where she began touching herself. Bryce continued to push her on, driving her to the brink.

She looked once more toward the stranger at the entrance of the alley, and saw his hand on the fly of his pants. She watched the zipper lower, then saw the flash of white as he freed his cock. She'd never done anything like this before and knew that her orgasm, when she had it, would be explosive.

Bryce slid his warm palm up her thigh to her ass and rubbed it lovingly, seductively.

"I want your cock, Bryce, fucking me hard."

Bryce growled deep in his throat. The sound freed her, and she reached for his hips, bringing them up against her. There was no way she was going to be able to wait till they got back to Bryce's house. She wanted it right there, against the wall, Bryce pounding deep inside her, the stranger watching them, getting aroused by what he saw.

"Let's pretend we're strangers," she whispered seductively against his ear as she stroked his cock, "and you've brought me back here to fuck me."

With a choked growl, he pulled her dress down all the way so that she was totally naked. Bryce lifted her leg so that the ball of her sandal rested against the hard edge of his thigh. She stroked her clit, knowing Bryce was watching, knowing the stranger was watching, too. The rush that sailed through her body was like nothing she'd ever felt.

"How bad do you want my pussy?" she asked.

"Bad. Since the moment I saw you in that sundress, I've been imagining the feel of your cunt. The taste of it."

She shivered against him as she held his rigid cock in her hand.

"So are you going to fuck me?" she asked in a voice that was smoky with desire.

"Oh yeah." His finger slipped between her creases. "Thoroughly."

"Condom?"

He reached into the back pocket of his jeans and produced a square foil wrapper.

"If you want it on, *bella signorina*, you'll have to be the one to cover my cock, because I sure as hell do not want to feel anything between us."

She made quick work of sheathing him, trying to make it sexy as she did it. Bryce was in too much of a hurry to let her play. He rolled the rest of the condom on and parted her swollen folds, entering her in one hard thrust. She gasped. Her breasts swayed back and forth and he fondled them more roughly than he ever had before. His palms captured them and he pressed her breasts together, kneading them in time to his strokes. His breathing was hard, and so was hers. They were almost panting and Jenna reached out and steadied herself by holding on to Bryce's shoulder. She cried out again as Bryce took her even deeper, filling her, stretching her all the way.

"Take me, Bryce." Her lips parted on a moan as he lifted her leg higher and pressed his strong fingers into her thigh. He thrust into her, rocking her body against him, and all she could think about was more.

"Harder," she groaned, gripping his shoulders as he pumped into her. And then she was coming and falling apart in his arms. Pressing her face into his shoulder, which was damp with sweat, she let herself get lost in the sensation of her body spasming around Bryce.

He was gentle, whispering soft words into her ear as he rubbed his palm down her spine. She heard footsteps and looked up from the tangle of her hair to see the retreating back of the stranger.

"Oh, my God," she breathed, then leaned once more against Bryce. "That was so beyond hot."

"Five-alarm hot," he murmured.

She lifted her head and looked up at him. "My gelato melted."

He smiled and closed his eyes. "I'll get you another one. Chocolate. And I'm going to eat it off your body."

Twelve

"This is so beautiful." Jenna sighed as Bryce came up behind her and wrapped his arms around her waist.

"I've seen things more beautiful. Like this morning, waking up beside you."

Jenna closed her eyes and rested her head on Bryce's chest as she watched the sun rise above the horizon. With a smile, she thought how right it was to have accepted Bryce's invitation to stay for another day. Last night had been the best, cuddling up together and falling asleep in each other's arms. They had both been so exhausted, not to mention jet-lagged, that neither one of them had moved. When they woke up, it was to find their bodies were still locked together.

"A penny for your thoughts?" Bryce asked as he kissed the top of her head.

"Just thinking."

"About?"

Us. But she couldn't really say that. Even though things seemed wonderful, Jenna couldn't allow herself to think that everything was the way she wanted it to be. Bryce had made no commitments.

"Last night," she whispered instead. "In the alley."

"Mmm," he murmured. "I thought of that most of the night, too. I've never done that before, and I couldn't stop thinking about how glad I was that the first time was with you."

Jenna smiled at that and let herself indulge in the warm cozies that came with Bryce's confession.

"Are you hungry, babe?" Her stomach suddenly growled and he patted it with his hand. "You're speaking my kind of language. Let me cook you something."

"Let me help."

He glanced at her, thought for a moment, then smiled. "I usually don't like any interference in my kitchen, but I'll make an exception for you."

"Well, don't get too excited. My specialty is toast."

"I love toast," he said with a grin.

They made their way to the kitchen and Jenna studied Bryce as he pulled open the fridge door and stuck his head in.

"We've got eggs, pancetta, some fresh herbs." He straightened and glanced over his shoulder. "How about an omelet?"

"Great." Jenna took a bread knife out of the butcher's block. Unwrapping a loaf of rustic Italian bread from a gingham napkin, Jenna started cutting off thick slices. "I'll start on the toast, then."

With a nod, Bryce gathered his ingredients, pulled out a bowl and started cracking eggs with one hand.

"How come whenever I try that I always get shells that fall in?"

He grinned, his dark eyes flashing at her. "It's an acquired skill. Took me a couple of tries before I got the hang of it."

"What's your favorite thing to cook?"

He thought for a minute, then frowned. "Anything, I guess. I go in phases. Sometimes I like to experiment with pastas or specialty cuts of meat. And desserts are always something I like to create. You know me and my sweet tooth."

"What don't you like about cooking?"

"That's easy," Bryce said as he began chopping up the pancetta, "people who don't eat."

"Everyone eats, Bryce."

"Okay, then, people who don't enjoy eating. I'll cook anything just as long as someone is going to dig in and take pleasure from it. I don't have to ask if you like cooking."

"It's not hard to know the answer to that, especially since I just confessed that toast is my specialty."

"Good thing I like cooking. Otherwise we might starve."

Jenna looked away to hide her confusion. He was talking like they were a couple.

"But if you did like cooking, what would you like to learn how to make?" Bryce asked.

"Bread. Nothing feels more like home than walking into the kitchen and smelling homemade bread baking in the oven."

"I can teach you how to make bread."

"And slather it in butter?"

"Is there any other way to eat warm bread?"

"Not in the McCabe house there's not."

Bryce laughed and Jenna watched as he whisked the meat into the eggs before turning to a pile of herbs he had placed on a cutting board. "You like rosemary and thyme?"

"Sure do."

"What about oregano?"

"I love anything you make, Bryce."

"Yeah? Well, I love cooking for you, Jenna. For real," he said when he caught her frown. "You like food. I like food. You appreciate my skills and that makes it such a joy to cook for you. You know, you're the only woman I've ever really cooked for? I like this, cooking for just one special person."

Jenna felt her heart miss a beat. It was definitely something special to her, too.

"So, what do you want to do today?" he asked as he chopped the herbs fine and dumped them into the egg mixture.

"Doesn't matter. I am at your disposal. Whatever you want to do, I'm game."

"That's a pretty big statement, babe," he teased as he gave her a wink. "You sure about that?"

"Within reason, of course."

He smiled, flashing her his sexy dimple. "Well, first off, we're heading to the market. I love market day. They have more than produce and meat, and I think you'll enjoy it. Then I thought we could have a picnic up on the hill. I know a great spot that overlooks an olive grove and a vineyard."

"Sure. Sounds great."

Jenna climbed up on the counter and crossed her ankles, letting her legs swing as she waited for the first slices of bread to pop up from the toaster. Bryce was already over at the cook top, making their omelets.

She watched him, amazed at how effortless he made it look as he held the frying pan by the handle, gave it a little shake, and flipped the omelet. He looked right at home in the kitchen, not to mention sexy, wearing only his jeans.

"Grab a plate. This is done."

Jenna reached above her head and pulled out a plate. Bryce slid the omelet onto it, and Jenna reached for the toast, which had just popped up. He held a fork out to her and she tore into the omelet scented delicately with fresh herbs.

"You're the master," she said as she closed her eyes in surrender.

"Yeah, I know," he teased.

She held a bite out to him, and he moved to stand between her legs. He let her feed him that bite. And then another, until they'd eaten it all. In between bites he gave her little kisses on her nose, her cheeks, until he was kissing her after almost every bite.

It was the best breakfast Jenna had ever had.

Bryce took the plate from her and helped her down off the counter. "Shower time?"

"Definitely."

"You don't mind some company?" he asked as he followed her out of the kitchen.

"You're gonna have to catch me first," she laughed as she took off for the bathroom.

Bryce had her in two strides. She squealed as he picked her up and carried her to the bathroom.

"Whatever I want to do, right?" he reminded her.

"Within reason," she said, batting her lashes. "A girl has to have some boundaries, you know."

"And a guy has to find a way to break them."

Oooh, Jenna thought as he set her down in front of the shower, *this is going to be one fun day.*

Bryce picked up a bunch of basil and held it to his nose. He couldn't get enough of the pungent scent. How come everything smelled better today? Was it because he was in Tuscany, or was it because Jenna was beside him, shopping with him?

"Let me smell," she said. He held the bunch out to her and she stood on tiptoe to smell it. "Mmm. Now what would you do with that?"

"Anything, but I'm thinking of using it with tomatoes and olive oil to make a sauce. It's called pomodoro and it's light and fresh. How about that for supper along with a bottle of Chianti and a loaf of crusty bread that we make together?"

"Over rigatoni?" she asked.

"Of course," he said, knowing it was her favorite kind of pasta. He tossed the basil into the basket that Jenna was holding and reached for her hand. "Let's go to the cheese and meat. I want some of that for our picnic."

Jenna followed him through the meandering stalls. She clutched his hand tightly, and Bryce felt an overwhelming protectiveness steal over him. When he looked over his shoulder, she gazed up at him and smiled. His breath caught in his chest. She looked beautiful today, dressed in a simple cotton sundress. She was wearing her hair down, like he'd asked her to, and it was blowing softly around her face in the warm Tuscan breeze. She wasn't wearing any makeup and he decided she didn't truly need it. Her skin was flawless and he liked the way her coppery lashes shone without mascara to hide them.

He stopped, gazed down at her, then cupped her cheek. *"Bella signorina,"* he murmured as he kissed her in the middle of the market, where dozens of locals clamored to buy their groceries. But Bryce didn't see any of that. He only had eyes for Jenna.

"What?" she asked, perplexed.

"Do I need a reason to stop and look at you?"

She blushed prettily, turning her complexion from cream to peaches and cream. With the pad of his thumb, he followed the path of the flush that crept into her cheeks.

"You look so right standing here in the market. It's as if this is all routine between us, as if we'd been doing this for years," he found himself saying with a hint of surprise.

And why should it feel strange? This was Jenna, after all. They'd done this a hundred times over the course of their friendship, but never had they gone to the market after sharing breakfast and making love in the shower.

He wanted to do this every Sunday afternoon with her: take her to the market and shop, then stop at a quaint café for a latte, then home, where he'd make her a fantastic dinner, which they'd share over a bottle of wine.

"For the lady?"

Bryce pulled his gaze away from Jenna's face to see an old man wearing a beaten straw hat. He was holding out a ring with a black onyx stone. Bryce contemplated it for a fraction of a second before taking it.

"*Si*, for *la bella signorina*."

Bryce slipped it on her finger. When he was done, he smoothed his thumb over her hand and smiled. "Looks good on you, Jenna."

Why he placed it on her wedding finger, he had no idea. It just seemed a natural thing for him to do.

"Jenna," he murmured as he cupped her face in his hands, "I'm ready for a committed relationship. Just me and you, no one else. And not just sex, either. I want a real relationship—both sides."

Jenna's expression was clearly shocked.

"I know you said you weren't looking for anything more than sex, and I thought I wanted the same thing, too, but now I know that I want more with you."

The smile that lit her face melted his heart. When she threw her arms around his neck, he twirled her around and laughed.

"Is that a yes?"

She nodded and squeezed him tighter. That was when he caught sight of a man with a camera aimed toward them. He was dressed like a tourist, but the camera he wore around his neck said otherwise.

Trey must have set this up.

Shit, he didn't want this moment ruined by a flash. He also didn't want Jenna to know that they were being followed.

"C'mon, I want to take you somewhere."

Throwing some euros onto the man's table to pay for the ring, Bryce grabbed Jenna's hand. Then he practically dragged her through the market and out onto the stone terrace of the piazza.

When he looked back over his shoulder, he no longer saw the photographer.

"Where's the fire?" she gasped as she ran to keep up with him.

"In my pants," he teased.

"Then we'd better head to the lake and get you out of those clothes."

"Funny, that's exactly what I was thinking." He was hard at the thought of skinny-dipping with Jenna.

By the time they got to the lake, which was down the hill and sheltered by the tall stone wall of the piazza, they were tearing at each other's clothes while they kissed as though they were starved for each other.

Jenna unzipped his fly and pulled his jeans down, freeing his cock.

"I want to do it in the water."

Good suggestion. Bryce made short work of her sundress and the lacy panties and lifted her high into his arms. He carried her into the lake until he was submerged to his waist. Jenna's legs were wrapped around his waist and she was rubbing her pussy against his cock.

"Let's go slower," he murmured as he pulled her hair off her neck and wound it around his hand. "I want to savor you in the sunlight."

He nuzzled her neck, then found the sensitive spot that made her mewl and rock into him. With his free hand he brushed his fingertips along her spine, sensitizing her skin until he felt goose bumps and she was writhing on his thigh. He grabbed her hips, watching them move in his hands as he moved his leg between her thighs. Her rhythm was slow and sensual, and watching her like this, naked and hot for him, was a powerful aphrodisiac.

"Bryce," she pleaded, pressing her mound into him in blatant invitation.

"Not yet."

He wet his hand in the water as it lapped his thighs, and brought his fingers to Jenna's breast, letting the cool water trickle over her nipple. It went hard, and Bryce tugged it, flicking it gently until he felt her shudder against him.

"Cold or aroused?" he asked.

"So turned on," she whispered. She rocked backward and he supported her with his hand as his mouth moved down the valley of her breasts. The sun was warm on her body, and the way it highlighted the blush of her skin made Bryce trace the shadows that danced over her breasts.

She reached for his head, directed his mouth to her breasts and sighed when he circled her with his tongue. With little flicks of his tongue, he made her nipple crinkle. When she was begging him, he took her in his mouth and suckled her until she was pulling at his hair and grinding against him.

When he finally reached between her thighs and stroked her, he felt how aroused she was. Dipping his fingers in, feeling her cream, he spread it on the secret spot he wanted to explore on Jenna's body. She was hot enough to let him in, he thought as he watched her lips part invitingly. He just hoped he wouldn't ruin the moment. But he had to get inside her—everywhere.

When he tested her with his finger, she didn't tense up, but moaned and fluttered her lashes, pressing her ass back into his hand for more. Bryce swore he grew another inch just knowing she was receptive to trying out something different.

His hand swept down her back until it was sweeping along her ass, soothing her as he slid his finger in a little more. "Okay?"

She nodded, rocked against his thighs, rubbing her clit on his thigh as he kneaded her ass and fingered her.

"That's it, Jenna," he whispered as she pumped up and down. She had the sexiest ass, perfect for this kind of sex play. He watched the way the sun lit her body, the way her hips were writhing. Christ, she looked perfect like this, with her head tossed back, her hair swinging down her back. He captured her breast and sucked hard as he fully penetrated her with his fingers.

She cried his name in a deep groan, and reached down between their bodies and began stroking him, spreading his precum all over the head of his dick.

"Take me, Bryce."

"No barrier. Just you and me." He nudged his cock in her pussy.

He panted as he filled both her openings. He supported her with his arms as his finger and cock kept up the same rhythm until he was thrusting up hard and she was begging him for more.

With her thighs, she gripped him, then ran her fingers down his back as she came apart in his arms. He barely remembered in time to pull out of her. When he did, he lived out yet another one of his fantasies and pumped himself between the cleft her breasts, coming all over her in an endless stream.

Next time, he promised himself, he was going to come inside her and feel her pussy gripping him, wringing him dry.

Jenna placed a piece of salami and a square of Furlano cheese on a piece of bread. God, everything tasted so good. Maybe it was all the sex they were having that made her so ravenous. Maybe it was just being here with Bryce, knowing that there really was something more than just sex between them.

"You want a grape?" he asked.

"Sure." They were big black grapes that they'd bought that morning at the market. The taste was out of this world. Everything about Tuscany was magical, most especially Bryce.

"Here try this. It's peach juice," he said.

"I love peaches."

"I know," he said grinning. "That's why I bought it."

Jenna took a sip and smiled. "Oh, that's good."

Bryce laughed. "That's what you told me last night. Now I don't know what to think. Am I only as good as peach juice?"

Jenna smiled as she thought of the previous night, and their recent bout of skinny-dipping, and the places on her body that Bryce had touched. "I think we both know you're better than just good."

"Yeah? Well, a man doesn't mind hearing that from time to time."

"Really? Are you saying you like your ego stroked?"

He shrugged. "Among other things."

"Well, let's just say I've never screamed before during sex, so the fact that I scream every time I'm with you is telling."

"Never?" he asked, his eyes sparking in the sunlight.

"Never."

He kissed her and popped another grape into her mouth. She watched as he changed position and leaned against the cypress tree that was shading them from the early-afternoon sun.

"So, tell me about your client."

"You remember when I landed that deal with Duchess Lingerie? Well, I made a mistake and gave James the job of coming up with the ad campaign."

"Why? Seems like something a woman should work on."

Jenna flushed. She didn't want to tell Bryce the truth and spoil this perfect afternoon. So she just shrugged and said she was busy with another project.

"So Jimmy screwed it up, did he?"

"The long and the short of it is, he took a product that celebrates the beauty of voluptuous women and draped it over a chair. Needless to say, the passionate Gabriella Giancomo was incensed that her plus-sized lingerie garnered the attention of a chair and nothing else."

Bryce winced. "I can see how she wouldn't like that. It's like me making a wedding cake, and having only a picture of the topper make the magazine."

"I know. It was a dumb move on my part and I've been working like crazy to make amends. I came to Italy to pitch my ideas in person.

Gabriella loved them. Now I just have to find the means to execute the plan."

"And what is that?"

"A gorgeous plus-sized model and a handsome stud to pose with her."

Bryce suddenly grinned. "That's why you were with that guy at the café?"

"Of course. He's a model, and I'm trying desperately to secure him for the campaign. What did you think I was doing with him?"

"Doesn't matter, does it?" Bryce asked as his finger brushed over the ring he'd bought her. "Because I've got you now, Jenna McCabe. It's committed relationship time. That means no more Italian studs for you."

Jenna actually had to quell the giddiness that threatened to erupt inside her.

"Well, Eduardo is the industry's most sought-after male. He doesn't come cheap. It's not going to be easy, considering the budget we're working with."

Bryce appeared startled. "Her father is one of the most successful designers out there. How can the budget be tight?"

"Because Gabriella wants to do this on her own, without Daddy's help."

"I can understand that. I've bought two oceanfront properties, one on the East Coast, one on the West. I've gone to the bank for a loan to open the restaurants. It's not looking good for financing. Basically the advice I was given was to call on my dad. I'd rather eat glass than do that. So I know where Gabriella is coming from. She wants to be a success on her own. As do I."

Bryce had bought properties? Jenna felt her heart sink. Where did he plan on living, then? Either coast was more than a thousand miles away from her. And what was going to happen to her—to them? Long-distance romances never worked.

Maybe he was thinking short-term commitment, just until he moved out to the coast.

"Hey, beautiful," he said, brushing her windblown hair from her cheeks, "what's the frown about?"

"Nothing," she said, forcing a smile to her lips. It was best not to dwell on things. Protect her heart, she kept telling herself, because she knew that Bryce was soon going to break it.

"Come here." He held his hand out to her and pulled her up so that she was sitting against him. "I want you to see something."

He settled her against him. Her head rested beneath his chin and his hands were crossed over her belly. She tried not to think of the future, of how it would feel when Bryce took off for the coast and a new life. A life without her.

"What does the view remind you of?" he asked.

She studied the shades of green pasture in the valley below them. Saw the cattle roaming free, grazing beneath the sun. The perfect rows of grapevines reminded her of the cornfields on her parents' farm.

"Home," she said quietly. "It reminds me of Lucan."

He squeezed her tight. "I've always thought the same thing. I came here my first year of cooking school to visit with Maria. I fell in love with the place at first sight. It reminded me of Lucan, of the hills and valleys and the farms and orchards. It reminded me of you, and how much I missed you and the farm. Ever since, I've always thought that Lucan could be Tuscany. I mean, look how much tourism Tuscany has. Sure, they have architecture and cathedrals, but what most people come for is the markets, the countryside, the relaxed way of life. Lucan has all that. It just needs to be cultivated."

"Well, good luck," Jenna grumbled. "Lucan is going to be the location of the next Bargain City store—right on my parents' farm."

"*What?*"

Jenna turned in Bryce's lap. "My parents are in financial trouble, Bryce. There's a foreclosure on the farm."

Bryce paled. "No way."

"Afraid so. It's been in the McCabe family for three generations and this will be the last one."

"They can't take the farm."

Jenna sighed. "Yes, they can. The farm has never really made any money. And with this economy, well, it's just not feasible anymore."

"What will your parents do?"

Jenna shrugged. "Dad says he'll become a snowbird and move down south like everyone else his age, but I know he's only saying that so we won't worry. Truth is, I don't know what he'll do if he can't farm."

He hugged her tight. "God, I'm sorry, Jenna. I love that place as much as you do and don't want to see it go."

"It may be a losing battle, but it's not over yet. There're a few more avenues to check." Namely the loan she'd applied for, which she should be hearing about any day.

"Is there anything I could do to help?"

"No, but thanks for asking. Besides, this helps. Just talking about it and feeling you hold me helps."

He kissed the top of her head and held on to her tightly. For long minutes they just sat there, listening to the sounds of nature surround them. It really did remind Jenna of those times on the farm.

A peace stole over her and she could have sworn that Bryce felt the same way.

"It's so beautiful here," she murmured. "But then tomorrow, it'll be back to normal, won't it?" Jenna didn't even want to contemplate that. Today was like a fairy tale. She actually felt as if she and Bryce had something real.

His hands clasped the sides of her face. He looked into her eyes with such emotion, such intensity, Jenna felt the urge to shrink away.

"I'll always treasure the memory of these two days. I think we have something really special."

Swallowing hard, Jenna nodded. He seemed to be waiting for her to say something, but she couldn't speak. A cloud shadowed them, turning everything a little bit darker around them, but not the wonderful green of Bryce's eyes as they held her gaze.

"When we get back home, you're not going to forget me, are you? Or what we've found together?" he asked.

She couldn't answer him, not truthfully. Because the truth was, these two days with Bryce had made her fall more in love with him than ever. And that scared her to death.

His gaze seemed to soften as he trailed his fingers down her cheek, along her neck and over her shoulders, where he slowly untied the straps of her sundress. The thin cotton fell to her waist, baring her naked breasts. She tried to think of something sexy and risqué to say, but he silenced her with the brush of his fingertips along her mouth.

"*Shh,*" he murmured, "it's OK. You don't need to say anything, Jenna. I think we're past words."

With breathtaking tenderness, Bryce reached for her, bringing his mouth down to hers. His breath was warm against her lips and she closed her eyes, waiting for his kiss.

His lips came down softly against hers and she sighed, letting her body sway into his chest as she straddled his thighs. He groaned, deepening the contact, sliding his tongue between her lips, circling her tongue with his as he slanted his mouth over hers. Gently he fanned his thumbs along her cheeks, brushing her skin, caressing her— cherishing her.

He pulled away, his gaze slowly rising from her mouth to her eyes. "Make love to me, Jenna."

Thirteen

"That was such a fabulous meal, Bryce," Jenna said as she sat back in her chair.

"To the chefs," he toasted, raising his wineglass.

"I hardly did anything."

"You were my inspiration. Plus, it was highly enjoyable watching you knead the bread." Jenna saw his gaze slip down to her breasts. "Although, I'd never let you step foot in the kitchen at Cravings. God only knows what Mark and the others would do if they saw you handling dough."

Jenna stuck her tongue out at him and he winked back. "Of course, you may knead anything you want in *my* presence. I thoroughly enjoyed the show."

"You're a pervert."

"No, merely charmed by your ample assets."

Why *had* he suddenly taken an interest in her "assets"?

All evening long she'd been going around in circles, chasing her thoughts, wondering why, after all these years, Bryce was suddenly hot for her. She'd had this body since she was eighteen, and he was just admiring it now?

Jenna worried her bottom lip for the millionth time. Part of her wanted answers to her questions; the other part just wanted to live in blissful ignorance with her sexy chef.

"Want to walk to the gelato shop?" His voice broke into her thoughts.

"Sure. Although the last thing I need is a gelato."

"Ah, we'll walk it off."

Jenna got up from her chair and followed Bryce out of the kitchen. He stopped suddenly, turned back to her and asked, "I have to ask you something."

"Sure."

"Are you regretting this . . . I mean, us?"

"No, why?" *Are you?* she thought.

"Because every once in a while I see you nibbling your lip. You do that when you're nervous or not sure of something. I wanted to make certain it wasn't me or my commitment you were worrying over. Because you can trust me, Jenna. I hope you know that."

The worry she was feeling suddenly lifted from her shoulders. She took his hand, squeezed it and forgot all about those niggling thoughts that had distracted her earlier.

"Let's stay in," she said, draping her arms around his neck.

"I don't know. I was looking forward to seeing you in something chocolate."

"You're the chef extraordinaire," she said with a smile. "Improvise."

* * *

"Chocolate body sauce," he said with a wicked grin as he let the velvety brown syrup run in streaming ribbons from his spoon.

"And just what do you plan to do with that?" Jenna asked.

"Pour it all over you and lick it off."

He reached for her waist and lifted her up to the kitchen counter. With skilled hands, he undid the tie of her silk robe and parted it. She was naked beneath, and his hazel eyes seemed to grow more green than brown in the candlelight that surrounded them as he studied her breasts.

"Do you like what you see?"

He looked up and smiled while he caressed her face. "Oh, yes. I like it. Love it, in fact."

Jenna curled her fingers into her palms. *Love it.* Well, that was a start.

"Will you take it off?"

"And sit on this countertop naked in front of you?" she gasped in mock outrage.

Shimmying out of her robe, she let Bryce pull it out from beneath her and toss it onto a nearby chair. She was totally naked, her body glowing in the warm yellow candlelight and the silvery radiance of the moonlight that poured in through the window.

"There's a treat in that basket for you," Bryce said. "Why don't you see what it is?"

Jenna reached into the wicker basket and pulled out the yellow box. "Cherry blossom? God, I love these."

"I know." He smiled wickedly. "And I love watching you eat them. Ever since that night at my restaurant when you were licking that plastic sword, I've had a fantasy of licking cherry syrup off your body."

"These are awfully messy and sticky. Are you sure you want me to eat this here? You know how the cherry syrup just runs out of it and dribbles everywhere," she said suggestively.

"Quit talking and start showing me."

Jenna unwrapped the foil and took a big bite out of the chocolate. Coconut, chocolate and nuts bathed her taste buds as the cherry syrup ran down her chin. A pink drop splashed down onto her breast, and Bryce caught it with his tongue.

"Mmmm, this is sooo good," she moaned, licking the syrup from her hand.

"Jesus, you're a picture. You make eating such a seduction. I could cook for you and feed you forever—you know that?"

She opened her eyes and stared into his beautiful face. "Bryce—"

He wouldn't let her finish. "Keep eating that cherry blossom. I'm going to start on a treat of my own."

Jenna picked the cherry out of the chocolate nest and curled it on her tongue. "What treat would that be?" she asked as she swallowed the glistening cherry.

"You, drenched in Toblerone. I'm gonna start with your mouth, Jenna, so close your eyes."

She did as he commanded. His finger brushed against her lower lip, and she felt some of the warm chocolate drizzle down to her chin. She felt Bryce's tongue lapping it up and snaking along her lips as she swallowed the remainder of her chocolate. He moaned as her throat moved against his mouth.

"I want a taste," she whispered, and he lifted his head and gave her his tongue in a kiss that was slow and sensual.

His fingers painted a line down the column of her throat. He broke the kiss to lick the melting path of chocolate as it ran down her neck and splashed onto the crest of her breast.

He licked her clean, and Jenna let her weight rest back on her hands, and her head drop to her shoulders.

"Can I watch you?" she asked, cracking open an eyelid.

He was looking at her, his hair rumpled from where she had run her hand through the silky length. "I thought it'd be sexier for you if you had your eyes closed. That way you could imagine whatever you wanted."

"Nothing my imagination would conjure up could be half as sexy as watching you."

His eyes turned greener, and when he flashed her a grin, his dimple was showing. She gave in to temptation and leaned forward, kissing his dimple, then dipping her tongue in the groove.

"I like your eyes on me," he whispered. "I like your hands on me. I like your body on me, Jenna."

"Good, because it's the same for me, Bryce."

"Lean back. I'm dying to taste your nipples covered in chocolate."

She did as he asked. Tilting her head, she watched him swirl his finger in the bowl until it was coated. Then he brought it to her areola and stroked the pink skin until he had the circle and nipple covered. He kept stroking her, even though her nipple was completely covered.

He wanted her harder, and he kept it up until she was moaning, begging him to take her into his mouth. Then he bent his head and slowly, erotically, so Jenna could see his tongue working, licked it off her.

"God, you taste better than the finest French chocolate, Jenna."

Jenna reached for his hand and brought his finger to her mouth, sucking off the remnants of the chocolate. "So do you."

As he looked into her eyes, he painted a line of chocolate with his thumb down the valley of her breasts to her belly, which she tried to suck in.

"Don't."

Their gazes met and she saw only passion in his eyes. "This isn't the most flattering of positions for a woman with a little bit of a ponch."

"Who told you that?" he asked as he swirled his thumb around her navel. "Whoever did was wrong. But then again, whoever did never saw your body drenched in chocolate. If he had, he would have worshipped you. But his loss is definitely my gain."

He lowered his head, trailing his hot tongue along the path of chocolate, licking it up until he got to her belly, where he paused and kissed her. She couldn't help it—she ran her fingers through his hair, feathering it away from his temple as he tongued the flesh around her navel. She'd never felt something so deliciously wicked in her life.

"An erogenous zone?" he asked without looking up. "I can feel you shaking."

He put his tongue in her belly button again while his hand kneaded her. Definitely an erogenous zone. She was ready to come, and all from the lavish attention Bryce was spending on her belly.

"Spread your legs, sweetheart."

He covered her pussy in chocolate, swirling it around, soaking her.

Jenna was beyond thinking as his hands slid up her thighs. His lips followed the path of his hands as he reverently went to his knees and kissed her as though he were worshipping her.

He looked up the length of her body, his eyes dark with passion. "Will you do something for me, Jenna?"

"Anything," she said on a breathy sigh.

"Cover your nipple in chocolate and let me watch you lick it off."

What a bad boy he was, and Jenna loved it. Dipping her finger in the chocolate, she brought it to the nipple that Bryce had only moments before sucked clean. She covered the tip, slowly, drawing it out, watching it harden. Bryce was watching too as he licked her sex. She felt wanton and liberated, and so sexy—more sexy than she ever had in her life.

"Taste it," he rasped in a voice laced with desire.

Their gazes met, and Jenna lifted her breast, stuck out her tongue and, with the pointed tip, flicked the chocolate off.

With a growl, he finished her within two licks, then drank her in, voraciously sucking and licking. She screamed as she came, and he drew out her orgasm by fingering her pussy, and playing with the crease of her buttocks.

"I want to be inside you," he murmured as he slid up her body.

She nodded, unable to even speak in the aftermath of her orgasm. He helped her down from the counter, and together they sank to the floor. Jenna straddled his hard thighs as he reached for her hips and brought her close to him. Beneath her swollen sex, she felt his cock widen and thicken and begin to pulsate. He was already sheathed and waiting to crawl up inside her.

"Look," he said, directing her gaze to the mirror on the wall to her left. She gasped at what she saw, them, together, naked, arms around each other, Bryce's palm stroking up and down her spine. "We look good together," he said. "I'm going to show you just how good."

Bryce steadied her with his hands on her waist, allowing them to trail along the hourglass of her figure as he let his gaze roam liberally along her body. He took his time studying her in the moonlight, which kissed her flesh. His gaze flickered along her hips and the reddish blond thatch of hair between her thighs. He brushed his palm over her, feeling the soft hair tickling his skin, feeling the heat of her body, smelling the scent of her arousal mixed with chocolate. He could still taste her on his tongue and he wanted more.

Letting the sensations envelop him, he continued his exploration until his palm was moving over the round mound of her belly. He kneaded the soft flesh, watched his hand on her, feeling a strange instinct overwhelm him as she moved restlessly on his lap.

His gaze left her belly, moving up toward her breasts. The nipples were reddened and distended from his mouth, and thinking to soothe them, he circled the areolas with his fingertips, comforting them, before capturing both breasts in his hands. She looked so damn hot and wanton in the mirror, her pale body undulating in time with his tongue, her hands tangling in his hair. He'd never get enough of her. He'd always want her.

He loved her.

He thought the realization would be earth-shattering, but it wasn't. It just felt right. As right as having his hands full of Jenna.

Reaching out, he let one hand ease from her breast, only to trail his fingers along the indentation of her waist and up and over her hip. Slowly, he sipped her nipple into his mouth, suckling her, all the while watching in the mirror as his hand roamed along her alabaster flesh. She was watching, too. Their gazes met in the mirror, and Bryce saw the love shining in his eyes, and thought he saw that same emotion in Jenna's.

"You're so beautiful," she whispered to him.

"Only when I'm with you, Jenna. Only for you."

Gooseflesh sprung to life beneath his fingers and he felt Jenna sway into him, the movement mirrored in the glass. His hand at last found her perfect ass, the skin silken beneath his palms. He squeezed it, sucking her breast harder, making her moan and writhe so that he felt her hot, wet cunt rubbing his cock.

He listened to her breathing, felt the ecstasy rise in her body, scenting her flesh so that it was like a heavy cloud of incense in the room. The aroma drove him to the brink. He wanted her, in the most primal way. His body was now ruling him, and he let his desires, his instincts, be his guide.

Freeing his mouth from her nipple, he tipped his head to the side so he could see his finger skimming down the crease of her bottom before disappearing into the curls that were already damp for him. He studied the sway and roll of her hips, the way her back arched as she met his deep strokes. Together they touched and licked, tasting each other's skin, exploring each other's body.

"Slide down—slowly. Watch in the mirror. See how beautiful it is."

He never talked this way, but God, Jenna's body loving him was a sight to behold, and he never wanted to stop watching her or to stop feeling this deep connection with her whenever their bodies joined.

Slowly, she lowered her hips, feeling his cock slip easily inside her hot, tight pussy. She gasped and clutched on to his neck, her breathing hard against him as her hand moved to her belly.

"You take me so deep inside you this way, baby. It feels so damn good, but if it's hurting you—"

"Don't you dare withdraw now, Bryce Ryder!"

Their eyes locked and he rocked against her, filling her all the way with his cock. He watched her lips part, heard the sigh of satisfaction escape from them. His hands roamed all over her body as she matched his rhythm, and he clutched at her, growing hungrier, needier.

He knew he was lost, accepted it. This was love, and he was just going to ride it out, to savor the feeling. He wasn't going to hide it any longer. He loved Jenna McCabe, and hopefully, she felt the same way.

With one final stab, he came hard and fast, pouring himself into the condom. She clutched at him, holding him tight to her breasts as she shivered and trembled in his arms. He felt moisture on his shoulder and looked up to see another drop trickle from her eye.

"I hurt you."

She shook her head and buried her face into his chest. "No, it was just . . . it was . . ."

"Beautiful?"

She nodded, and he smiled into her hair. "I told you we looked good together. Maybe now you can believe me."

When she looked up at him, her eyes misty and her body still quivering, he cupped her face and kissed her with everything he had, with every emotion in his heart. When they parted, they were both breathing hard.

"I want to take you to bed and sleep beside you all night. I want to wake up to your body beside me. I want to kiss and cuddle in the morning and make slow, lazy love. What do you want, Jenna?"

"The same thing."

He drew her close and held her tight. "Thank God."

Soaring in the air in the 747, Jenna drew her gaze from the window and glanced to her right. Bryce was there, dozing quietly, his laptop open on the little seat-back tray.

She was exhausted. So was Bryce. But she wouldn't have traded these past two days for anything. She swore that every moment she fell deeper and deeper in love with him. Glancing down at her hand, she smiled when she saw her ring. Already she was used to the weight of it on her finger. It was a familiar, comforting sight, and whenever those pesky insecurities about Bryce's intention threatened to sneak up on her, she looked at her ring, and reminded herself of what it represented. Bryce's commitment to her.

He stirred in his seat, and shifted his weight onto his other hip. His long legs stretched, bumped the tray and nearly toppled the laptop onto the floor. Jenna caught it in time and righted it on the tray. Thinking to shut it off, she turned the computer so that the screen was facing her. It was open to his e-mails, and right away the subject line of one caught her eye:

I'm fucked but can be saved by Project Jenna McCabe.

She couldn't help it. She had to open it, despite a gnawing certainty that nothing good was going to come out of it.

She started at the bottom, the original source. Bryce's e-mail to Trey about Greenwood Financial and his inability to get backing until his reputation was once more on track. She read Trey's cynical advice on how to win back his fans and mollify the bank. And then Bryce's reply: *You're a genius.*

The hair on Jenna's nape rose as she put the pieces of the puzzle together. She knew just how it was all going to play out. Four weeks of courting the plain Jane, just until his reputation was restored and he got his money, then a big fat adios as Bryce headed for the coast and his latest four-star restaurant.

And wasn't she just a fucking idiot to have fallen hook, line and sinker for everything he had said—everything they had done?

She was too hurt to cry. Too stunned that Bryce and Trey—but most especially Bryce—could be so cruel.

She sat back in her seat and let out the breath she had been holding while thoughts tripped through her mind. Humiliation. Shame.

Those feelings inundated her until she needed to stand up and climb, awkwardly, over Bryce so she could go to the bathroom and hide till she figured out what she was going to say to him.

"Hey, babe," he asked sleepily as she climbed over him, "where are you going in such a hurry?"

His hands were cupping her ass, and she brushed them away, not wanting to feel his touch. "The bathroom."

"Want some company?" he said with a sexy smile.

Asshole.

She made a beeline for the bathroom and practically lunged for the door when she saw a woman unbuckling her belt. She made it just in time and locked the door before she sat down on the metal toilet and hung her head between her hands.

Great. Now her mascara would be running and she'd have raccoon eyes. Oh, who gave a shit, anyway? It wasn't like Bryce would care. He only had to pretend to desire her for another couple of weeks.

How long she sat there and cried, she didn't know. She heard the knocks, the muffled sighs, the groans of frustrations, but she couldn't move. Couldn't make herself stop crying over Bryce's betrayal.

"Jenna?" Another light rap on the door. "Sweetheart, are you in there? It's been nearly half an hour."

She saw red when she heard him call her sweetheart. Yeah, right. What a rotten liar he was. "Leave me alone."

"Let me in," he said, sounding concerned.

"Go to hell."

"Pardon?"

"Oh, don't act surprised," she hissed as she unlocked the door and threw it open. Thank God, she had already wiped her black mascara streaks from her cheeks.

"Why are you crying?"

"Haven't you figured it out yet?" She snapped. Pulling the ring from her finger she shoved it into his chest.

He barely caught it before it dropped to the floor. He looked at it in his hand and frowned. "What's going on, Jenna?"

"The name's Jane. Plain Jane. You know, when I agreed to help you get your rep back, it wasn't by surrendering every shred of dignity I have."

His face went white as he finally met her gaze.

"How could you?" she said. "I never thought you could be this cruel."

"Jenna, wait," he pleaded, reaching for her elbow. "Let me explain."

"Excuse me," the stewardess said behind Bryce. "But you both need to take your seats and put on your seat belts. We've started our descent."

Jenna brushed past Bryce and returned to her seat. He tried to reach for her hand but she pulled away. She wouldn't look at him either, and finally he just gave up.

Well, that was easy. He barely put up a fight.

As the wheels skidded on the asphalt, Bryce leaned into her.

"This is *not* over, Jenna."

Fourteen

"I'm telling you, Jen, he wasn't using you."

"Sarah, I'm not listening."

"Ugh!" Sarah groaned as she followed Jenna out of the kitchen. "Why won't you listen?"

"Because I don't care, that's why."

"How many times do I have to tell you, Trey only sent that e-mail as a way to give Bryce a nudge in your direction."

"Yeah, well there're other plain Janes out there."

"Argh!" Sarah growled. "Trey doesn't think you're plain, and neither does Bryce. He was just goading Bryce to *see* you."

"Well, he saw me all right. As a way to fix his rep."

"Morning, girls," their mother called from her bedroom. "Did someone put the coffee on?"

"Yes, Mom. Sarah did."

"Jenna," her dad yelled from the kitchen, "phone for you."

"Tell whoever it is I'm not in."

"Too late. Already told them you were here."

Jenna rolled her eyes and made her way to the hallway, where an old rotary phone sat on a table. She knew who it would be, and she needed a measure of privacy to tell him off.

"Hello?"

"Hey."

Her heart started a mad dance as she heard his voice. *Stop it*, she told herself. It was ridiculous how she was acting.

"So, you ready to talk yet?" Bryce asked.

"Yep, I am. So here goes. You used me and made me feel like a total moron. I think you're a creep and I never want to see you again. Ciao."

Slamming the phone down, Jenna took a deep breath and smiled with sheer malice. She felt better already. Coming to Lucan had been the right idea. So what if she was licking her wounds? She had every right to.

Padding down the hallway, she stopped at the front door to open it and let in the early-morning sun and the warm spring breeze through the screen door. She stifled a scream when she saw someone leaning up against the jamb, looking down at her through the screen.

"I told you before, you ever decide to run from me, you'll only find me right behind you."

Bryce.

She reached for the door latch, but he beat her to it and pulled the door open so she couldn't lock it. She grabbed the handle, then fell into him as he pulled the door open wide. He caught her and held her tight.

"I knew it was only a matter of time before I could get you out here for a little chitchat."

"I'm not going anywhere with you."

"Yeah, you are, and you'll come nicely, or I'll haul you up and put you over my shoulder and carry you to my car."

He would do it, too. And no doubt her family would be watching from the living room window.

Giving in, she let the door close behind her. "Go ahead."

"Come to my car. I want privacy and I'm sure your two sisters are hiding out, listening to every word."

"I don't keep secrets from my sisters. They both know you're a son of a bitch."

He didn't flinch when she called him names, she noticed. He only looked more determined, and that ticked her off. She wasn't good at being nasty to people. It wasn't in her nature. But damn him, she didn't want to be nice to him or let him off gently.

He started walking to the car and she followed him. When they were inside, he turned to her, looking tired and pale.

"I want to explain."

She held her hand up. "No need."

"Yeah, there is a need. It's not what you think."

She snorted and looked out the window.

"Jenna, how can you not give me a chance?"

"Like you deserve one."

He ran his hands through his hair and rested his head back against the seat. "When I got that e-mail from Trey, I was at your house. Remember that night I cooked the steaks for us. I . . . I wasn't in my right mind. I wanted you, and it was all new and confusing, and you hadn't answered my calls. . ."

He was rambling, and Jenna glanced over at him, watching the frustration pour out of him.

"I did not start this with you in order to get my reputation back. I swear it."

"Why did you start it, then?"

"Ever since I saw you sitting across from me at my restaurant, I couldn't stop looking at you, or thinking of you in my bed. I've always thought you were pretty, Jenna, but that night . . . I don't know. You made me sit up and take notice, and my eyes, and thoughts, have never left you since."

"What about the e-mail, Bryce?"

"That fucking e-mail," he growled. "Look, it means nothing. I don't know what Trey was smoking. I knew he was way off about you, but it made me realize how much I wanted to be with you. All I could think of was you, having more of you, wanting you. When I said he was a genius, that's all I meant. I wasn't agreeing to his 'plan,'" he scoffed. "I never even thought about it. I sure as hell haven't implemented it. Oh, God, Jenna, give me one more chance. Please."

"Why should I?"

He reached for her hand and held it steady in his. "Because I love you."

Slowly she turned to look at him. Surely he wouldn't stoop so low as to say he loved her just to get himself out of this.

He touched her face, caressed her lips with his fingers. "I knew I loved you when I went chasing after you to Italy. I knew I'd always love you that morning when we shared our omelet. Jenna, I've never told any woman this, but I'm telling you now. And I mean it. Christ, I mean it," he whispered, forcing her to look him in the eye. "How can you not believe me when you can see how much damn pain I'm in right now? I can't sleep. Can't eat. Every time I close my eyes I see you, and I only love you more."

"I . . . want so badly to believe you," she whispered through trembling lips.

"You can, Jenna. I swear it."

She bit her lip and glanced down, giving a little shake of her head.

"I'll teach you to trust me again. If you'll let me."

"I don't know, Bryce."

"What about now, here in Lucan? This is the best place for us to start."

Here? In the sleepy little town where she and Bryce had grown up? That same sleepy town that had nothing better to do than gossip?

Oh, hell, no!

Her parents, not to mention her sisters, would make too much out of it. And Bryce's parents? The whole town would be thinking wedding bells and babies.

"No, I don't think so."

"Jenna, are you trying to tell me that you don't want to be seen with me?"

"You know Lucan. People will talk."

"So?"

"So?" she asked, her eyes narrowing. "You can't tell me you want the entire town talking about what we're doing."

"What, having a relationship? Last I heard, it wasn't a sin."

"Well, it will be in Lucan when nothing comes of it. Oh, come on, Bryce," she said when he frowned. "You know small towns. If we appear together everyone is going to think something is going on between us—"

"Isn't there?" he asked. "I just told you that I love you, Jenna. I think that's a lot going on between us."

"Bryce—"

"I'm just asking for a chance, that's all."

"Lucan isn't the place to do it."

"Why not?"

"Because when it doesn't work out, everyone will talk. God, Bryce, don't you see that?"

"Then that's all the more reason to see that it does work out, isn't it?"

"God," she groaned, reaching for the door handle.

"Jenna, I'm not going to go away."

"One more chance," she snapped, "and there had better not be any more lies."

She started to open the door when he asked, "Aren't you going to invite me in?"

"You know everyone is going to be gossiping."

He skimmed his fingers down her cheek. "I want you back, Jenna. No amount of gossiping will stop me from having you." He pulled her toward him so that she was leaning over the gearshift and her top was gaping open at the neck. "I miss you. I miss your touch and your smile. I want to make love like we did in Tuscany."

Her body officially forgave him despite the warnings from her brain. She was still leery, and probably foolish for believing him so easily. But she missed him, too, no matter how hard she tried to deny it. And she wanted to make love, too.

"You know my parents. They're pretty conservative. I ... don't know what you expect from staying here."

He smiled and caressed her bottom lip with his thumb. "I know your parents. But I can be pretty quiet when I want to be. Can you?"

She smiled suddenly, the first time in the two days since she'd been home in Lucan. "I don't know. You do tend to make me scream."

"And I love hearing those screams."

"I think we better not plan to be sneaking around. My mother can hear for miles, and my dad has a nose like a bloodhound. They'd only find out what we're doing and it'd just be awkward, you know."

"I know," he said, brushing her hair back over her shoulder. "Trust me, I can think of other places to seduce you than under their roof."

"I'm sure you could."

He laughed. "I'm thinking my car might be a good start."

"Oh, Bryce, not now. Sarah and Emily are watching from the window, and I need a shower."

"Any chance they'll be out of the house so we can shower together?"

"I doubt it. Mom will be busy getting lunch ready for Dad and Ashton."

"Surely she couldn't hear us over the spray of the water?"

Jenna gave him a doubting look. "You want to bet on that?"

Bryce laughed and drew her to him, and Jenna allowed herself to sink into his bone-melting kiss.

"Thank you for giving me another chance, Jenna. You're not going to regret it."

As they got out of the car, Bryce gave a huge sigh of relief. With a glance up at the sky, he gave silent thanks. He hadn't been sure if Jenna would give him another chance, but he knew he had to try. He loved her, and even though she hadn't said it back, he was certain she felt the same way. She was just hurting right now and couldn't risk her heart by telling him. He knew he had a lot to prove before Jenna told him the words he longed to hear.

As he went around to the trunk to unload his suitcase, he heard Jenna's breath catch and looked up. Four men in black suits were coming around the corner of the house.

Their gazes caught and she shrugged, trying to pretend she wasn't upset. "Guys from the bank, I guess."

Bryce looked again. An older man, graying and wrinkled, led the pack. Bryce felt his stomach fall to his feet.

It was David Cullen; he worked for Bryce's father.

A sickening thought filtered through his mind and he glanced at Jenna. "Do you know who's interested in buying the farm?"

Jenna shook her head. "I just know the bank is going to foreclose and whoever wants the land is willing to pay for it."

Bryce thought back to his appointment with Greenwood. Was

the fifty-acre parcel of land that was "close to home" the McCabe farm? Was that why old Greenwood had mentioned it?

"Well, you ready to go in? It's after nine and the morning chores will be done. That'll mean Mom has breakfast ready. And I'm starved."

"Sure," he mumbled, "but first I need to make a call."

"You need to check on the restaurant?"

"Yeah," he said. "It won't take a minute. You go on in and I'll be right behind you."

She sauntered up the lavender-lined garden path and up the old steps of the veranda. He watched her enter the house, heard the sounds of happy voices from inside, before he pulled his phone from his pocket and dialed.

"Hello?"

"Hi, Mom?"

"Bryce, darling, it's so good to hear your voice."

Either his mother had been into the gin this morning, or she was with her cronies, pretending to do charity work.

"What am I doing?" she asked, her voice getting louder. "Why, you know I always run the auxiliary booth for the festival. I'm just here with the ladies setting up."

That explained it. She was with her friends and she wanted to play devoted mother.

"So, where are you, darling?"

"I'm willing to play along with this charade, Mother, but only if you're willing to answer my questions."

"Oh, that sounds lovely."

"Where is Dad?"

"Your father left for the city. He had a business meeting early this morning. He'll be disappointed that he missed your call."

"Not likely," he muttered.

"Is there a message I could give him, sweetheart?"

"Now you just sound unbelievable, Mom. Cut back on the endearments or they'll know what a phony you are." He could almost see her seething on the other end. "As for Dad, is he planning on buying the McCabe farm?"

"Why, yes, he is," she said with enthusiasm, knowing he'd be devastated by the news.

"Well, you can tell him that it's not a done deal. Tell him to give me a call when he gets back. We need to talk." He snapped his cell phone shut.

"You heard the news?"

Bryce could hardly believe his eyes as he whirled around. "Trey! What the hell are you doing here, man?"

"I'm scheduled in New York for a magazine interview next week. Thought I'd take a detour and lend a little moral support to your cause."

"So, how'd you get here?"

Trey shrugged and put his hands in his pockets. "Sarah picked me up at the airport."

"What? Sarah never drives in the city."

"Yeah, I know, but the things she'll do for her sister, you know."

Bryce gave his brother a hug, "It's good to see you, man,"

"You look like shit," Trey said, slapping Bryce on the back. "Heard Jenna found our e-mail."

"Not one of my better days, I tell you. I think I finally convinced her to trust me and give me another chance. Hey," Bryce asked as they strolled up the walk, "how did you hear that Dad is trying to buy this place?"

"I ran into one of his buddies at the coffee shop this morning. I didn't realize that the McCabes were going to lose it."

"You know what he'll do with the land, right?"

"Of course," Trey said. "He'll develop it and it'll become his next shopping mall."

"I won't let that happen."

Trey gave Bryce a sidelong glance as he held the screen door open. "What, you going to try to buy it from Dad?"

"Yeah, I just might," Bryce muttered. Even if it cost him everything he had, including his restaurant.

They entered the house and the smell of bacon and coffee made his stomach grumble.

"Ah, the smell of home," he said appreciatively.

"Yeah," Trey agreed. "Nothing better than bacon in the morning."

"Bryce, Trey," Mrs. McCabe said with a welcoming smile, "come in and have some breakfast. It's nice to have you both home again." She hugged them both and dragged them into the kitchen. Mr. McCabe, Ashton, Jenna and her sisters were already seated at the long table covered with a blue-and-white-checked tablecloth. Bryce smiled and said hello to everyone, but he only had eyes for Jenna. Despite the stress of the past couple of days, she was glowing. She looked utterly perfect seated at the table, smiling and laughing as she sipped her coffee.

Home, he thought. This was what it was like to be home, to be part of a family. And God, he wanted that. To walk into his own kitchen and find Jenna sitting at the table drinking her morning coffee.

"Good to have both of you staying with us," Wayne McCabe said from his place at the head of the table. "Ashton and I were starting to get run over by females in this house."

"Oh, c'mon, Daddy," Emily teased, "you love your girls."

"That I do, but it's nice to have some male companionship. I'm tired of being outnumbered all the time. Well, then, boys, grab yourself a seat. Eggs are getting cold. Ashton, hand me that basket of biscuits, will ya?"

Trey took the empty chair beside Sarah so that Bryce could sit beside Jenna. Mrs. McCabe poured some steaming coffee into his mug. Unable to resist, Bryce reached for Jenna's hand and gave her a quick kiss.

Jenna's dad looked up from buttering his biscuit in time to catch the kiss and Jenna's pretty blush. His gaze lowered to where Bryce was holding Jenna's hand and brushing his thumb along her knuckles.

"You got those spare bedrooms in order, Angie?" Wayne asked Jenna's mother as he watched Bryce with his daughter. "Because I got a feeling we're going to need them."

"Dad," Sarah groaned. But Wayne McCabe was clearly not going to be dissuaded. He even stopped staring at Bryce to take an interest in Trey, who, it seemed, kept stealing looks at Sarah, who kept brushing his arm with her chest. It was unconscious, of course; the seating arrangements were tight. But that didn't stop Wayne from lifting a questioning brow as Trey's gaze slid down into forbidden territory.

"Better get *both* these boys rooms," Wayne muttered as he cast a glance from Trey to Bryce before digging into his eggs. "Looks like they might be staying for more than a night."

Bryce's arms held her tightly as they stood together under the steady stream of water. Jenna let it flow down her head and over her shoulders and back. Let herself melt into Bryce's strength. She felt like she couldn't stand up on her own and he was her steadying rock.

It wasn't just exhaustion and jet lag; it was emotional fatigue as well. And Bryce seemed to know it, to understand. She felt it in the way he rubbed his hand down her spine in soft, soothing sweeps. It was in the way he kissed her, soft undemanding brushes of his mouth against her temple, her cheeks, her shoulder. It was in the way he held her closer and whispered to her as he felt her body tremble.

Jenna couldn't hide the cascade of tears that fell from her eyes. She'd tried to keep them in check, but Bryce's tenderness was her undoing.

"I'm sorry," he murmured over and over. "I'll make it up to you, Jenna. I swear it. God, I never wanted you hurt like this."

Without looking up, Jenna pressed her face into his chest, wound her fingers through his wet hair and wept against Bryce.

"I'm here, Jenna," he kept saying. "Let me in. Let me fix it."

She cried for the love she felt for him, for the ache she had to make a life with him, a life like this, full of closeness and support. She wanted it so badly, but fear still had a steady grip on her heart. Even though she loved him, she couldn't say the words. She was too afraid, too uncertain of the future.

And now she had to face the loss of her family home. The only place on earth where she could truly be herself. The place where she'd been born and raised. The place where she'd fallen in love.

"Talk to me, Jenna. Is it me? Is it the farm?" He held her tighter so that they were molded together by skin and warm water.

She nodded, hardly able to speak. "It's everything. The farm. The ad campaign. Gabriella has said no to every model I've proposed. I don't know what I'm going to do, Bryce. I can't lose this account. It's not just the money. It's the product. I believe in what Gabriella is doing. I want to be a part of it."

"I've just thought of someone who I think would be a perfect woman to model for Duchess Lingerie."

"Who?"

"Let me work on it, and I'll get back to you. Promise."

"Did you sleep with her?" Jenna blurted out. Because if so, she wasn't interested in working with her. In fact, Jenna knew she'd hate her on the spot.

Bryce laughed and lifted her up so that Jenna's legs wrapped around his waist and his hands cupped her bottom. "No, I haven't slept with her. But I have known her for a long time. Trey knows her, too, and being that he's a famous photographer and he knows women like the back of his hand, I thought I'd get some advice from him as to whether she'd photograph well before I get your hopes up."

She eyed him suspiciously. "Do I know her?"

"I don't know."

"How come you're being so secretive?"

"Am I? And here I thought women liked guys who were mysterious."

"Not when it comes to their livelihoods."

"Trust me, Jenna," he said, kissing her neck. "Let me worry about this, and the farm, too. I want you to just relax and not have a worry in the world."

"Easier said than done."

"Maybe this will help?"

Bryce reached behind Jenna. He took the ring from the silver soap dish and pulled her hand from where it rested on his neck. He slid the onyx ring back on her ring finger. Their gazes met, and he rubbed his finger along the ring in a possessive manner he hoped Jenna understood.

"You're mine, Jenna. Now that I've admitted it to myself, I'm not letting you go. I'm also not letting you out of the house without some sort of sign that you're taken."

She smiled and kissed him. "I'm feeling better."

"But are you relaxed? I know something that would melt your bones."

"Oh really?"

"Yeah, really."

"What would that be?"

"This."

Bryce slid into her, stretching her wide. He was thick and hard and Jenna closed her eyes as he took her. Would she ever tire of this, feeling him slowly filling her, giving her all of him? She didn't think so.

He took his time, thrusting gently, caressing her ass, and Jenna reveled in how magical it all felt. The feel of him inside her was . . . perfect. As the water beaded on her breasts, trickling off her nipples, Bryce caught the drops with his mouth, all the while keeping up a slow, unhurried pace inside her.

"I've missed you so much, Jenna. When I thought I'd never get you back . . . I just . . . fell apart."

She clung to him, holding him, making love with him, freeing her mind, not thinking, only feeling as she clung to his neck and kissed him behind his ear.

He made love to her long and slow, pleasuring her with his gentle hands and loving, whispered words.

"Is it safe to come inside you?" he asked between pulls on her nipple.

She shook her head. "No, it's not the right time of the month."

"All right," he murmured as he pressed her against the wall and sunk into her a bit harder. "But you'll let me know when you want that, right?"

She caught his expression through her wet lashes. She could have sworn that was disappointment shining in his eyes. Did Bryce really want to come inside her? They had no protection. She wasn't on birth control. He couldn't possibly mean—

"You'll tell me when you're ready for that step, right? Because . . ." He swallowed and Jenna watched him look up at her. "Because I'm ready for that, Jen—more than ready."

She touched his face, stroked his mouth with her fingertips. He kissed her fingers and closed his eyes. God, how she loved him. She wanted to tell him now, but she still wasn't sure. He might mean it in the moment, but she couldn't take the risk that he would change his mind, so instead she just said, "Yes, Bryce, I'll tell you."

He pulled out of her and pressed his erection into her belly. He found her clitoris and stroked her as he poured himself onto her. She came not long after him, and he stifled her cry of pleasure with his mouth—a mouth that was at once soothing and demanding.

"Jenna." The knock on the door made them break off their kiss. Bryce was breathing hard against her neck as she answered.

"Yeah, Mom?"

"Are you okay, honey? You've been in there a long time."

Jenna stroked her hand down Bryce's broad back and kissed his forehead. "Yeah, Mom. I'm perfect."

He looked up at her and smiled. "That you are, Jenna McCabe."

Fifteen

That evening, after they'd returned from the planting festival, Jenna went to her room to work on the ad campaign for Duchess Lingerie. Bryce and Trey headed down to the dock with a six-pack and watched the sun slip below the horizon.

The first thing Bryce did was call and check in with Mark. The restaurant was busy, and he was managing just fine. In fact, Bryce wondered why he'd never left Mark to run the place before. Of course, he'd never had a good enough reason before to leave his beloved restaurant in the capable hands of his sous chef. Not until Jenna.

Jenna was the best reason there was. If they were going to make this relationship work—forever—then he needed to learn how to hand the reins over to someone else from time to time. There would be times Jenna would need him, and times he would need her. He had to start thinking of them as a team, because that was what they would always be.

No longer would he live in isolation, and the feeling was like having the world lifted from his shoulders. Now all he needed to do was convince Jenna of his sincerity and his love. He thought he was doing a pretty good job of it, but every once in a while, he caught her looking at him with sad, worried eyes.

He had her body back; now he just needed her heart to follow.

"Whatcha thinking about?" Trey asked.

"Nothing."

"I bet."

Bryce grinned and rested his head against the wooden railing of the dock. Beneath him, the water lapped softly, the dock swaying gently with the rhythm of the water. It was growing dark, the sky a blanket of blue velvet. The sound of crickets and frogs filled the air, while the occasional hoot of an owl or a cry of a newborn calf from the barn could be heard over the insects. Even a firefly or two lit up the blades of grass.

It had been a long time since he'd seen fireflies. Just another thing you missed out on when you lived in a big city. He thought of how he and Trey used to sneak out of the house in their pajamas and bare feet, the feel of the moist grass beneath their toes.

Armed with big glass canning jars, they'd catch as many fireflies as they could; then with the tips of scissors, they'd punch holes in the metal lids, trying not to let their parents hear. Then they'd put the jars on the windowsills in their bedroom and watch them all night long as the flies lit up their room.

Of course, in the morning the jars were gone and they were grounded for a week. Their mother never went in for nature, unless of course it was from the balcony of a five-star resort.

Trey drained his beer, and popped open another one. "She forgive you yet?"

"I think so, but I'm still trying to make amends. I banged up her pride pretty good. Damn it, why did you have to send me that fucking e-mail in the first place?"

"You needed a push, little brother, and I know which head you usually think with."

Bryce glared at him. "It's not just about sex, you know."

"I know," Trey said with a smile. "And *that's* why I sent you the e-mail. Because I've known all along what you didn't: You love Jenna. You just needed your eyes opened."

"Well, they're opened, and now I can't see anything but her, and our future together. I swear I'll never do anything to fuck up what I have with her."

"Love's that painful, huh?"

Bryce shook his head. "I just don't want to lose her."

"I don't think you will. Sarah told me all along that Jenna would come to her senses."

"So Sarah was involved, too?"

"Of course. I had to cover my tracks in case the e-mail got out. I didn't want that she-devil thinking that I'd trashed her sister. We came up with a plan together and executed it perfectly, if I may say so."

"Yeah. Except you forgot to tell me to destroy the evidence."

Trey laughed and they sat for a moment, just watching the sky in silence.

"This place is so quiet. It's like it's dead."

Bryce lifted his head and glanced at his brother. "No way. This place is full of life."

Trey snorted in disagreement. "I can't think of anything that could tempt me to put down roots in a backwater like Lucan. God, did you see that miserable excuse for Art in the Park today? Pathetic. There is zero culture in this town."

"It is different from the city—I'll give you that. But I like it. It's so peaceful. It's like everything has suddenly fallen into its rightful place."

"Whoa, who are you and what have you done with my brother?"

Bryce drained the rest of his beer and tossed the empty bottle onto the grass. "Okay, I know Lucan can't compete with London, but you seriously don't think this place has something?"

"Yeah, a lot of rednecks and women with big asses and bad dye jobs with black roots."

Bryce glared at his brother. "That's a bit harsh, isn't it? Even coming from you."

"Sorry," Trey muttered. "But take a look around."

"I have, and I think this place has something special, this farm in particular. I mean, we both loved to hang out here."

Trey grunted and took a long swallow of beer, then wiped his mouth with the back of his hand. "I came to the farm with you because I hated our old man and I was looking for an escape—not because I liked it here."

Liar. "You never liked coming here—not at all?"

"It was just the lesser of two evils as far as I was concerned."

"You're saying you didn't like this place as much as me?"

Trey gulped back his beer. "Well, I never had the warm reception you always got."

"C'mon, that's not true. Mr. and Mrs. McCabe have always wel-
comed you here."

"I wasn't talking about them."

Sudden understanding hit Bryce broadside. He found himself
looking up to the house, to a bedroom window that faced the pond.
"You mean—"

"I think I must be drunk. I think I'm going to shut the fuck up
right now."

Bryce took the hint. He'd change the subject, but he wasn't going
to stop thinking about it. Well, wasn't this an interesting turn of
events?

"I went to see Dad today," he announced, hearing the bitterness
in his own voice.

"Yeah? How'd that go?"

"He's not going to cut me any slack. He won't make it easy for me
to buy this place."

"Are you sure you want to? I mean, it is a farm, Bryce—what the
hell do you know about farming?"

"I know that a cattle farm could sustain a four-star restaurant. I
know that the house, once it's fixed up and furnished with some an-
tiques, could be a killer bed-and-breakfast."

Trey looked at him as if he were speaking in tongues. "You really
serious about this?"

"Yeah, I am. I think this would make a really great romantic retreat. I mean, I'd open up my restaurant, maybe hold some cooking
classes, couples cooking classes, even. There's lots to do here, in all

four seasons. Ashton's got a great idea about adding some horses—did you know that there are trails back there in the bush? We've got the pond for swimming or boating. In the winter we could have skating and sleigh rides. Shit, I'm even thinking that we could bring the set of *Heating It Up* out here, and I could tape it from a new studio built by the barn." Bryce stopped when he saw the shocked expression on Trey's face.

"Is this what you really want? Or are you doing this just to prove yourself to Jenna?"

Bryce held his brother's gaze. "Trey, I want this more than I've ever wanted anything in the world. I want to make a success of this place. These are my ideas, not Jenna's. Hell, I haven't even told her. She doesn't know I'm trying to buy the farm."

Trey looked out at the water, his expression still guarded. "If this is what you truly want . . ."

Bryce huffed in frustration. "I know we don't want the same things, but I'm not crazy. I want a future with Jenna. Here. I want kids," he said tentatively as he watched a pair of fireflies circling around a patch of crabgrass. "With Jenna. She's my future, Trey. And so is this place. I know now what I need to be happy."

"I don't fault you, Bryce."

"But you think I've lost it, don't you?"

"I've always known that you ached for what the McCabes have. You want that sense of belonging. You want the closeness of a real family, an actual home. If you didn't, you wouldn't have spent so much time here."

"But the part about me wanting kids?" Bryce asked, his voice getting thick with emotion, "I mean, when I think of how we always vowed never ever to have kids . . ."

Trey leaned his head against the railing and looked at Bryce. "I've always known what you wanted, little brother. It was in your eyes whenever you looked at Jenna. And just because I don't want that for myself doesn't mean I don't think you should. We're different men, Bryce. I don't want a wife and kids. It doesn't interest me, being tied down, making sure other people are happy. I'm selfish, I guess, like Mom. But it's okay if you want that. I get it. And you know, I think you'll be a great husband and father."

"Thanks, man."

Trey finished his beer. "So, how bad does Dad want this place?"

"Bad. He's got big plans for it, and most of what you see here is going to be an asphalt parking lot for a big shopping mall. He's quite pleased about bringing Lucan into the twenty-first century, as he says. I pointed out that by bringing Lucan forward, he's going to kill the downtown businesses. He didn't think it was a problem, and he sure as hell wasn't concerned."

"His friends who own those businesses might think differently."

Bryce grunted. "Dad cares about himself, and making more money. He's never given a shit about anyone. And neither has Mom. Whatever keeps her in diamonds and furs and expensive vacations is what she wants."

"So how shy are you from meeting the price that Dad has offered?"

"I'm not. Trouble is, my money is tied up in real estate. I have to sell the two coastal properties and the house in Tuscany. Unfortunately that takes time. I've talked to Greenwood already. He won't back me on the speculation of the properties selling. Dad's got the ready cash. I can't beat that."

Trey winced. "Man, you're giving up a lot on a vision that might not work out."

"No. It'll work out. Lucan is a perfect town for escape. Lucan could easily become the North American Tuscany. It's got that old-world charm with the quaint shops on Main Street and the food markets. And don't forget the two wineries that recently started operations. Where there're wine and gastronomy and good scenery, there're always visitors looking for a weekend retreat."

Trey nodded and glanced around. "That barn would make a kick-ass restaurant—you know, rustic and romantic with beamed ceilings and dark lighting. Something *Food and Wine* would love to run an article about. Maybe you're right. Lucan could become the North American Tuscany."

"And the farm could stay intact because it could sustain the restaurant. Farm fresh everything. That's what everyone wants these days, eating local."

"You know, I could take some shots of the place and Jenna could draw up a marketing plan with them." Trey seemed to be catching some of Bryce's excitement. "And how about this? You could even tape shows about the making of your new endeavor out here, and what it takes to get a restaurant off the ground. That could be huge for promotion. And with Jenna's marketing, yeah—you could really sell this place. After all, it's what? An hour out the city. Yet it feels like it's out in the middle of nowhere. The distance alone is attractive."

Bryce nodded enthusiastically. "It wouldn't take much to start it up. Now, if only Dad would quit being such a prick, I could start making plans. I could tell Jenna, too. I haven't wanted to get her hopes up. The properties are already on the market, but if they don't sell by week's end, I'm screwed."

"Don't worry about things, Bryce. I've got a feeling Dad isn't going to be that difficult to handle."

"What makes you think that when he's never been anything but?"

"I've got an ace in my back pocket. Don't worry. And look, here comes your future wife, looking all wifey in a bathrobe."

Bryce flashed a huge smile. God, it felt so good to hear that, and to see her walking toward him in the moonlight wearing nothing but a thick white robe. Jesus, when did terry cloth become sexy?

God, he just wanted to bring her into his arms and hold her all damn night while they looked up at the stars and made plans for the future—their future.

"Well, I'm outta here," said Trey.

"Why? Stay and have another beer."

"Nah, I'm good. I'll let you two lovebirds be alone. Who knows? You might want to go skinny-dipping, and then I'd just be in the way."

Bryce laughed, his gaze devouring Jenna as she walked across the grass toward them. He thought of sliding that soft terry cloth down over her shoulders. Thought of her naked underneath. Thought of the water sluicing over her curves, making her skin glisten. Imagined what she'd look like as he made love to her in the water, beneath the moonlight.

"You're right, Trey. Get yer ass outta here, man."

Sixteen

Trey crossed the long grass, thinking Bryce would be happy here. He'd make a success of this new business. And Jenna, well, Jenna would be the best partner Bryce could ever want.

"Hey, Trey," Jenna said as she neared him. "Where are you going?"

"Oh, just heading in. This country air makes me tired."

She laughed and Trey could see why his brother had fallen so hard for her. She was sweet and honest. A natural beauty without needing to be all made up. She was comfortable, and she'd make his brother's life just as comfortable.

Lucky bastard. Trey had a fleeting wish to find himself a little slice of heaven, too. To come home after a long day at work to the comforts of a home and a woman who cared.

But then he'd ruin it with his coldness. He just didn't feel the way other men felt. It was like he was wired wrong, like all warmth and feelings had been omitted from his makeup when he had been created. He was numb. And being numb and emotionless didn't make for good relationships.

In the end, he'd just fuck everything up. He didn't deal well with people. Now photographs, they were different. He never fucked up those.

"I bet you're bored stiff out here, especially after living in London for so long," Jenna said. "I know it's not much, but if you're interested, Ashton is heading into town for last call at the Caddy. There's always something going on up there after a night of drinking."

Trey tried to keep his expression neutral. The mention of Ashton Wilson made his teeth clench. "Nah, I'm good. I think I've had enough already."

"Okay, then," she said, squeezing his arm briefly. "Night."

"Night."

He watched her run the rest of the distance to Bryce, who was standing with his arms opened to her, welcoming her. She jumped up into his arms and wrapped her legs around his waist. His brother's hands were already on her ass and they were kissing like they hadn't seen each other in a year.

Lucky bastard.

Restless, Trey decided to walk around the old Victorian farmhouse. It needed some work and a significant amount of updating, both outside and in, but with a little money and lots of elbow grease, it could be just as stunning as it was in its heyday. The stained-glass windows were original and in good repair. The porch just needed the paint scraped and a fresh coat applied.

And with a few modern improvements, like some Jacuzzi tubs in the rooms and turning the walk-up attic into a luxury honeymoon suite, this old farmhouse could be turned into a beautiful hotel.

Climbing the steps to the veranda, Trey shook the railing. A little loose, but not bad. The wooden floor slats, from what he could see, were in good repair. This would be a perfect place to offer the guests late-afternoon cocktails with some of Bryce's appetizers, or even afternoon tea. The front garden, thanks to Jenna's mom, was stunning. And with a water feature and some more plants, it could become the focal point for a relaxing twilight stroll.

"What? Seeing if Daddy dearest is getting his money's worth?"

Trey's heart jumped. *Such hatred in that sweet voice,* he thought. And Sarah McCabe always had the sweetest, sexiest voice he'd ever heard.

"So you know?" he asked, keeping his back to her.

"Of course. He had the nerve to come to the Caddy for lunch today with his investment banker. He made it very clear that I could kiss my family home goodbye. That within the year it'd be a Bargain City and a fast-food restaurant. Wonder if he'll choose a pizza joint this time instead of Value Burger."

Trey heard her sniffle and turned. Saw her on the porch swing that was suspended from the ceiling of the veranda. She was wearing a light-colored sundress, the moonlight backlighting her figure, giving pretty much everything away.

He swallowed—hard. He'd like to take her picture, just like this—with the curved outline of her breast, the hem of her dress riding up over her knees, her bare feet, with her pink toenail polish, making little circles on the hardwood while her blond hair whispered softly across her cheeks.

Sarah looked away from him and he saw her swipe her hand across her cheeks.

"My sisters and I always dreamed about getting married out in the garden. We thought we'd have our reception picnic-style in the backyard." She laughed, but it was full of heartache. "I'm sure you're thinking how hillbilly that sounds. But that's the difference between you and me. I love my home and my family. And you don't care about anything but yourself."

"That's not true."

"Whatever," she muttered. She climbed down off the swing. He held out his hand to help her but she pushed him away. She never wanted him near her. Never had.

"Jenna, Emily and I used to sit in the hayloft and talk about what it would be like when we'd come back to the farm after we were grown," she said as she slipped her feet into a pair of sexy sandals. "Our kids would play together, running around and laughing and getting dirty, just like we used to. We thought of all the long weekends we'd have, and the fireworks. We thought about tucking our kids into beds—the beds that used to be ours. And now all those dreams are being bought up by some money-worshipping bastard who thinks that we're nothing but a bunch of sentimental hicks."

Trey's heart was beating rapidly. Laughter. Fun. A sense of belonging. She'd had it all, her whole life. And he had always been on the periphery, standing alone and apart, watching and trying so desperately not to wish. To want. While Bryce laughed and teased, he had remained silent. Bryce had always been family, while he had always been the guest.

Headlights drifted over them, illuminating the veranda, where they stood side by side. Gravel crunched beneath heavy tires. The purr of a diesel engine idling in the driveway coasted over.

"I gotta go," Sarah said.

Before he knew what he was doing, Trey reached for Sarah and grabbed her by the arm. "I'm not an unfeeling asshole, you know."

"Of course not," she spat.

He pulled her closer, feeling those big, gorgeous breasts brush against his chest.

"I don't know what I ever did to you to make you hate me so much."

"Let me go."

"What if I don't want to?" He had no idea what she saw in his expression, but she recoiled from his touch and the closeness of his body. Damn her.

"Why do you hate me, Sarah?" he repeated, despising the confusion he heard in his voice.

"I don't hate you. I just want my home to be safe. I want my family close by. I want a husband who I can love and who will love me. One who will want me just as I am. I want a houseful of laughing children. And I want, just once, for you not to laugh at that."

"So you're going to hop into that diesel with Ashton Wilson and make your fondest dreams come true—is that it?"

"What if I am?"

"Mrs. Ashton Wilson, is that what you want? Really? A lifetime chained to a farmhand?"

"There's nothing wrong with working hard for your money."

"But will he still want you after four babies, Sarah? Will he still come home to you and that houseful of laughing children?"

"He's a good man. He's responsible, honorable. Something you wouldn't know anything about."

"He's the wrong man for you, Sarah. He can't save your farm. He can't give you your dreams."

"And you can?"

Trey finally allowed himself to drop her arm. "Forget it."

The horn honked. It was followed by the deep drawl of Ashton's voice. "C'mon, gorgeous," he called. "Time's wasting."

"I have to go."

Trey watched Sarah run down the veranda steps. Ashton jumped out of the truck and caught her around the waist. He bent down and whispered something in her ear. Sarah looked over her shoulder— back at Trey. And all he could see was the way she went so easily into Ashton's arms. As he dialed a number on his cell phone, he told himself he was doing this for his brother. For a chance for a future for both Jenna and Bryce. The other McCabes, while he liked them well enough, did not figure into this. This sacrifice he was going to make was for Bryce only. He kept telling himself that, but deep down, he knew it wasn't true.

"Hello?"

"Lance Ryder?"

"Yes? Who's this?"

"Your son."

"Which one?"

"The oldest."

"Bryce?"

"Bastard."

"Trey, then."

"That's right."

"Haven't talked to you in years. What do you want from me?"

"Your promise to quit busting Bryce's balls."

A deep-throated chuckle reached him through the phone. "Why should I?"

"Because I'm an influential person now. I've got an excellent reputation, and a pile of money in the bank."

"And I give a shit because . . . ?"

"Because I have two interviews lined up in the next week. One with *Maxim*, and the other with *GQ*. Both publications are global. And I'm feeling decidedly melancholy in my old age. I once had a therapist who told me that what I needed was closure and I'm thinking he was right."

"You—"

"That's right, old man. If you don't back off and let Bryce buy the farm, I'll sing like a fucking canary, and I'll be hitting all the high notes, if you know what I mean. Not sure what the good folks in Lucan or your cronies at Greenwood Financial would think about your dirty little secrets."

"You wouldn't dare."

"I would dare."

"What does that shit pile mean to you?"

"Nothing, but it means something to my brother, and my brother means everything to me. Now back the fuck off, or find our personal history spewed on the glossy pages of those magazines. Got it?"

"You don't have the balls."

"I've grown a set over the years, old man. I wouldn't test them. Tomorrow, by noon, I want the deal called off. Or I'll talk, and you'll go down."

Clicking his phone shut, Trey took a deep breath. Well, at least he'd saved the farm. There was no way Lance Ryder would risk his secret coming out. The man was, and always would be, a coward.

He'd done it for Bryce, Trey reminded himself, even as he brought his hand to his nose and inhaled the sweet country-flower scent of Sarah McCabe's soft, luscious skin, which still lingered on his fingers.

"I swear, you must have ESP."

The bedroom door clicked softly in the dark. Jenna approached the bed, where Bryce was propped up with pillows, wearing nothing but a white cotton sheet over his lap.

"And why would you say that?"

He smiled and reached out to her. "Because I was just thinking of you coming in here, wearing something slinky and sexy and having your wicked way with me."

"Seems we're wired alike, because I was thinking the same thing."

He pulled her down and she straddled his thighs. His hands, warm and soft, went to her ass. He pulled her panties up so he could caress her intimately.

"And what wicked thing were you thinking of doing?" he asked.

She shrugged, purposely letting the strap of her red nightie slip down her shoulder. The crest of her breast was freed, and Bryce put his face to her, inhaling her scent, kissing her with slow calculation. "Maybe I was thinking of watching you jerk off. Maybe I was going to take your cock in my mouth and suck you dry."

His brow arched and he pinched her butt. "Your vocabulary has undergone such a change, Miss McCabe," he teased. "I wonder who could be the bad influence."

"I wonder."

"What a quick study you are," he said, pulling her panties aside so he could dip his fingers into her pussy. Jenna moaned as she felt the fluttery strokes of his fingers. "Ah, Jenna, your cunt is so wet and warm."

She closed her eyes as he circled her clitoris. "And waiting for your cock, Bryce."

"What about your mom and dad," he asked, baring her breast to the moonlight, which was coming through the lace curtains.

"I think it's safe," Jenna whispered. She pulled the filmy negligee over her head. Bryce caught it in his hand.

"I intend to make you scream, Jenna," Bryce said as he reached for her hands. "I want to hear you cry out. But I don't want Mom and Dad to come rushing in here, because what I'm going to do is totally X-rated." He took her wrists and tied them behind her back with her negligee.

"What are you doing!"

"Playing."

Her body trembled as Bryce ran his hand down her side. Her back was arched, and the position pushed her breasts out, right in front of Bryce's face. "Have I told you how much I love your tits?"

"Only a dozen times," she laughed.

He circled his tongue along her areola before flicking her nipple. "Have I told you how much I love the way you taste? The feel of you on my hand. On my mouth."

She was breathing hard. His seduction was too slow, too lazy for her needs. She wanted him fast and hard, swiftly taking her.

"I love going down on you, Jenna. I love knowing I'm the only man who has."

"God, yes, Bryce, I want . . ."

"What do you want, baby?" he asked darkly as he caught her breasts in his hands and met her gaze. "What do you need?"

"You know," she said, her face growing hot. It was one thing to say she wanted him to fuck her, but something else entirely to say that she wanted his mouth on her pussy.

He followed her glance as her gaze drifted to her spread legs. He smiled wickedly as he ran his fingers along her folds. He grinned up at her as he rubbed her clit.

But he didn't do what she wanted. In frustration, Jenna groaned and shoved her hips toward him. He laughed and lay on his back, capturing her hips in his hands.

"You'll have to tell me what you want, babe."

She would have swatted him if her hands hadn't been tied. But then, she wouldn't have the wicked feeling of being bound up.

Her nipples beaded more tightly and he pulled on them, bringing her down until her breasts were directly over his mouth. His tongue reached up and flicked the nipple in a way that only inflamed, not soothed, the ache between her thighs. His fingers continued to play in her folds, grazing and stroking, building until she was restless.

He was sucking her breasts, kneading them, until she couldn't breathe. Her face was hot, her cheeks burning as he looked up at her, challenging.

"I want you to taste my cunt."

With a smile, he reached for her hips and brought her up his chest, toward his mouth. "Let me go to work, then."

When Bryce brought her sex down to his mouth, she cried out at the pleasure of his tongue lashing out over her sex.

He was wild beneath her, she was crazed atop him, panting and mewling, and trying hard not to scream in pleasure. With her hands bound, she felt at his mercy, and it heightened her enjoyment until all she could think about was coming.

He brought her to orgasm within moments, and Jenna found herself shaking, then crying out, as he pulled her down and slammed into her still quivering pussy.

"God, you feel so damn good," Bryce growled as he gripped her hips and thrust up inside her again. He was taking her hard, stretching her wide as his fingers held tightly to her hips. "Fuck me," he commanded, and Jenna did, riding him hard, just like she had the first night they'd been together.

When Jenna felt the silk freed from her wrists, she shook the negligee off and captured Bryce's face in her hands, kissing him with all the love she had harbored in her heart.

Their tongues danced and darted, growing more frantic. His hands were everywhere on her body as she took him deep within her. Then suddenly he flipped her onto her back, loomed over her, thrusting into her slow, measured. Their hands were entwined above her head, their fingers lacing tightly, holding on to each other, never wanting to let go. Bryce watched her, their gazes locked as he increased his rhythm, possessing her with his cock as he watched her body taking him in.

"Will you let me?"

Jenna knew what he was asking. "Yes."

He closed his eyes for the barest of seconds, then opened them. With one final stroke, he came inside her, pouring himself in pulsating strokes until he emptied deeply inside her with a shudder. He pulled her against him, gathered her in his arms and squeezed her so tight.

"I love the way your pussy holds on to me," he murmured against her throat. "It's as if your body doesn't want me to leave it."

"It doesn't."

He looked up at her and smiled. "Mine doesn't want to leave yours, either. Stay with me tonight, Jenna. Stay with me forever."

Seventeen

"Oh. My. God."

Everyone glanced up in time to see Emily close her eyes. "This is soooooo good."

Jenna's gaze shot to Bryce, who was sitting beside her at the breakfast table. He was grinning like a schoolboy bringing home a report card full of A's.

"Thanks, Emily."

"I love strawberries. And French toast. Put them together with cream cheese, Bryce, and I am your servant."

"Really, Em," Jenna laughed. "You've got to get out more."

"Have you tried it, Jen?" Emily asked. "It really is to die for. I'm bringing a piece to work for Beth. She's going to love it. Besides, it's her day to do inventory of the new stock; this little treat will make it more tolerable."

"How go things at the Lucan Library?" Bryce asked.

Emily's cheeks grew pink. "Okay. It has its good points and bad points, like any other job."

"Yeah, it's a real downer tracking down those overdue books,"

Sarah teased. "Besides doling out late fees, the highlight of Emily's day is when Donny Whilton comes in."

"It is not," Emily gasped in outrage.

"Yeah, it is," Sarah countered. "I know you and Beth spy on him when he goes upstairs to check out the 'lifestyle' section," Sarah said, using air quotes.

"Emily, you don't," her mother scolded, shocked at the very thought of one of her daughters doing something so underhanded.

"Of course she does, Mom. She and Beth do it all the time. She told me his favorite is the kama sutra. That's probably because he can't read—you know it has all those *pictures*."

"I told you that in confidence, Sarah."

"Nothing is ever a secret when it's shared over a pitcher of mojitos. You know that, Em."

Emily glared at Sarah over the black rim of her glasses. "Just for that, I'm not saving you a copy of the new Raven Midnight when it arrives today."

Now it was Sarah's turn to blush. "Em."

"Who is Raven Midnight?" her mom asked as she wiped her hands on a tea towel. "And is that her real name?"

"Oh, no one," Sarah said at same time Emily let the bomb drop.

"Raven Midnight is an erotica writer. Sarah's been devouring her dirty books as though they were chocolate brownies."

Dishes clattered in the sink. "I beg your pardon?"

"*Emily!*"

"Here, now, what's all this noise about? It's louder in here than the henhouse," their father grumbled as he breezed through the kitchen.

He poured himself a cup of coffee, took a sip and grimaced. "Coffee tastes like it's got flavoring. Guess that's what happens when you got a gourmet chef staying with you."

"I made the coffee," Sarah grumbled. "And it doesn't have flavoring. It's just a different type of bean."

"Angie, where is the Taster's Choice, for God's sake?"

"Will you watch your temper, Wayne," their mother scolded. "Your blood pressure—"

"My blood pressure will be fine once I get a decent cup of coffee, and none of that artsy-fartsy fancy-beaned coffee, either. Just the regular high-test stuff that gets me going in the morning."

Jenna couldn't help but laugh. "See, nothing much changes around here, Bryce," she said, smiling at her dad. "We're still the same old McCabes."

"And I love every minute of it," he whispered to her.

Jenna felt her toes curl. God, she loved him. And what was more, she loved sitting here with him in her mom's kitchen, her boisterous family surrounding them.

"At last," her dad said as her mother passed him a cup of instant coffee. "You might want a cup of good old instant, Ash—" He stopped, his mouth agape as he looked at Ashton, who had his back to the table. "What in the hell happened to your face?"

"Nothing."

"Nothing? Your eye is swollen shut."

"I'll be fine," Ashton growled.

"Oh, wow," Emily muttered, then nodded toward the hall. Jenna heard Sarah suck in a breath. Trey was standing there, shirtless.

Wow was right. Who knew Trey was that stacked? And tattoos? Jenna had never figured the reserved, refined Trey for the tattoo kind.

Jenna's gaze, just like those of her two sisters, she knew, traveled over Trey's form in appreciation. He looked totally different with this bed-rumpled look than he did in his dress clothes. *Good boy gone bad,* Jenna thought.

"Good morning," Trey murmured. "Sorry. I didn't know there was anyone in the kitchen. I'll get my shirt."

"Don't be ridiculous," her father said. "Come get yourself a cup of coffee and have a seat. Might not want the crap in the pot. Sarah made it."

Trey, Jenna noticed, had a big purple bruise on his chin and a red mark over his ribs. She watched the way his gaze drifted over Sarah, then turned to Ashton. The two of them were staring each other down like two competing bulls getting ready to charge.

Well. This was interesting. Obviously there was a story here somewhere. And by the way Trey kept glancing over at Sarah, the story must involve her little sister.

Weird, because Sarah had always despised the cool and aloof Trey.

"C'mon, Ash," her dad said at last, "time to start milking."

Ashton nodded, wiped his mouth with the back of his hand, then left. Jenna didn't get a real good look at his face, but her mother did, and from her expression it wasn't pretty.

"When you're done with the chores, you come back in the house, Ashton. You need ice on that face."

The screen door swung shut, muffling Ashton's reply.

"Coffee is good," Trey said as he leaned his hip against the kitchen counter. Sarah ignored him, and Jenna kicked her beneath the table.

"Thanks," Sarah muttered.

"You want some breakfast?" Bryce asked his brother. "Strawberry-stuffed French toast, your favorite."

"Nah, thanks. I'm good."

Bryce nodded to where Trey was fingering his ribs. "Looks like you might have run into something last night."

Trey shrugged. "Guess I was sleepwalking."

Bryce's eyebrow shot up. "Uh-huh."

"Emily, mind if I come with you into town? There's a book I'm looking for. Maybe the library will have it."

Emily sat up straight in her chair and pushed her glasses back up her nose. "Sure, Trey. But I have to leave in about five minutes."

"No problem. I'll get my shirt."

"Oh, that's okay," Emily said with a giggle as she followed him out of the kitchen. "I don't mind you without your shirt."

"You girls," her mother gasped. "Bring a couple of handsome boys into the house and you act like twelve-year-olds."

"They're hardly boys, Mom," Sarah said, rolling her eyes. She was trying hard not to watch Emily trailing behind Trey, but Jenna saw her gaze shoot over to the door until Emily had disappeared around the corner.

"Well, they are to me. I hope you don't mind, Bryce, but you and your brothers will always be the 'Ryder Boys' to me."

"I don't mind."

"And my apologies for Emily's behavior today. I don't know what has gotten into that girl lately."

"She needs a man," Sarah said.

"That's enough out of you, Sarah."

Bryce winked at Jenna and slid his palm down her thigh. "So, what are you making, Mrs. M.?"

Jenna's mother sagged with relief as Bryce changed the topic. "I thought I'd make a pie for dessert tonight."

"It wouldn't happen to be my favorite one, would it?"

"Well, I don't know, Bryce Ryder. You'll have to wait to find out."

"In that case, I'll just sit here and watch you. Besides, I've been waiting for you to show me how to make pastry like that."

Jenna watched her mom's face grow pink as she batted her lashes at Bryce. What a seducer he was.

"I'm quite certain those French chefs showed you how to make a proper crust."

"Yeah, but it never tasted quite as good as yours."

"You're such a shameless flatterer, Bryce."

"Bullshitter is more like it," Sarah mumbled.

"Sarah Anne McCabe, that dirty language is not appropriate," her mother warned with a narrowed gaze.

Bryce leaned across the table and whispered to Jenna, "Better not tell Mom what you were saying to me last night, huh? That was very dirty language, Jenna Lynn."

"Nice girls do not speak in such a way," their mother lectured.

"Personally, I love it when nice girls say bad words," Bryce whispered to Jenna.

"Yeah, but you're a pervert," Jenna said.

"Just your pervert, babe," he said with a wink. "So, Mrs. M., are you making your famous coconut cream pie?" Bryce asked.

"I am."

"Mom, that pie is full of fat. Dad shouldn't be eating it."

Jenna's mom glared at her as she rolled out the pastry on the old Formica countertop. "Your father is under a lot of stress, Jenna. It's not the pie that'll kill him, but the thought of losing this old place. He can't sleep at night for thinking about it. Trust me, it's not my cooking that will bury your dad."

"Mom!" both she and Sarah gasped.

"Well, it's the truth."

"I'll make a bargain with you, Mrs. M.," Bryce said. "If you give me the original recipe, I can show you how to reduce the fat. Mr. M. will never know."

Jenna's mom put her hands on her ample hips. "Are you trying to worm your way into my good graces, or are you trying to steal my ribbon-winning pie recipe for your restaurant?" she asked Bryce.

"Both," he said, grinning.

She considered Bryce's offer. With a glance out the window, Jenna saw her mom track her dad's progression to the barn. She saw so much love in her mom's face, even after thirty years of marriage.

Bryce felt it, too, because he reached across the table for Jenna's hand and held it tight.

"All right," Jenna's mom said with a sigh, "and maybe while you're at it, you could help me modify a few more of his favorites?"

Bryce squeezed Jenna's hand before he got up from his chair. He walked over and placed a soft kiss on her mother's cheek. "I'd be happy to. I'm hanging around the house today anyway because I'm expecting a phone call. So, I'd love to cook with you."

Jenna's mother wiped at her eyes, trying to pretend that a fleck of dirt had crept in there. "Well, now, I don't have this pie recipe written down or anything. I go by memory."

Jenna watched Bryce with her mom and felt her heart fill. She'd never loved anyone more than Bryce. Bryce took the rolling pin from her mother's hands, floured it, shot Jenna a to-die-for wink and began rolling out the pastry while her mom looked on, clearly awed by his skills.

She'd never get tired of watching him cook, the way he always seemed to enjoy every little task, from chopping to peeling to rolling. He cooked with such love; he loved the food but most of all he loved to prepare it and share it with others.

Jenna realized that the majority of those creations were new ways of preparing old standbys. He loved comfort food. The kind of dishes that were meant to be passed down from generation to generation and served on long, scarred wooden tables with lots of people laughing and enjoying their meal. That was why he loved Italy so much. For Italians, food was a celebration of love and family. Dining together brought closeness—something that Bryce's family had severely lacked.

Jenna knew that in the Ryder household, mealtimes were not shared. The boys had been fed first, in the kitchen; then their parents would sit in the dining room with a fancy tablecloth and eat off the good china. There had been no laughter. No warmth around the Ryder table.

That was why Bryce had always been at her place. Why he had jumped at her mom's invitations to eat supper with them. This was the real Bryce. The one who loved her. The one who had always seemed to be part of her family. The one who always would be a part of her—forever.

Well, right now he was mighty busy rolling pastry and flustering her mother. She needed something to do other than ogling Bryce. "Anyone know where the newspaper is?" she asked.

"Dad took it out to the barn, and I don't think he brought it back. But there's a news magazine that Sarah picked up at the supermarket yesterday. It's in the living room, on the coffee table."

Jenna sauntered into the living room and picked up the magazine. It would pass the time while Bryce was occupied cooking.

"Find it, honey?"

"Yeah," she mumbled as she returned to the kitchen, leafing through the glossy pages. The magazine fell open to the center spread and she froze in her tracks.

Sexy Chef's Latest Dish

There were pictures of her and Bryce in Tuscany, and—oh, God, there was one of them in the lake. Her chest was plastered against

Bryce's chest, but even though only her back was showing, you could still see the sides of her big breasts spilling out. And then there was one of them in the market, the day he'd given her the ring. He was looking down at her, cupping her cheeks, a look of adoration on his face. Beneath the picture was the caption "Ready for a committed relationship," as if his words had been rehearsed and caught on tape by an interviewer. And maybe they had.

What the fuck was this?

She skimmed the article, growing more and more incensed as she read the story of their time in Italy. The writer played up the fact she wasn't the sort of woman he usually cavorted with, and if he used the phrase "girl next door" once, he used it a dozen times.

"Jenna?"

She looked up from the magazine. She felt ugly. Stupid. Betrayed. The longer she stood there, the more ridiculous she felt.

"Honey, what is it? You've lost all the pinkness in your cheeks."

"It's nothing. Mom. I'll be all right."

"Babe?" Bryce's beautiful face showed bewilderment. She wanted to scream *You've been found out, asshole*, but she didn't have the strength to yell and not burst into tears.

His expression fell, and Jenna saw him reach for the dish towel. Saw him wipe his hands, the same hands that had done so many wicked and wonderful things to her body—the same hands that had left imprints on her heart and soul. He tossed the towel aside and started toward her, reaching out to touch her.

She couldn't let that happen. She didn't want to be near him. Not yet. Not until she knew what she was going to say, how she was going to act. Because there was no way in hell Jenna was going to show Bryce that he'd ripped her heart from her chest and left her bleeding to death. She had given him another chance, and that was her own stupid mistake.

"Jenna?" he asked, then stopped. His gaze suddenly shot to the magazine that had fallen to the floor. His face paled as he recognized the pictures of them together in Tuscany.

"Jenna, no," he said, coming toward her like a bullet. She backed away, her bottom lip quivering. "I can explain. Let me explain."

She turned and ran then. Heard him following after her, his bare feet slapping against the hardwood floors.

"Fuck!" he yelled, following her down the hall to the front door as he struggled to shove his feet into his shoes. "Let me explain. Jenna, don't do this, not like this."

But she was out the door and running down the path toward her dad's beat-up pickup truck as fast as her flip-flops would carry her. He always left the keys in the ignition and Jenna prayed they'd still be there, because Bryce was catching up to her.

The screen door slammed shut on its squeaky hinges. Jenna ran faster, until she was crying and gasping. Jumping up into the cab of the truck, she had just enough time to lock the doors before Bryce reached her.

"Jenna," he roared, trying like a madman to open the door. "Don't go. I don't want you driving. C'mon, Jenna," he ordered as he glared at her through the window. "Get out of the truck and give me a chance to explain. Or, if you don't want to talk to me, then that's fine. I'll leave. Just . . . don't drive away. Not like this."

He didn't deserve anything from her, most especially a chance. Not trusting herself to speak, Jenna put the truck in reverse. The gas pedal hit the floor and the old Chevy fishtailed a bit, then barreled back down the gravel drive. Stones and dust flew up around her, blinding her along with her tears. As she spun the truck around and headed down the road, she saw Bryce standing alone in the evaporating dust.

Her heart crumbled, just like the dust, and she drove faster, not knowing where she was going. Only knowing she had to put as many miles between them as she could.

Everything they had done had been a lie. He'd used her. Had made her think that she meant something more to him than a means to an end. She had actually believed him when he told her he loved her.

What a joke. She was a joke. And this whole thing—the idea of them together—was the biggest joke of all.

Her cell rang, the ring tone letting her know that it was Sarah. Jenna pulled the truck over and fished her cell phone out of her pocket.

"Jenna?" came Sarah's frantic voice.

"I'm here," she said through sobs. God, she was so pathetic.

"He just wants to know that you're safe," Sarah said. Then she lowered her voice. "He's . . . ah . . . he's pretty much climbing out of his skin, Jen."

"Too damn bad."

"Jenna, you've terrified him."

"No, I haven't. He's just worried because he's been found out, that's all. He's wondering how he's going to get his rep back after wasting nearly half of his four-week deadline with me."

"He loves you, Jenna. You should see him. If you could see how he looks, how heartbroken he is, you wouldn't doubt his feelings."

"If there's one thing I've learned this past week, Sarah, it's that Bryce Ryder should have been an actor."

"Where are you going?"

"The Caddy for a margarita, and if you tell him where I've gone, I'll disown you. I swear I will."

"I'll meet you there in ten."

Jenna flipped her cell phone shut and rested her head against the steering wheel. For the first time in her life, she hated Bryce and everything about him. She hated herself, too, for making up that stupid plan in the first place.

Her phone rang again and she answered in a tone that was the furthest thing from civil.

"Miss McCabe?"

Jenna sat up straight and brushed the hair from her face. "Yes."

"This is Leonard Greenwood from Greenwood Financial."

Jenna's heart began to pump in overdrive. This was about her loan. *Oh, God,* she silently prayed, *let this be good news.*

"I'm afraid that I have to decline your loan. You've got excellent credit, and Global Marketing is really doing quite well for so new a company. But it's that newness that makes it a bit too unstable for our stakeholders. You might want to try for another loan in a year or two, once you have a bit more equity in your business."

Jenna didn't even say goodbye. The phone fell from her hand and landed on the bench beside her.

Not only could she kiss her friendship with Bryce goodbye—her entire family could kiss the farm goodbye, too.

There was nothing to save the McCabe farm from foreclosure. Nothing.

Putting the truck into drive, Jenna headed for the Cadillac bar. It was going to take more than one margarita to get over this.

Eighteen

"Here, I brought you up a treat."

Jenna reluctantly tore her gaze from the twilight sky to watch her sister flop down beside her on the haystack.

"It's chai latte. You'll love it. It's my latest addiction. And here's something else that'll take away the pain."

Jenna grinned even though a new flush of tears was welling in her eyes. "White chocolate macadamia nut cookies?"

"My world-famous," Sarah said as she handed her a ziplock bag full of them. "And still warm, too. Oh yeah," her sister murmured as she reached into her sweater pocket. "Thought you might be running low."

Jenna took the wad of fresh tissues and laughed even as the tears began to spill down her cheeks. "You'd think I'd be all dried up by now, wouldn't you? After those margaritas and crying on your shoulder all afternoon, I'm surprised I have water left in me."

With a sad smile, her sister reached out and hugged her. "You've got a right to cry as much as you want. I'm sorry I interfered with you and Bryce. It's just . . . Trey and I had both of your best interests at heart."

"It's not just Bryce," Jenna said through sniffles. "It's the thought of losing this place that is also breaking my heart. If only I could have gotten that loan against the business."

"You could never come up with that kind of cash, Jen," Sarah said. "Besides, you can't risk your future for this place. Even though we both want the farm to stay in McCabe hands forever, it's not realistic. The farm has been losing money for decades. And now improvements are needed, and there're no funds for that. It's a money pit. You getting the first loan is only a bandage on a gaping wound."

Jenna knew Sarah was right, but still she felt her heart split in two as she looked down the open door of the hayloft to the surrounding countryside. "You're the softie," Jenna said, through a laugh. "I'm the realist. I'm supposed to be telling you this stuff, not the other way around."

"Yeah, well, I've never left the farm, and while I'm a daydreamer, I'm a realist when it comes to this place. It's a lot of hard work for little return, Jenna. I'd hate to see you lose your business because you felt you owed it to Mom and Dad or your sisters."

"I wanted it for our kids, too, Sarah."

Sarah leaned her head in until it was resting on Jenna's shoulder. "I know, Jen, but it's not to be. We can forge new memories. It's not like the farm is what made it home for us—it was us, Mom, Dad and Emily."

"How's Dad?"

"Surprisingly okay," Sarah said as she sipped at her latte. "He hasn't told us who has bought the farm, but he has hopes that he can rent the land and still keep the cattle."

"He and the new owner have spoken?"

"I don't know. But when he called us all together and told us the farm had been sold, he said the new owner had no intention of razing the place to put in a big mall."

"Obviously Bryce's father was outbid."

Sarah shrugged. "I guess so. Dad said it's someone from the city who wants a chance at a quiet life."

"Well, he'll have that out here."

The crickets echoed her sister's nod. "Remember how we used to play house up here?" she asked, reminding Jenna of childhood days that now seemed like a distant dream.

"You always wanted to be the mother," Jenna teased.

"Still do," Sarah laughed.

"Remember how you always conned Emily into being the dad?"

"And I fricking hated it, too," called a voice from below. A few seconds later Emily's red hair could be seen from the top of the ladder, followed next by her glasses. "And I also hated how I wasn't allowed up here when you had your friends over."

Emily flopped down beside them and pulled a stray piece of hay from the stack. Twirling it between her fingers, she peered down the loft with Sarah and Jenna.

"I remember sitting on my window seat watching you two, dreaming about the day I could have boys up here."

"We weren't allowed to have boys up here," Jenna reminded her.

"Well, that didn't stop you from having Trey and Bryce up here. And don't bother to deny it, Jenna. I saw you guys. More than once."

"I admit it," Jenna said, holding up her hand, "I did have boys up here. But it's not like anything went on."

"Oh, *please!*" Sarah teased. "What about when I caught you and Bryce up here drinking?"

Jenna smiled at the memory of Bryce puking in a bucket as she held on to him, fearing he'd fall right out of the hayloft and down onto the baler below. He had been so drunk and unsteady on his feet. When he tried to stand up, he fell backward, landing on top of her. He grinned then and said, in a drunken slur, "I love ya, Jen."

It seemed like a lifetime ago. Yet the memories were still fresh, and the pain still raw.

Bryce didn't love her. Despite what Sarah said, he'd used her as a way to get his reputation back. But then, hadn't she used him, too?

"I had my first kiss in this hayloft," Sarah said on a wistful sigh as she looked around the rafters. "I still remember it like it was yesterday. I thought I was going to die, it was so perfect."

"Who are you kidding, Sarah? You're still getting kissed in the hayloft," Emily taunted.

Sarah glared at their baby sister. "You are far too nosy—you know that, Em?"

"Hey, that's what little sisters are for. Spying and tattling."

"Yeah, tattling is right. Remember how you ran and told Mom that we were smoking up here?"

"Well, at least I told them it was cigarettes. I could have told them it was pot."

Sarah and Jenna both burst into a fit of laugher. "Do you remember that afternoon? Oh, God, you were green, Jen."

Jenna laughed, recalling her first and last time experimenting with anything other than cherry whiskey and cola. "Who brought it up here, anyway?"

"Trey," Sarah sneered. "Who else? He was always the one with the booze and the pot and the dirty magazines."

"Oh, I forgot about those." Jenna smiled. "Remember how scandalized we were looking at those pictures of couples 'doing it'?"

"I remember. You were so embarrassed but you couldn't look away. Bryce was laughing at you."

"Well, I remember you blushing and covering your face when we turned the page to that centerfold of the naked guy with his package in his hand."

Sarah made a face, then laughed. "I was nearly a year younger than you. I wasn't ready for something so . . . so graphic."

"See, you guys always got the fun. By the time I was old enough for any of that, Jenna was away at school, and Sarah was working full-time."

"Aw, Em," Jenna said, "your time will come."

"But it won't be here, will it?" Emily said bitterly. "I won't have the same fun you guys had. Besides, my opportunity for those antics has come and gone. I am nearly twenty-one, you know."

"Maybe you'll have better opportunities, Em."

"I wouldn't count on it."

Emily sat back and put her hands behind her head as she looked up at the barn swallows that flew over their heads. A devilish smile crossed her lips as she thought of something. "I remember the first time Trey and Bryce came to the farm. Do you remember that? They were so out of their element. Remember, Jen, how Bryce slipped in that pile of cow manure? That was priceless. Even Dad laughed."

Jenna smiled at the memory. "What about when Trey and Bryce were helping us milk the cows, and they started the milk fight. What a mess. Dad was so pissed that they'd used the cows that way."

Sarah laughed. "I thought Dad was going to murder both of them. It was sweet justice that he made them muck out the stalls."

"Jenna?" Jenna stiffened as she heard Bryce's voice from the barn door. "Are you up there?"

"Tell him I'm not," she whispered to her sisters.

"She's not up here, Bryce," Sarah called down.

"Then how come I saw her from the window not more than ten seconds ago?"

Great.

He appeared at the top of the ladder, his hair mussed and his face covered in a sexy five-o'clock shadow. Wonderful, he would have to be looking utterly sexy and alluring. But then she would have to be more than angry to think him less handsome. She'd have to be dead.

"Jenna—" He stopped, swallowed. His gaze was busy roving over her face. Jenna knew how she must look. With her hair pulled back in a haphazard ponytail and her eyes red rimmed and puffy, she wasn't "hot girlfriend" material. But then again, she evidently wasn't, even on her good days.

Well, best not to think about all that. What was done was done. And frankly, she was tired of crying and feeling sorry for herself. It was time to accept that Bryce was a jerk, and she'd made a huge mistake by loving him all these years.

"Can I speak to Jenna alone, please?"

Sarah and Emily all but jumped up and vaporized into thin air. Traitors.

Jenna watched her support scramble down the ladder. When the barn door was pulled shut, Bryce took a step closer to her.

"We need to talk."

"No, we don't."

"Yeah, we do."

Jenna put her hands in the pockets of her hoodie so Bryce couldn't see how they trembled. She didn't want him knowing how much he'd broken her. How much her heart ached.

"Jenna. I want to explain—I *need* to explain."

"What?" she hissed, finally turning to look at him. "What do you need to explain? That you used me for sex and as a way to kiss up to your viewers? No, you don't have to. The e-mail was explicit enough, but the photos . . . well, they're worth a thousand words, aren't they? I can't believe you and Trey set me up like that. And I fell for it. How you must have laughed at how easily I fell for your lines. And saying you love me? Yeah, right. That was a low blow, Bryce."

He knelt beside her and tried to reach for her, but Jenna stiffened. She obviously didn't want his hands on her.

She stood up and brushed the stray bits of hay from her rear end as she glared down at him, showing him all the pain and hurt she'd tried so hard to hide. She pushed past him. He stood and reached for her. She neatly avoided him.

"I didn't ask to be photographed with you. Trey thought it would help with my rep, but he never told me. I only realized it when I saw the photographer that day in the market."

"And that's why you said you were ready for a commitment, because you knew your every word was being recorded. You saw a perfect way to be seen as something other than a playboy."

"Damn it! All I saw was you!" He touched her hair, ran his fingers through her ponytail. "I said what was in my heart, Jenna. I meant every word. When I realized we were being watched, I pulled you away. That's why I took you from the market. I didn't want you to know about the photographer because I was afraid this would happen—that you would think I'd set it up. I also didn't want what we had going on between us to be ruined by a flash of a camera. You took my heart that day, Jenna. When I looked at you in the market, I knew there would never be another woman for me."

"How do I believe you when you're such a convincing liar?"

"Jesus Christ, will you stop and listen to what I'm saying! I love you, and you love me, damn it!"

She turned and looked at him. "Maybe. But that doesn't mean I'll ever be able to trust you. And what is love without trust? Nothing."

Bryce watched Jenna run across the grass that lay between the house and the barn. Her hair was slipped from her ponytail elastic, spilling across her shoulders. His fingers ached to run through the soft silkiness.

He wanted to bring the thick locks to his face and smell her. To tilt her face up to his and kiss her swollen eyelids.

Goddamn it. How could he have made such a mess of this? Because he hadn't been thinking, he reminded himself. Ever since Jenna had come into his life he'd done nothing but eat, breathe and live for Jenna. He'd even neglected his restaurant for the first time ever, and all so he could spend every minute with the woman he loved.

She had to love him. He'd seen that love. He'd felt her love sneak into his soul and fill him with warmth and peace. And he wanted it back. Whatever it took, however long it took, he'd get it back.

"Hey, thought I might find you up here."

Bryce turned to find Trey standing behind him. "I was told that these were the cure for all heartache." Trey handed him a sandwich bag filled with cookies. "Macadamia nut."

Bryce gazed back at the house and Jenna's bedroom window. A light went on, and he imagined her undressing and slipping beneath the sheets, which had been hung that afternoon on the line to dry. They would be cool and crisp and smell like sunshine. And he wanted more than anything to be in them with her.

He looked down at the cookies in his hand. "Do they work?"

"I don't know, little brother. Depends on how bad the ache is."

"Pretty fucking bad."

Trey put a reassuring hand on his shoulder. "She'll come around. Let her sleep on it."

"And if she awakens in the morning hating me even more?"

"I don't think she will. Someone told me that she was up here rehashing old times. She wasn't cursing you, Bryce. She was laughing, and her eyes, I'm told, were full of love."

"Just love?"

Trey shrugged and put his hands in his pockets. "Well, hurt, too, but that's to be expected."

"You think I can save my relationship with Jenna, Trey?" Jesus, he sounded desperate—and scared, too.

"Yeah, I think you can."

"I hope you're right, because if I don't have Jenna in my life . . . I don't know how I'm going to deal with that. My chest is aching like a bitch."

"Why not tell her you've bought the farm? Maybe that will convince her you love her."

"No. She'd only assume that I was telling her as a way to make her soften to me. No. I can't tell her until she believes I want a future with her."

"You have a point. It could be construed as manipulation. I guess I didn't see it from where Jenna stands."

"Trust me, Jenna is suspicious of every move I make. I don't think there's a word that's come out of my mouth that she hasn't picked apart and analyzed."

"Still, though, I don't think it's going to take Jenna long to figure things out. She'll come around. I know it."

"I hope you're right, because every minute that passes with her not talking to me is torture."

Trey looked around the hayloft, then back at him. "You don't have any plans to demolish this barn, do you?"

"No. Why do you ask?"

"Believe it or not, I have some good memories of this place," Trey said, his voice suddenly growing quiet. "Some *really* good memories— probably the only ones I've ever had."

"Me, too. I fell in love up here."

Trey's gaze dropped to Bryce's face. "Chin up, buddy. She'll figure it out. If you need me, you know where to find me."

"Trey."

"Yeah?"

"Thanks, man. For everything. I know you were the one to get Dad to change his mind."

"It's nothing. Just don't fuck it all up by losing the girl."

"Trey?" Bryce said again. His brother stopped his descent down the ladder and looked up at him expectantly. "You gonna stay in Lucan for a while? You know, till I get this place up and running."

"I don't know. There's nothing here for me but bad blood."

"I understand. I'll leave it up to you. But I want you to know you have a place with me."

Trey didn't answer; he just climbed down the ladder. Before he climbed down himself, Bryce stole one last look at the empty hayloft. He could still see Jenna sitting there, her knees up to her chest, her ponytail slowly sliding out of its holder. She'd never looked more desirable to him, even with her tearstained cheeks and puffy eyes. His heart bled with every beat knowing he'd been the cause of those tears.

He just wished he knew what to do. Where to start.

He turned to the only place that could give him solace.

The kitchen.

* * *

It was well past midnight when Jenna tiptoed into the kitchen. She'd waited until the house quieted down and she was certain everyone was asleep. She couldn't wait any longer for a drink of milk and another handful of Sarah's cookies.

If there were even any left. She'd seen Trey with a plate of them as he'd disappeared into his room. With a frown, she contemplated the prospect of being heartbroken without anything sweet and fattening to provide relief.

Stepping into the kitchen, she stopped just in time to see Bryce standing shirtless at the kitchen counter, drizzling honey over something.

He stopped. She hadn't made a sound, but it was as if he felt her standing there watching him. As he looked over his shoulder, he put the honey down and wiped his hands on his jeans.

His gaze raked over her from the top of her head to the tips of her pink toes, which Sarah had painted for her only a few hours before. When his stare proceeded back up the length of her, Jenna recalled that she was wearing a translucent baby doll negligee that left little to the imagination.

"I just came for a drink," she muttered as she made a beeline for the fridge. But when she reached the door, he was standing there, looming over her, his hazel eyes almost black.

He didn't say anything, just reached out and grabbed her wrist, turning her until he had her trapped between the counter and his hard thighs.

She struggled, and the strap of her nightie slid down her shoulder. She froze as he put his face into the crook of her neck and pressed against her, his mouth moving slowly, almost imperceptibly along the column of her throat as his hands tightened hard against her waist.

"I've missed this, smelling you. Feeling you against me."

"Bryce, don't."

"Jenna, talk to me," he pleaded. His lips were nuzzling her ear and her traitorous libido began to wave the white flag. "We've always been able to talk to each other, no matter what."

"There were never lies between us before."

"Lies aren't the only thing separating us," he retorted. "You are."

She gaped at the accusation. "I beg your pardon? I'm not the one who plotted with my brother to date a plain Jane and get my picture taken with her to restore my reputation."

"I told you, I didn't know Trey was going to do that. He never meant to hurt you and neither did I. He thought he was helping me—helping us—by pushing us together. I don't know how to make you understand. Maybe if you stayed and had some dessert with me, we could talk, and I could convince you to believe in me."

She wasn't surrendering, and certainly not this easily. "I don't think so, Bryce. The last time you fed me dessert, I ended up sleeping with you—which is how we got into this mess in the first place."

He reached for the pie plate and showed it to her. "Whenever I'm stressed, I cook."

"Whenever I'm stressed, I eat."

"Then we make a good pair."

Oh, she was so not falling for this, for the words that were tripping so easily—too easily—from his mouth. She'd fallen for it in Tuscany, that day he'd been posing for the camera, and she'd been looking up at him like a lovesick fool.

"I came in here, not knowing what I was doing. Everywhere I looked, *everything*, it just brought me back to you. Everything in this house, this kitchen, is a reminder of you—of us. It's the memories of the past—it's the glimpses of the future."

There went that white flag again, waving like mad. Her thighs were beginning to tremble and she felt the first flush of moisture trickle out of her sex. He certainly was a master at more than cooking.

"Even when I closed my eyes, I could see you, hear you, smell you. So, I did the only thing I could: I put everything that reminds me of you into this dessert."

"I remind you of a pie?" Well, wasn't that romantic? A fattening piece of lard and sugar. She didn't know whether to laugh or cry.

Bryce reached up and pulled the elastic from her ponytail. Her thick hair tumbled to her shoulders and Bryce smoothed it back, caressing her collar bone. "The crust is made with buttermilk. It made me think of your skin: white, creamy, smooth, rich. The peaches are for how you blush. I've never been able to look at a peach and not think of you." As if to prove his point, he trailed his fingertips down her arms, and damn her, she felt her skin begin to heat up. "See, that's the peach glow I love so much."

"Bryce—"

He put his fingers over her lips. "The almonds, they remind me of the way you smell, the way your skin tastes when I trail my tongue all over you. And you know what the honey reminds me of. I can still taste your honey, Jenna, the way it drips onto my hand, my tongue."

OK, so that was romantic and the white flag was flying high again. But she still wouldn't let herself buy it, even though she was beginning to turn into a pile of liquid honey right there on the kitchen counter.

"Don't go, Jenna," he pleaded, his voice hoarse. "Please stay."

"We have nothing we need to say to each other."

"I've got ten years of things to tell you."

"I'm not interested."

"How can I tell you, Jenna?" he murmured against her throat as his lips trailed lower. "How can I make you understand what I feel for you? Do I just say the words? Will you even listen?"

No, she wouldn't. She couldn't. She couldn't allow herself to think of anything but that hated e-mail and those pictures. No words could erase what she'd read. Nothing Bryce could say now could make her heart stop bleeding.

"How can I make you understand?" he asked again, only this time his hand left her waist and traveled over to her belly, then slowly moved up until he reached the underside of her breast. "Do I show you with my body?"

Definitely not, she thought, already feeling herself begin to melt.

"If I make love to you, will you understand how much I need you in my life?"

She shoved at his shoulders but he didn't move an inch. "I'm not interested in falling into bed with you," she snapped, trying again to push him away.

"That's not what you said when we started this," he replied hotly. "Remember, Jenna? Hot, sweaty, anytime sex, with no strings."

"*Damn you!*" Jenna slapped him against his shoulder. "How could you throw that in my face after the way you and your brother plotted against me?"

"Stop it!" He tried to keep his voice steady, though he felt himself shaking with emotion. "I told you, I was not plotting with Trey!" He ran a hand through his hair, struggling for control. "He sent that e-mail to push me into seeing you as the woman I loved. He knew I'd balk at any matchmatching stuff, so he worded it in such a way that I'd never suspect what he was up to. You see, since Chrisy—" He licked his lips and Jenna felt his fingers dig into her waist. "When Chrissy left I began to fear that I had nothing to offer, that I could never make a woman happy. Especially a woman like you."

"But you replied—"

"I know what I said. But try to understand how I felt. It was all so confusing. We were friends. Then we were having sex. Then before I knew it, I was falling in love with you. But I had no idea how you felt about me. I was afraid that maybe it was just sex you wanted, after all. That scared the hell out of me, but I decided to go along with it. I was gambling that eventually you'd develop the same feelings for me that I had for you. I didn't give Trey's e-mail a second thought. I should have taken the time to correct his assumptions, but all I could think about that night was getting you alone. I've never been so out of control, Jenna. I was going out of my mind for you."

"But you're the one who used me—"

"Enough! It's truth time, Jenna. You weren't honest with me

about your feelings, and I wasn't honest with you. Can you admit that we both made mistakes? That out of insecurity and stupidity we screwed up?"

"I thought . . . I thought . . ." Oh, God, was she really ready for this? Ready to confess her feelings even though he'd betrayed her?

"Truth time," he repeated.

Their gazes met, held. His never wavered. She felt that penetrating stare right to the very core of her being.

"I only offered you the sex because I thought you wouldn't be scared off that way. I kicked you out of my apartment that night because I thought you'd be apprehensive about anything that smelled of a real relationship. I knew you weren't ready for that. I didn't know if you would ever be ready for that. And that's . . . all I've ever wanted. But I thought you'd only want the sex."

He lifted her face in his palms and looked down into her eyes. "I love you, Jenna." His voice was dark and husky as the words drifted between them. "I love you so much. I want everything from you, not just your body."

Jenna cast her eyes down and her hands fisted against his shoulders. Her heart was beating so hard, it was difficult to breathe. When she finally looked up, it was to see his eyes wet with unshed tears. Now she was robbed completely of the ability to draw air into her burning lungs.

"I love how we laugh at the same things, think the same way. I love how comfortable you make me feel in my own skin. I'm myself with you—something I've never been with any other woman in my life. You don't know what a gift that is, Jenna. You can't imagine how I want to kick myself for not seeing you this way before. But I am seeing you now, and I love what I see. I love you. Why can't you believe that you've done the impossible? You've made me want a relationship—the kind that comes with a wedding band."

Her mouth wouldn't work, but then her brain couldn't come up with the words, anyway. She just stood there, looking into Bryce's face.

"Marry me, Jenna. I'm ready to be a husband. I'm ready to be a father. Hell, I'm ready to be a farmer."

"Pardon me?"

Oh, boy. Here goes. "I bought the farm."

"You what?"

"I sold the two oceanfront properties and the farmhouse in Tuscany to buy the farm."

"You didn't! Bryce, those restaurants were your dream."

He brushed his fingers along her cheek. "It means nothing if I can't share it with you. Besides, this place is my dream. I bought it for us. For our kids, Jenna."

Jenna's heart went into overdrive. She felt like she was going to pass out; her head was swimming.

"What do you know about farming?" she asked skeptically.

"Nothing except that it's hard work and I'm damn glad your father and Ashton have agreed to help me out. But this isn't going to be just a farm, Jenna. This is going to be a vacation retreat for couples. And that barn, it's going to be my next four-star restaurant, and this house is going to be a luxury bed-and-breakfast. And I'm going to fight like hell to get my show taped out here, too. I'm hoping you're going to have a damn good marketing plan to get this up and running."

"My business," she muttered, trying to take it all in. "I know I wanted the whole marriage and kids thing, but I want to work, too. I'm not the stay-at-home type."

"I know. I'd never ask you to give your business up. Actually, I was thinking that maybe you could divide your time between here and your office in the city. I'll still need to go into the city a few times a week to Cravings. I thought we'd commute together."

She looked up at him. "Are you sure?"

"About everything except your feelings for me."

Jenna buried her face against the smooth skin of his chest. "How could you not know how much I love you? I've loved you all my life!"

He pulled her back and looked down at her. "Then what do you say? Will you marry me?"

"Oh, yeah."

"Shall we seal the deal in your bedroom?"

"Are we bringing this?" Jenna asked, lifting the pie from the counter.

"Absolutely." He grinned as he lifted her into his arms.

"We've got a lot of time to make up for."

He put her down and patted her bottom. "Then let's get started."

As soon as the bedroom door shut behind them, his arms were around her and his face was buried in her hair. "Are your mom and dad asleep?"

"Hmm, I'm not sure."

"What'll happen if you get caught?" he teased.

"I don't know. I'll probably be grounded," she giggled.

"I've been dreaming of doing you on that twin bed," he said naughtily in her ear.

Together they laughed. Jenna led him to her bed by the hand and he fell on top of her.

"Where is that pie?" Jenna asked as he kissed a path to her breast.

"Why, babe?"

"I just had a yen to eat some strategically placed peaches."

He looked up from her body, his eyes glowing. "It's going to be such a pleasure to grow old with you, Jenna."

"And I'm going to be so well fed."

He pulled a sliver of peach from the crust and dangled it over her mouth. "In more ways than one, I think."

She smiled and caught the peach slice between her teeth. "You are so bad, Bryce Ryder, and I love every sinful inch of you."

"Good, because I love every beautiful inch of you, Jenna McCabe."

Epilogue

The rain was coming down hard in straight lines. Forked flashes of lightning illuminated the black sky, while thunder rumbled overhead. Tucked up in the hayloft, Jenna snuggled back against Bryce's chest as they watched the thunderstorm together.

She sighed as his hand began to roam over her belly, then sneak beneath the waistband of her shorts. He started caressing her pussy with slow, languid strokes, as if he had all night to bring her to orgasm.

"You are such a tease," she moaned.

"You are so damn impatient," he said back. "Just rest your head against me and enjoy this."

"I don't think the groom is supposed to be feeling up the bride the night before they get married."

"Well, I don't care what the tradition says. This groom is dying for a feel of his bride."

"Oh, Bryce," she purred as he found the right spot—the spot he had been purposely avoiding since he'd started teasing her.

"Don't stop," she whispered, arching against his palm. "Please don't stop."

"Stay the whole night with me, up here."

"I'll do anything if you just give me that orgasm you're teasing me with."

"You promised. Remember that," he whispered as he finished her with just three more strokes. She screamed—his name—and he chuckled. "I'm expecting the same favor, you know."

She collapsed against him and hugged his arms around her waist. He nuzzled her ear. "Look at the horizon, babe. The storm is clearing. Our day should be perfect tomorrow."

"Yeah. I just hope Sarah and Trey can get along for the day. It's not very nice when the maid of honor and best man can't stand to be together."

Bryce pulled away and looked down at her. "What makes you think Trey doesn't like Sarah?"

"Well, he's such a bear when he's around her. Oh, c'mon," Jenna said as Bryce frowned, "you've heard them going at it. They're going to tear each other's throats out if we leave them alone."

"I have something to show you."

Bryce lifted his T-shirt from where it lay in the hay and passed Jenna the white envelope that had been beneath it. "Trey gave these to me because he knew your designer would love them."

"They're all of Sarah," she said as she looked through the photos that were inside.

"Yep," Bryce murmured as he nuzzled her ear.

"My God, they're gorgeous. *She's* gorgeous."

"Gorgeous enough to be the face of Duchess Lingerie, don't you think?"

"Oh, my God, I need to show these to Gabriella. She's going to love them. And you're right. Sarah is perfect for the line."

She tried to get up, but Bryce held her firm in his arms. "Tomorrow, after the wedding, you can show her, babe. Tonight you're mine."

Jenna flipped through the pictures once more and frowned at one in particular. "This is an old one, at least two years ago."

"I know. I found it interesting, too. Maybe we should leave them alone. Maybe there's something there we don't know about."

"I doubt it. My sister has something going with Ashton, and he's totally nuts for her."

"We'll see," Bryce said.

"Seriously, Bryce, I don't know what you have planned, but I don't think you should be counting on Sarah falling for Trey. She's never liked him, and I don't think she ever will. Besides, I caught Sarah and Ashton up here last night. From the sounds of things, it was hot and heavy."

"Speaking of that," he said, rolling Jenna over and looming over her, "is it getting hot in here or what?"

"Definitely hot," she said with a smile.

"We better get you out of those clothes, then, Miss McCabe."

"Did you bring any chocolate?"

"As a matter of fact, I did. It's your turn to lick it off me."

"I don't think so. I might not fit into my wedding gown and Gabriella will have a fit if she has to make an alteration the morning of the wedding."

"Then it will be my pleasure to lick it off every delectable inch of you," he said with a healthy glance at her body.

And he did just that. Jenna was certain she'd died and gone to heaven as she cried out beneath him.

"I love you," he whispered in her ear. "And I can't wait to start our life together, Jenna."

She gathered him in her arms and held him tight. She was never letting go of her sexy chef.